PANIC YEARS

DANIEL DIFRANCO

This is a work of fiction. Names, characters, businesses, places, events, locales, and incidents are either the products of the author's imagination or used in a fictitious manner. Any resemblance to actual persons, living or dead, or actual events is purely coincidental.

Tailwinds Press
P.O. Box 2283, Radio City Station
New York, NY 10101-2283
www.tailwindspress.com

Published in the United States of America
ISBN: 978-0-9975742-2-7
1st ed. 2018

For Ellie

and

To everyone who, while pursuing their art,
has ever humped gear up a flight of steps
in the middle of the night—
this is for you.

PANIC YEARS

PART 1

CHAPTER 1

Gooch quit after our gig in Amarillo. He said he couldn't deal with the shit anymore. It's always the singer or drummer. It's always the guitarist. It's always someone when you're strapped to a van, humping your gear back and forth across the country, waiting for a break—just for a fucking chance.

When I came back from loading up the van, Gooch and Jeff were arguing. Again.

"We have to reach out to everyone," Gooch said. "I'm just the drummer. No one wants to talk to me."

"I went to the merch table right after our set," Jeff said. "You were at the bar getting a drink."

"We're in a fucking bar. That's what people do in bars."

I've been listening to Gooch bitch about this for two weeks. It's been a slow burn. You really get to know someone when you spend this much time with them. I found out he's one of those guys who expects people to think like him and act without provocation. My mother, when she was still married, used to yell at my dad. "I'm not a mind reader," she would say.

Laney came back with our advance from the promoter. She played guitar and acted as our manager. "One hundred and fifty bucks," she said.

"Gooch quit the band," Jeff said.

"What?" Laney said.

Gooch didn't say anything.

"Dude," she said. "You gotta stay until New York."

Gooch could be a dick to Jeff or me—but never to Laney.

He mumbled something and looked away.

Laney looked at Jeff. This was their band. They'd started it in Baltimore before moving to Philadelphia. Gooch was their seventh drummer. I met Jeff and Laney through him when their last bass player took a full-time job with an insurance company two weeks before the tour. I was in between bands and jumped on the chance to play again. It was in my blood and bones. Always had been. It was either do this or scrape by as a fucking bartender serving drunks, cleaning bathrooms, and mopping floors for the rest of my life.

It had to be this.

"Whose turn is it to drive?" I asked.

"I'll drive," Gooch said. "I haven't had a drink tonight." He said that like the proud owner of something found.

"Let's find a motel and sleep it off," Laney said. She took out her smartphone. Early on the tour, Jeff and I discovered we had the same beat-to-shit flip phone. We bonded over that and our mutual appreciation of Andy Kaufman, Mitch Hedberg, and Marc Maron.

"There's a Motel 6 about twenty minutes away," Laney said, looking up from the screen.

"Give me your drink tickets," I said to Gooch.

Jeff smoked. I used to. I took one from his pack and lit it and went to the bar. I pulled up a stool and ordered a stout and a whiskey. Sitting alone at the bar with a cigarette, chairs up, near darkness was about as much of a break as there was on the road. I'd be twenty-nine at the end of the year and playing bass was the only thing I was good at. Being a musician was the only thing I'd ever wanted. I joined Qualia because they were a good band with a shit-ton of underground buzz. If I was going to make it, this was the best shot I'd ever had.

Tom Waits' "Christmas Card from a Hooker in Minneapolis" came on the house system. I laughed to myself. It was almost too perfect. Sitting in Texas, in the middle of the night, far away from home, miles ahead, a band on the verge of breaking up, dreams slipping—sing it, Tommy.

Laney made peace between Jeff and Gooch and talked Gooch into staying. There have been fights before. It would have been a miracle if we made it down the coast and out and back again without getting on each other's nerves. But no one had quit. I hoped that Gooch could ride it out for the rest of the tour. We had already done nine weeks. Three more shouldn't kill him. But time has a way of standing still when you're rambling from town to town. It seemed like only a blink ago I was outside of my apartment with my bass and amp waiting for them to pick me up—it seemed like a lifetime ago.

I woke up first, showered, and walked across the parking lot to the gas station to buy a coffee. The sun was up and high and hot. The rest of the guys were getting ready. I went to the van, a used rental they picked up for two grand at an auction, courtesy of Laney's uncle. I packed my bag away and sat in the driver's seat. We had a gig in Santa Fe that night and needed to be there by five to load in our gear, and wait.

We still had an hour's drive before we were out of Texas. The drive was lonesome. I thought that yesterday too. I never realized how small a town could be until I drove through Texas. The vastness of the landscape was intimidating and the small stretches of a main street, a gas station and a few odd shops seemed to cower and disappear. If they were shook, they would roll over and turn up a breath of dust.

We crossed into New Mexico and traffic grew heavy as we approached Santa Fe. It was half past five when we found the club. We threw on the hazards. Laney went inside to sort out where we should load in. Gooch, Jeff, and I unloaded the van and stacked all the gear on the sidewalk. Gooch took the keys and went to find a parking space.

"What the fuck got into him last night?" Jeff said. He took out a cigarette and tilted the pack towards me. I took one.

"He's been like that since Jacksonville," I said. "Going on about the same shit. I had to calm him down outside the club."

"That's what was wrong with him last week?" Jeff said, pushing his hair away from his face.

"I guess. He's a funny dude. I didn't think he was like that."

"Laney and I thought you knew him. You were his friend."

I leaned against the wall and slid down till my ass was on the ground.

Laney came outside. She was wearing shorts and hadn't shaved in a couple of days. Legs like pepper. Everything's got a bit more grit this close to the ground.

"We can load in through the front. Amps on the stage, drums, guitars, and keys backstage. We're on at 10:30. Forty-five minute set," Laney said.

"Oooh, a backstage," Jeff said.

"I think it used to be a kitchen."

"I'm hungry," I said. "Let's get this shit inside."

I looked up at Laney and held my hands out like a toddler with a cigarette hanging from its mouth, "Mama?"

Laney pulled me up off the ground.

"You're acting weird," Jeff said.

"Perhaps it is the way you perceive me that is weird," I said and flicked the cigarette into a ceramic pot filled with sand.

I was getting punchy. It wasn't a long drive, but that much time in your own head can get to you after you've played to tens of adoring fans. It was a good thing Laney arranged for an advance last night. The promoter really fucked up by booking three out-of-town bands on a Thursday. We had a single in rotation on the college stations and some rock stations in most towns. Amarillo wasn't one of them. We hadn't been playing well the last few nights, and an empty floor doesn't help the cause. Tonight had to be better. We needed it to be.

We started the tour with Lunchbox and Thermos. They were signed to a major label and the crowds were big, we played well, made fans. We'd been on our own since

Savannah and were meeting up with another band, Spectacular Death Extras, in San Francisco for a few dates. They had a huge single on the underground stations and a real catchy video online. We had to stay sharp and not get comfortable with just getting by. You always hear stories of bands that have been together for years and then break up the first week on tour.

We went to get some takeout from a Mexican joint around the corner. Gooch said he wasn't hungry and stayed at the club.

Laney and I ordered food. Jeff ordered a margarita and shot of tequila.

He put back the shot as soon as it was poured.

"You gonna be all right?" Laney said.

"I'll be fine," Jeff said.

"We've got four hours still. We can drink after at the motel."

"I'm thirsty now," Jeff said with the straw between his teeth.

It started to become a chore lately making sure Jeff didn't drink too much before we played. When that happened, he forgot the words or talked too much in between songs, slurring all over the goddamn place. We had had to track him down a couple of times the past week, minutes before we were about to go on. He drank the last half of the margarita in one long pull from the straw when our food was ready. We walked back to the venue and Gooch was sitting at the bar drinking a club soda.

Jeff walked up and slapped him on the back. "Gooooooch," he said.

Gooch looked at us.

I shrugged my shoulders.

Jeff sat down next to him. "Listen man, I like you a lot. You're a good guy," he said and then ordered a beer.

I felt like telling him to cool it. I felt like it wasn't my place.

"Last one," Jeff said to us over his shoulder. "I promise."

Jeff slid up closer to Gooch and started talking. He pulled out a cigarette and lit it.

Laney and I went backstage to eat our food and meet the other bands. Only one had shown up. They were a local rockabilly-bluegrass band playing a small circuit for the weekend. They called themselves the Cracker Rogers Gang.

We talked with them for a while about the scene in Santa Fe and where we could get a reload on some pot. Their violin player, a guy with a beard, was going to join us for our closing number. It was a ballad with an indie rock flare to it—whatever the fuck that means anymore. I played keyboard and bass on the song, which I liked because I got to show off. Jeff called it a country song. I thought it was a good song no matter what we called it.

The doors opened and the other two bands weren't there. One called and said they broke down two hours away, and the other wasn't responding. We got bumped to 9:30, playing after Cracker Rogers. The venue got their house blues band to play the rest of the night.

I sat with Jeff at the bar while Gooch gave his drums a last-minute tune and Laney warmed up on her guitar.

"So now we're opening for the house band?" Jeff said.

"Isn't that the dream? Friday night, home before 11?" I said.

"Not my dream. No one wants to hear the blues dads play their hot licks."

"Some people might. It's still a Friday. Maybe we'll move some merch since we won't get shit from the door."

"Your optimism is bringing me down, Paul."

"Just trying to stay positive," I said. "We lost a step after Jacksonville."

"Well, that happens when the promoters fuck up and fuck over the bands." Jeff shook his head. "And when the drummer wants to quit."

He flagged down the bartender and ordered a beer.

"Hey man," I said and looked at his drink.

"We're on in an hour," he said. "I'm fine. I'll be fine."

Some people did show up. The Cracker Rogers Gang went on and played well. The room was half full with people sitting in booths and at the bar and shooting pool. Some were on the floor, here for the music. We set up as the other band broke down. We shared drums and amps so it'd be a smooth switch. Jeff set up the keyboards and wrapped white Christmas lights around the stands on both sides of the stage while we got in tune and set our levels. The sound man came over the monitors on the floor and asked each of us to test our instruments, one at a time. The bass was thunder and the drums were full and snapped.

We were on in two minutes. Jeff jumped off the stage and went to the bar. He came back with three beers. He put one in front of me and one in front of Laney and swallowed half of his. "Set beers," he said and smiled. He grabbed the mic.

"Hey guys, we're Qualia. Thanks for coming out." He took another big drink. "Let's get everyone up front. I want to see your faces. We're at a rock show." A few people moved forward. "There you go. You guys in the back, come on up, let's get real close tonight." His voice echoed clear throughout the room. He liked a good amount of reverb. Not Jim Morrison cathedral reverb, but enough to give depth, and a little more—just enough to keep the listener at an inviting distance.

More people came up front. Jeff was persistent. "We drove all the way out here from Philadelphia to play for you and see you. Why are you hiding from us? Only our drummer bites. Promise." We had half the room.

Jeff winked at Laney and she gave Gooch the nod. Click, click, click, click and we were off. We had to hit them with a power set, starting hard and fast and staying that way. The crowd didn't want to be there. We had to prove them wrong—they were supposed to be there.

We tore through the first three numbers. Gooch and I were locked in, bass and drums laying it down. Laney's guitar broke into syncopation with delayed melodic runs on top of the music. It created an edge and an atmosphere that gave a sense of warm danger. Jeff was on until the fifth song when he forgot the words and laughed. The audience laughed with him. When the song was over most of the crowd was up front and clapping. Jeff had been working on the other two beers during the few seconds between songs and during the intros.

He held up a beer to the audience. "Thanks guys. We're Qualia from Philadelphia. We've got two more and then we want to come out there and meet you and hang out and drink with you. Stick around."

He turned to us.

"Let's do 'Peoria,'" he said.

We hadn't played that one since Cincinnati.

"Let's stick to the set," Laney said.

"We gotta move," Gooch said.

"I'll play guitar," Jeff said.

We were wasting time. Laney relented. "Fine."

She handed him the acoustic guitar and went to her keyboard.

Jeff spoke into the mic, "Hey guys, we're gonna try something for you. Haven't done it in a while but we think you're gonna like it."

The audience clapped and yelled. People like to see a band trade up instruments on stage. It adds to the mystique of the rock star—that not only are we up here playing, but that it's easy for us and we can do whatever we want, that the audience is in capable hands.

Jeff started the song by himself and the chords were clumsy. He sang and his voice was clean and cut and emotive—almost enough to make up for the guitar. Laney started on the upbeat of four. I followed my ears and Jeff's hands. The song was buried somewhere in me. I was just going to lay the root and lock in with the bass drum—keep it simple, and live to fight another day.

We plowed through the bridge and it didn't sound bad. Laney and Gooch knew their parts. Jeff focused on his singing—which was good. The song needed a voice. All the great songs would fall apart without one. You'd never make it to the solo in "Stairway" if Plant sounded like shit. All the flutes in the world wouldn't save it.

We finished the song and I nodded to our bearded friend from the bluegrass band. He climbed onstage as the audience's applause died down. He plugged in and tuned up his violin.

Jeff took off the guitar and the headstock whacked into the mic stand—a loud clang of metal and wood. He handed it to Laney and picked up her electric.

"All right guys. Thanks for coming out. Stick around," he said

Laney barely had the guitar on before Jeff counted off the song. I set up at the keyboard. My right hand on the keys and my left on my bass.

Jeff played a melodic line on the electric that I doubled on the keyboard. The violin entered and it was beautiful and I thought we'd make it out of the gig unscathed. The drums entered with my bass and Laney's guitar.

Something was wrong.

A low bass note was out over the E chord. The song was in E. At the next pass I moved up an octave to another string. It was still out. I listened. It wasn't me. I looked at Jeff. He was playing and singing and he looked at me sideways. I shook my head. Laney was playing, eyes down. Gooch could hear it and raised his eyebrows and then pounded harder as the song built.

Laney finally heard it. She looked up and kept chunking out the chords. It sounded bad. For three minutes that chord hit and I knew the audience could hear it and see it on our faces. The song ended with a crash on E and the violin player didn't know it and his melody hung over the silence, but this guy was fucking good and he gave it a little more, and then a slow turnaround. Gooch and I picked it up and ended with him on a plaintive note, trying to salvage those last moments.

Jeff looked at Laney, not bothering to back away from the mic. "You've got to be fucking kidding me."

CHAPTER 2

We packed up our equipment, had a drink with the bluegrass band, and hung out with some people before putting the merch away. We sold a few things, but didn't come close to the amount we needed to stay afloat. Jeff didn't talk to Laney and downed a few beers before going to the van while she squared things up with the promoter.

Gooch said he'd drive. We had a gig in Flagstaff the next day and decided to put some miles behind us before we found a motel.

Jeff was in the passenger seat and turned around to Laney.

"Now that we're back in the van as one big happy family," he said, "you want to explain why you were out of tune for a whole fucking song?"

"Chill out," she said. "I didn't know."

"Everybody in there knew," Jeff said.

"I thought it was Paul or you."

"Well, it wasn't."

"I think it went out when you took the guitar off," I said. "The headstock hit the mic stand."

Jeff looked at me.

"It wasn't even my fault," Laney said, "and you're going to yell at me instead of being a better front man and not getting drunk during the set."

"Be a better front man?" He shot back at Laney. "What the fuck does that mean? What the fuck." He shook his head. "And, I had three beers Laney. Three."

"Not counting the ones you had earlier."

"That was hours before you decided to not tune up before the song."

"You threw the guitar at me and were rushing through songs before I had a chance."

"You could have still asked to hold up to fucking get in tune."

"And you could have not fucking yelled at me onstage in front of everyone." Her voice cracked.

"All right, all right," I said. "We'll get it together tomorrow night."

"We fucking better," Jeff said.

"We will," I said.

Laney looked out the window and put earbuds in. Jeff sat with his feet up on the dash and flipped through the satellite radio stations—the rental place never disconnected the service. Each day we were expecting static. He shut the radio off and wound down the window and lit a cigarette.

I was tired of the fighting and welcomed the silence. Sometimes that's better than a resolution. Gooch drove with his eyes forward and mouth shut. I could feel him counting down the days.

We found a motel a few hours outside of Flagstaff and parked around back. Gooch looked at me and shook his head when we unloaded our bags. Laney and I went to the front desk and checked in. One room, two beds. Gooch and I shared a bed while Jeff and Laney shared the other. I wasn't sure if they were ever together before, but a band is a real enough relationship. Fighting is common. Silence is common. Breakups are common.

We didn't talk much. Jeff slept on the chair.

We woke up and had coffee and breakfast sandwiches at the gas station near the motel. Rule One of the road is to never eat where you get your gas. That's a good way to get fat and diarrhea. Rule Two is to spend as little as possible and try to come out ahead at the end. These rules don't often jive.

Jeff and Laney didn't talk much. They seemed to have made up, if not by agreement, then by mutual understanding, to let it slide. Laney drove the rest of the way into Flagstaff. Jeff sat in the back with his eyes closed. He kicked off his shoes.

"Jesus Christ, man," I said from the front.

"What?" Jeff said.

"Your feet stink."

"I just got a shower."

"Not with your shoes on you didn't."

"They're not that bad."

"It's like fucking mustard gas."

Gooch held his breath and made gagging sounds. He opened his eyes wide and put his hands to his throat like he was choking.

"*Fein, fein,*" Jeff said in a stiff, guttural German accent.

Jeff emptied out a plastic bag full of napkins and pistachio shells and put his shoes in the bag and tied it shut. He shoved the bag under the seat.

"Better?" he said.

"We'll get you some new shoes soon," I said.

We hit traffic five miles out of Flagstaff. Our Never Lost GPS, which we dubbed the "Forever Lost," put us on the main interstate into town. The one locals know to avoid at rush hour.

We made it to the venue just in time to load in. We lined our gear up against the back wall of the stage. It was a big place and the music over the house system was tight and balanced. It felt good to be there. Laney talked to the promoter and got the final details about the night's line-up. It was Saturday and we should expect a big crowd. The local openers had a draw, and our single was getting serious airtime over at the local rock station and its sister internet station.

Jeff and Laney were wearing shorts and went out to the van to change into pants. They had a rule about short pants on stage, which was, in short: Don't Fucking Wear Them. Jeff came back with his old shoes on.

"The front row is lucky the stage is only two feet off the ground," I said.

"Ah, they're not that bad," Jeff said.

Laney handed out our drink and meal tickets.

"Drink and food vouchers?" I said. It was unusual to get both.

"Real class place we've got here," Jeff said.

We sat at a table in the dining area of the venue.

Laney ordered a water.

"Same," Jeff said to the waitress. "Gotta stay hydrated."

We ate and then watched the opening acts. The air was clear and the floor was sticky—the markings of a good venue. The house was full and when it was our turn we played a good set. Jeff was sober and spot on. Gooch and

I kept the rhythm section tight to allow Jeff and Laney to take over. We ripped through our songs and finished before our allotted time. It's good to leave them wanting more. Laney met with the promoter and got our cut. Between merch sales and door money, Flagstaff was a success. We drank with some fans and the other bands, and then found a little motel not too far north. We had the next day off and wanted to see the Grand Canyon.

We stayed up late smoking pot and drinking beer in the motel room. Things seemed to be ok. Even Gooch smoked with us and let us throw cheese balls into his mouth from across the room. We made plans to bring the acoustic guitar and some percussion instruments the next day and record a live set for whichever social media apps Laney was using. We shut the lights off and put Jeff's shoes in the closet.

We drove out to the Grand Canyon and decided to hike around a bit before setting up. When the canyon came into view it seemed there were two horizons—one sky and the other rock.

"There's wisdom in that there canyon," I said to the guys.

"Who are you, 'Poncho Paul'?" said Gooch.

"Who is 'Poncho Paul'?"

"You. With your six shooter and mule."

Gooch raised his index fingers and thumbs in the air and made gun-shooting sounds.

"I'd ride a mule into the canyon. That's the way I want to go," I said.

"It wouldn't be very fast," Laney said.

"That's fine," I said.

We walked along the trail and looked out. Slim arms of rock reached out and thrust into the void. You could walk on them. You shouldn't be allowed to, but I guessed the park service expected common sense to prevail over building a fence around the entire thing.

"Let's go out," Gooch said.

"I don't know," Jeff said.

"Come on," Laney said. "Where's your sense of adventure?"

"On solid ground," he said.

We held onto a tree branch and stepped down onto a dirt trail that led out to a ledge. Gooch and I went first. Laney followed right behind us. Jeff took little steps and almost crouched to the ground. We got to the limb. It was maybe seven feet wide. We walked out slowly and sat down at the edge with our feet hanging over. All I saw was red, and orange, and tan. Blue sky. It all blended in and distorted my perception. A small breeze came through and I mentally drilled my ass to the rock. I looked over my shoulder at Jeff. He was crawling on his hands and knees.

"What are you doing?" Laney said.

"Respecting the canyon," Jeff said.

Two birds flew past us. They dived into the depths of the canyon and pulled out and up, high above and twisted through the air.

"No respect," he said and crawled backwards.

Back on the trail we walked past tourists and I had a gross feeling that we were also tourists—visitors that didn't belong. I developed an instant bout of self-loathing at the thought that we were doing the same thing thousands of people do every day—that I thought our experience was unique.

We grabbed some gear from the van and found an alcove. We played a couple of songs with acoustic and percussion, and I ran my bass through a little battery powered practice amp. We set up the camera on a rock and some people stopped to listen. Families, Eastern Europeans, Australians. A group of monks walked by, or people I assumed were monks. They were bald, Asian, and wearing bright orange robes. I wondered if they thought we were assholes, and if monks thought anybody was an asshole.

On the way back to the van I saw one of them out on a ledge with the wind blowing through his robes. Just standing there.

CHAPTER 3

We left the Grand Canyon and drove down to Phoenix where we had a gig the next day. We took a nap at our motel before heading out to catch the bands on the bill that night. We stopped at a print and copy store and made flyers to hand out. The venue was a bit of a dive but had a reputation as a place to catch good local and touring bands. Laney explained who we were to the doorman. The promoter came out and he looked Laney up and down. He let us in without paying the cover.

We talked about the show and handed out flyers. We had to be our own street team whenever possible. The venue had ads in the paper, and the radio station promoted the show, but a Monday night is a Monday night unless you're a major act. Ideally we'd want to stay as close to the weekend as possible, but that's not realistic on the road. This is the stuff Gooch was talking about in Jacksonville. In truth, we weren't going after each opportunity as hard as we could. It's easy to get worn down and lazy. You play a few good shows and you expect people to come out in the next town.

We mingled and Jeff didn't drink too much. Gooch talked to people in the crowd. I sat at the bar and talked to the bartender and some people. The promoter was talking to Laney. He was smitten and kept looking at Laney and checking her out. He had hairy arms and I thought we should be careful with him. He didn't seem like he'd be trouble, but we had a problem once early on the tour outside of Cincinnati. We were playing a real shithole, getting our chops warm before hooking up with Lunchbox and Thermos. We booked ourselves under the name Merlin's Grundel as a joke.

When we finished our set, Laney went to collect from the promoter, who was also the sound man and stage manager. That's usually a bad sign. The place was packed out and the advance we were promised wasn't great, but it was enough to get us over to Chicago to officially start the tour with the national act. Jeff, Gooch, and I were talking to some girls. I looked over to Laney and the promoter had his hand on her back, right above her ass. He slid it down and grabbed her and then leaned in and whispered.

She pulled back.

He said something else.

She slapped him.

I nudged Jeff and we ran over to her.

The promoter pushed Laney hard, off her barstool.

"What the fuck man?" I said as Gooch helped Laney up.

"Cunt slapped me," the promoter said.

"He said he wouldn't give us our advance unless I sucked his dick," Laney said, fixing herself.

People around us looked over.

"Fuck off," he said.

The bartender came over.

"What's going on Larry?" she said.

"Nothing," he said.

"He wants me to suck his dick to get paid," Laney said.

The bartender rolled her eyes, "Quit being a pig, Larry."

"Yeah, Larry, quit being a pig," I said.

Larry looked over at me. I didn't know much about the guy except that he was huge and could probably kick my ass.

"Fuck you," he said.

Being from Philly, one has a certain appreciation and acceptance of the "F" word. It's in our blood. It rolls off the tongue easy like the "d" in "wooder ice." But him grabbing and pushing Laney didn't sit well. Something in me shut off.

"Fuck me?" I said and got in his face. "Fuck you, fat guy. Why don't you suck your own fat fucking dick you fucking fatso?" He wasn't even fat.

He punched at me and I ducked, but not enough and he got me right in the forehead. It hurt. Gooch and Jeff grabbed him. The bartender yelled and the doorman came over and broke everything up.

"You guys have to go," the bartender said. "Give them their cut, Larry."

Larry pulled out the money and counted off a bunch of ones and threw them at Laney. He walked away and went to the other end of the bar.

"Sorry about that," the bartender said to Laney. "He's a dirtball, but he's ours."

"Let's go," said Jeff.

"Can I get some ice for my head?" I asked the bartender.

"Make it quick." She gave me a plastic bag and nodded to the kitchen, right next to the door where we loaded in.

Larry was commiserating with some locals and I got the sense it would have been best to get out of there soon.

The guys left through the front and pulled the van around back to pick me up. I didn't want Larry to catch me alone on the way out.

I filled up the bag with ice and left the kitchen. On the way to the back door I noticed a metal case with foam padding to the left of the backstage, storing all the house microphones. I looked around the corner. The bartender was occupied and Larry was still sitting at the other end of the bar.

I took the microphones out and dumped the ice in the case and unzipped my pants.

I bolted through the back door and jumped into the van.

"Go," I said, holding up a bag.

Gooch tore off.

"Here you go, Laney," handing her the bag over the back seat. "A big old bag of dicks for you to suck."

She took the bag. Jeff opened it up with her. "You fucking steal these?" he said and laughed.

"There was a flight case that really needed to be filled, and I really had to go. It would have been rude to leave the microphones in there," I said.

"Did you shit in there?" Gooch yelled.

"I don't know what you're talking about," I said.

We all laughed. The wind blew through the van and the night wasn't so bad. Laney leaned over the front seat.

"Thanks, dude," she said to me.

I winked at her. "You got it, mama."

Jeff looked at her and then me. He cleared his throat. "Laney," he said. "We need to talk."

"About?" she said.

"Whose dick would you suck for this band?" Jeff said, and then cracked up.

"Definitely not his," Laney said.

CHAPTER 4

The next day we drove around downtown Phoenix and passed out flyers at the local record and coffee shops. It was an all-ages event and pre-sales were light. Even bigger indie acts still have to hustle to make a buck. Despite how many talk shows they go on and how many people have their t-shirts and CDs, their apartments and bills and health insurance, if they have any, resemble that of pretty much every other nine-to-five working stiff. Most bands make virtually nothing off records if they're signed to a major, and often end up in debt even if they move a couple hundred thousand copies.

A band makes its money from the road. From selling t-shirts and stickers. The only difference is the potential for that road to be wider and longer with support from a major. In that regard, on paper at least, we resembled a fairly successful unsigned rock band. We were self-sustaining on the road with a growing fan base. But it wasn't enough. It wasn't enough by a fucking long shot. No one can keep up this kind of exertion without something giving out. It's only a matter of time.

Gooch and Laney split off to go look in a pet shop after we finished plastering the town with flyers. Jeff and I walked back to the van. He was wearing sandals. I've struggled with having respect for a man who chooses to wear sandals as his daily footwear. In college, for the two years I went, the only people who wore sandals were spoiled suburban kids with popped collars who listened to jam bands and spent their parents' money. This association has stuck.

"Nothing good has come from a man wearing sandals," I said.

"Jesus wore sandals," he said.

"I stand by my statement."

"One of these days you'll be a sandalman."

He pronounced it like one would "craftsman" or "boatsman." If you liked pepper you were a "pepperman." A few weeks ago he got a haircut from a place that made wigs. He said he preferred his barbers to be "wigmen."

He took out a cigarette.

"Give me one of those," I said.

"We gotta knock this shit off when we get back," he said, holding up his cigarette.

"When did you start?"

"Seventeen. Senior year of high school. You?"

"Fifteen. Started with weed first."

"Damn gateway," he said and leaned back against the van.

"I don't believe that shit," I said. "I think you're either going to make bad decisions or you're not."

"I think it's got merit."

"Oh, pot definitely has merit."

"No—the gateway concept," Jeff said. "You grow up being told it's this awful thing that you shouldn't do. That if you smoke pot, you'll end up giving handjobs out on the freeway while your family starves."

"That's what you were taught?"

"I came from a very progressive family," he laughed. "It's all bullshit. You know what happens? You end up smoking and laughing your ass off in your friend's basement and eating a bunch of Doritos. So, you get thinking, 'Well, that wasn't so bad. I wonder what heroin is like?' "

"You ever done heroin?" I asked him, raising an eyebrow.

"Fuck no," he said.

"Coke?"

He looked down. "Uh," he said. "I dabbled for a bit."

"What, like at parties?"

"Like almost every day for a while."

"That's a hell of a dabble."

"I'm straight now. Laney put me in check when I got bad," he said. "What about you?"

"I'm not built for it. This singer from one of my first bands got into the heavy shit and started living the rock and roll lifestyle without the rock and roll."

"What happened?"

"He got to the point where he was banging lines of coke off his dashboard doing 80 in this Monte Carlo from the mid-70s. He picked me up for a gig and it was the most frightening experience of my life."

"What did he do?"

"He started banging lines of coke off his dashboard doing 80."

"Fuck," Jeff laughed. "How was the gig?"

"Not good."

"What did you sound like?"

"Exactly what you'd imagine a band from the mid-2000s to sound like with a deep-voiced singer and a guitarist that played licks."

"Like Creed?"

"Not far off."

"Oh, man, I want to hear that."

"No you don't."

"What happened with the singer?"

"He ended up in rehab after almost getting himself killed about a year after the band split up. He was in some dude's house, graffiti on the walls and people fucked out, lying on dirty mattresses and shit. He was looking for crack, found some, and the next thing he remembered he was crawling on the floor under smoke, down stairs and out into an alley. Some people followed him and some didn't."

"Fuck," Jeff said.

"The place burned down. People died," I said.

"How long ago was that?"

"Eight or nine years now, I think. Maybe ten."

Jeff looked at me. He blew out the cigarette from the side of his mouth, away from me. "How old are you?"

I put on my best, disgruntled cop voice, "Too old for this shit."

"Nah, man. Page was twenty-six when he formed Zeppelin. Manzarek was like fifty when he formed The Doors."

"I'll be twenty-nine in a few months."

He waved away my response and shook his head. "There's time, man."

Laney and Gooch came around the corner. Gooch was holding a small round tank. The kind a kid would put a goldfish in.

"You bought a fucking turtle?" I said.

Gooch smiled. "Yes."

"That's a big responsibility, Gooch," Jeff said. "You're going to have to feed and clothe it on your own dime."

"His name is 'Dunk,'" Gooch said.

"Why'd you name him that?" I asked.

"Look."

We all watched the turtle. It stood on a little rock sitting in the pool of water. It stuck its head in the water and pulled it back out. It did this a few times and then stopped.

"It's pretty much all he does," Gooch said. "He's cool."

"He looks just like you," I said.

"Oh, I'm Poncho Paul and I got jokes," Gooch said and put his free hand in the air and made gunshot sounds.

"Paul's first band was a Creed cover band," Jeff said.

Laney looked at me. "That's gross."

I shrugged my shoulders. "I'm a gross person."

There was a group of girls walking across the street.

"Got any more flyers?" Jeff asked.

Laney handed him the remaining flyers. He ran across the street.

Gooch went around the side of the van and put Dunk in the backseat.

"He got a turtle?" I said to Laney.

She put her hands up. "I told him to wait."

"I hope it doesn't end up stinking."

"Can't get any worse than Jeff's feet." Laney looked at me out of the corners of her eyes. "Were you really in a Creed cover band?"

"People knock them, but they were the biggest band in the world for a few years," I said.

"But you were in the band covering their songs—not their band."

"Maybe."

"So you were or you weren't?"

I smiled and looked over to Jeff talking to the girls.

"Yo, come on," I said.

He looked over and held his finger up. One of the girls was writing on a flyer.

He started jogging back and fell. Laney doubled over. Jeff got up from the middle of the street. The girls were laughing. He waved back to them. "I tripped on my sandal," he said and then looked at me. "Not a fucking word."

"Dude," I said. "Your foot."

He looked down. He was bleeding where the big toe meets the foot.

Laney grabbed some paper towels from the van and gave them to him. She drove back to the motel. When we got back to the room, Jeff's foot was still bleeding. Laney ran out to the drugstore around the corner for some bandages and antiseptic and fixed him up. We took a nap before we had to get to the club. Gooch put Dunk on the desk in the room. I could hear him sticking his head in the water if I listened hard enough.

We woke up and Jeff and Laney changed into long pants. We got to the club and loaded in. The promoter smiled when he saw Laney and gave her a hug. Backstage, Gooch looked at Laney.

"Aw, bellissima," he said, trying to hug her. "I am ze hairy one. You are my one true love, bellisima." She pushed him away and Gooch stumbled after her with his arms out.

Jeff intervened. "Knock it off."

Gooch put his arms down.

Jeff lifted his arms, "Bellissima," he said, and grabbed Laney and licked her face. She screamed and pushed him away.

"That's disgusting," she said, wiping her face.

"But you're just the most precious thing there ever was," he said.

"Shut up."

The other bands were loading in when we went out to the bar. They looked like kids. They had their friends with them carrying gear, and the doorman stopped them and checked ID's and gave out a lot of yellow "no drinking for this one" bracelets. None of the bands talked to us. We probably looked ancient to them. I was only a couple years older than the rest of Qualia, but I definitely had ten years on some of these guys coming in. I was playing clubs when I was sixteen and this is probably what I looked like to the older guys. I went backstage to introduce myself and see about sharing gear.

"Which band are you guys?" I said.

"We're Speculoos," said one kid.

"We're Pilkington," said a good-looking kid with a square jaw and clothes that hung on him like they do on the dudes in magazines. I was a little jealous.

"Cool," I said, "I'm in Qualia." I reached out and shook their hands.

"We know," said the kid from Pilkington. "You guys are awesome."

"Thanks, man," I said. "We checked out your stuff online yesterday on the drive down. Good shit." That was a lie, but you need to say something back. They seemed like nice guys.

We sorted out what gear we could share. The drummers wanted to use their own kits, which was probably for the best since their drumheads were beat to shit. A lot of young rock drummers are all aggression. The harder the better. No room for finesse. I'll give Gooch that—for all of his mental deficits he was one damn good drummer and understood that he had to play to the song and give it what it needs. Sometimes all a song needs is silence. A great song is a gift, an accident, and it takes grace to be able to receive it. Take "Lover, You Should've Come Over," by Jeff Buckley—that is a perfect song. Vocally, lyrically, instrumentally—everything is where it should be. Musicians could spend their whole lives trying to write a song like that. Chasing it. And it might not even exist within them. It's fucking frightening.

The first band, Speculoos, went on. They were loud and out of sync. There was too much cymbal and yelling, and all of their songs were a rip-off of a 90s grunge song. I watched with Gooch, off to the side, out of the way of the front line speakers blasting the room with sound. We played a game seeing who could name the song they were copying. "My Wave," "Rape Me," "Pretend We're Dead"—I got those first. Gooch got the rest—"Them

Bones," "Lump," "Interstate Love Song," and then some song he swore originated with the Gin Blossoms. They closed with "Kashmir."

The second band went on—they showed up a half hour before they were scheduled. They said they got lost, and when they walked by us they smelled like pot. They tried to shuffle through the crowd with their gear but gave up and asked to use the first band's backline since the place was packed out. The guitar player took off his shoes and started playing licks for three minutes while the other guitar player tried to get in tune, not realizing his guitar wasn't plugged into the tuner. I walked away.

I was impressed and even a little shocked at the turnout. I ran into Laney and she found out from the promoter we had over half the room there for us. Seven bucks a ticket. We got the door after twenty heads, and with merch sales we should expect a great haul. Only thing left to do was play a great set. We found Jeff at the bar.

"Let's go outside for a cig," I said.

"Ok," he said. He swallowed his beer and stood up. The three of us went outside.

"How you feeling?" I said.

"Fine, I guess," Jeff said.

He gave me a cigarette and pulled one out for himself.

"Big crowd tonight," Laney said.

"Almost as big as Jacksonville," I said.

"Might be bigger."

More people were lining up at the door. Jeff leaned against the wall.

"What's wrong, dude?" Laney said to him.

"Eh," he said. "I got to thinking about what got me into music after me and Paul's talk earlier. First bands. All that shit. I thought we'd be further now." He took a drag off his cigarette and exhaled slow. "I'm just in a mood, that's all."

"Dude, there's at least two-hundred people here. For us. On a Monday. In the middle of Phoenix," she said.

"Yeah, but I'm just thinking about when we were support for Lunchbox and Thermos. We were better than them and they had a fucking record deal. In a few days when we get to San Francisco and hook up with Spectacular Death Extras, we'll be playing bigger venues again because they made a trendy video."

"You know it's a fucking racket, man," I said.

"I know, I know. I'm just thinking."

Four girls got in line. They looked over to the fenced-off smokers' section. They waved at us. They were the girls from the afternoon.

"There's four good reasons why we got into this," I said.

"Looks like eight to me," Jeff said and elbowed me in the side. He waved at them.

Laney looked at me and shook her head. "Have fun, boys," she said. "I'm going to go find Gooch."

The jam band was finishing up, though I couldn't really tell where any of that music begins or ends.

Pilkington set up their gear. The handsome kid stood to the left of the stage with his guitar and microphone. The other guitar player and bass player stood at the right. The drummer was in the middle. I liked that. It was a good stage look.

Jeff and I found Laney and Gooch up front. Pilkington launched into their first song. They sounded like Al Green and Pixies had a baby raised by Radiohead. The rhythm section was tight. The singer had a clear, strong voice that was fragile when it needed to be. But not in that boy-band-airy-whiny-bullshit way meant to make little girls swoon, or in that pop-singer-songwriter this-is-clearly-my-airy-whiny-bullshit-voice meant to make little girls swoon.

I stood next to Laney and noticed her hair was different. It was pulled back, but it looked shorter.

"What?" she said.

"Different hair?" I said.

She touched her head. "I did this three days ago."

"Well," I said, "I noticed today."

She smiled and looked back to the stage.

Pilkington played a dynamic set full of energy and subtlety. The other members of the band left the stage and the singer closed with a solo performance of the Afghan Whigs' "My Curse." It was fucking good. I looked around at all the little girls in a swoon.

"Not bad," I said to Jeff.

"Yeah, I liked that," he said. He clapped me on the back. "Our turn, sir."

We pulled our gear onstage and tuned up. We did a line check. The sound was clear—the levels were balanced. It's always a good sign if the stage sound is right on. It doesn't mean the room sound is going to be perfect, but it sure helps—and so does slipping the sound man twenty bucks. We were on in five minutes. Jeff went to the bar. I went to the bathroom to take a piss. When I came out I saw Laney talking to the singer from Pilkington. She was laughing and put her hand on his chest. I felt a small, unexpected tinge of jealousy in my gut watching her talk to the Pilkington kid. I walked up behind him.

"Easy, tiger," I said in his ear.

He turned around.

"Oh, hey," he said and turned away from Laney. She looked away. She looked embarrassed. She looked like a girl.

"I'm just fucking with you," I said to him. "Great set, man."

"Thanks," he said.

"We're on in two minutes," I said to Laney.

I flagged down the bartender and ordered a double Tully and went onstage.

Gooch was up there adjusting his kit and pedals. He looked over at my glass of whiskey.

Jeff hopped up on stage and put his beer down. Laney was behind him. We retuned our instruments. Jeff grabbed the microphone.

"We're Qualia," he said. The crowd applauded and moved forward. Jeff looked at Laney. She began the intro to our first song. I stood back with Gooch. The light man dimmed the stage lights and put the spotlight on Jeff and Laney. Her guitar started thin until the delay effect cycled around, creating an internal harmony. She added a lower note that droned. Jeff closed his eyes and started singing. The intro was building to its breaking point. Gooch started in on the bass drum. Steady. I let a bass note ring and then again when the one came back around. We couldn't hold it much longer. The audience was watching patiently, listening. A few heads were moving. We were teasing them—they knew it and wanted it. A half second rest—a moment of silence—and the lights exploded on as the first chords and cymbals crashed down. Jeff's voice soared above the band, and we were pounding out the chorus. You can tell a lot about how a set is going to jive by the first song. We just created the whole goddamned universe.

The audience yelled and clapped and sang along. They gave us a reason to push harder and go beyond. Before our last song, Jeff gave us a wink and then turned to the audience.

"Thanks for coming out. We're Qualia. We'll be on the floor to meet you and drink with you."

The audience whistled and cheered.

"Thanks," Jeff said.

"One more," someone yelled. Then another. And another, until the audience picked up the chant.

"Thanks," Jeff said. "I think we have one left."

Laney gave him her guitar and she picked up the acoustic. We tuned up while Jeff talked to the audience for a few more seconds.

Then we played the shit out of the song.

CHAPTER 5

We all manned the merch table. One of the girls from earlier came over and talked to us. She kept touching Gooch's arms and talking about his muscles. She wouldn't stop saying "rock hard." He pushed her hands away, which made her laugh. I could tell Gooch wasn't amused, even though he was playing along and smiling. Jeff got swept away by a group wanting to talk music and buy him drinks.

We mingled for a while, talking with people, getting their email addresses and names. When it calmed down Gooch and I left Laney at the table to pack up the merch while we broke down and stored our gear.

"Not bad," I said to him. "Not bad at all."

"Yeah," Gooch said, "except Jeff went drinking right afterwards."

"He got caught up in the moment."

"He should have stayed at the table." Gooch shook his head and threw his bag of drumsticks off the stage.

"Relax, brother," I said. "He was sober for the stage and we played a good set. And look," I pointed to Jeff surrounded by people, all laughing. "Those people right there are having a great time. How many times do you get to hang out with the singer of the band you went to see?

Isn't that what you said he should be doing? Reaching out?"

"Does he have to be drinking?" Gooch asked.

"He's been better the past few days," I said.

"He should have been doing better the whole tour."

"Let's consider tonight a new start. Give the guy some credit."

"One night isn't change."

I put down the amp I was carrying.

"Goddamnit, man. We hustled this town and got a packed-out house. Probably made two grand. We played a great fucking set and made tons of new contacts. We've never done that."

"I'm not saying tonight wasn't good, but it's what I've been saying the whole time. We should always be doing this. We should have been fucking doing this nine weeks ago."

I picked the amp back up.

"Gooch, I love you. You're my friend. But right now you're whining and you're just going to keep saying the same shit over and over." I slid the amp in the van and turned back to Gooch.

"Because he keeps . . . " Gooch said, before I cut him off.

"Stop it," I said. "I'm done listening. I'm going to go enjoy the rest of the night, and the way I see it, you have two choices: come have fun with us, or fuck off."

I slammed the hatch to our van and walked away. I felt bad for treating him like that. I never spoke to him that way before, but fuck, he was irritating. There's nothing worse than being a perceived ally to someone hell-bent on hearing their own voice.

Inside the venue I saw Jeff with the girls from earlier. I went over to Laney who was with the singer from Pilkington. He told me his name was Layne.

"You're fucking with me," I said.

He took out his license.

"My parents met at an Alice in Chains concert."

"Let me see," I said. He handed his license to me. "Layne Thomas LeJeune. Born 1/07/96." I looked at him. "Ninety-six? Did they fuck at the concert, too?"

"Paul," Laney said.

"What? Do the math."

Layne laughed. "I never thought about that."

"Think real hard about it," I said.

He closed his eyes and shook his head, "I don't want to."

"Hey," Laney said, "Layne's gonna have people back to his place out in the desert past Scottsdale."

"The desert?" I said.

"My uncle's a big hotshot tech guy. I take care of the house when he's not there, which is like, almost always," Layne said.

"I'm game. When we leaving?"

Laney's phone buzzed. She took it out and showed it to me. A text from Gooch.

Went to feed Dunk. Text me and I'll come pick you up when you're done.

She looked at me. "Did he say anything when you left him?"

"Yeah. He got into whiny mode again and I told him to fuck off."

"What?"

I asked Layne to excuse us for a minute. We didn't need to air our dirty laundry in front of other bands. I told her all the shit Gooch was saying and how I didn't want to hear it again.

"Should we tell Jeff?" she said.

"I don't know. It's just three more weeks. Less, really."

"He said he was going to stay until New York. I thought he was just having a fit a few days ago."

"He's been having a fit for over a week. Ever since Jacksonville. Which is strange, because I thought he had fun at that gig. Especially with that chick with big tits that practically raped him in the bathroom."

"They didn't do anything. Well, he didn't at least," Laney said.

"How do you know?" I said.

She looked at me, confused. "You don't know?"

"I guess not."

"Gooch isn't having sex for a year."

"What?" I laughed.

"He told me before we left that he was going to be celibate for a year. Starting with the tour."

"You've got to be fucking kidding me," I said.

"I thought you knew."

"Does Jeff know?"

"Probably not."

"For someone as simple as Gooch, he sure is complex. This makes a lot of sense though."

"What do you mean?"

"Laney, our dear Gooch is getting frustrated."

"Frustrated?" She furrowed her brow and then her eyes and mouth opened. "Oh," she said.

"That's twice he's been hit on by girls and then flipped out afterwards," I said.

"Dude, do you think that's why he went back to the motel?"

"With the girl?"

"No, to like, be a boy?"

"You're a dirty girl, Laney."

"Me? It's you boys that can't keep your hands off yourselves."

I laughed and shook my head. "Let's find Jeff and Layne and go have ourselves a party."

"Ok, I'll text Gooch, see if he wants to come out." We found Layne and got his address. She took out her phone and sent a message. Her phone buzzed.

I'm good. Somebody has to drive tomorrow, he wrote back.

We piled into cars. I rode with Layne and some other people I didn't know. The back seat was cramped with five people. Laney climbed in and sat on my lap. I put my arms across her legs. I felt uncomfortable and a little excited in this half-holding of her.

"I apologize in advance for what may or may not happen," I said to her.

"I probably wouldn't even notice," she said.

"Ok, ok," I said.

The drive took twenty minutes and when we got there my legs were asleep. I almost fell getting out of the car and held on to the door as feeling slid back into my legs. Other cars pulled up in the driveway. I leaned against the door.

"Ever been in the desert before?" Layne asked me.

"Nope," I said.

"It's beautiful, but if you decide to wander around, there's one thing you have to remember."

"What's that?"

"Don't touch anything."

"What about wolves?"

"They come around. Probably not tonight with all the noise."

"Damn. I felt like dancing." I tried to shuffle my feet and almost fell. "Goddamnit, Laney."

They laughed. "See you inside," Laney said.

I stood there and saw Jeff get out of a car. He came over to me.

"Yo," he said and took out two cigarettes and handed me one.

"Thanks," I said, pained.

"What's wrong?" he said.

"My fucking legs are asleep. Bad. They might have to go."

Jeff kneeled down with a cigarette hanging out of his mouth. "Let's have a look."

He stared at my legs. "Yeah, these are pretty bad," he said and then started poking my thighs and grabbing my calves.

"Knock it off," I screamed. "Pins and needles, man. Pins and needles."

I managed to push him over. I stomped my feet until I could walk.

"Damn," I said. "That was the worst. Fucking Laney."

"Where is she?"

"She went in with Layne."

"Yeah?" he said. "Good for her."

"You think she likes him?"

"I've learned to never make assumptions about what girls think."

We walked up to the house. It was built into the side of a hill. The driveway was dirt and flanked by desert shrubbery and cacti. The sky was dark and wide open. It was almost a full moon and the house was glowing. Lights began turning on. Then music. A caravan of headlights on the driveway. I looked around. The next closest house was far down below in the valley.

"Jeff," someone yelled.

Jeff waved.

"Who's that?" I asked.

"Sounds like Rachel. Could be Max."

"Which one was hitting on Gooch?"

"I think that was . . . actually, I have no fucking idea." He laughed. "Last I saw, she was flirting with the bartender. Took us forever to get a drink."

Inside the house there were multi-tiered sections of carpet, hardwood, and stone. A fireplace was carved out of a rock that was part of the hill. The outer walls were glass and the terrace looked out over the landscape. It seemed to be part of the desert and sky—like you could just walk off and be a part of it.

It reminded me of Fallingwater out in western PA. Some rich guy had a birthday party there and wanted jazz in the background. I filled in for a friend, rounding out a trio. This house felt like that one, except I didn't have to stand in a corner and not touch anything, or talk to anyone.

People were filing in. Lots of faces I recognized from the bar. Beer and bottles of liquor turned up. Someone rolled in a keg. I've always been fascinated by the industriousness of people who want to party. It was one in the morning and things were just getting started. Jeff was hanging out with two girls by the fireplace. The ones I assumed were Rachel and Max.

I went out on the terrace and bummed a cigarette off someone. I could smell the pot happening. I saw Laney and Layne in a corner on the terrace. I walked over and stood behind them.

"I used to wake up every Saturday morning and drive an hour to a piano lesson," Laney said. "Once a month, on a Sunday there would be a recital in the afternoon. I missed a lot of sleepovers and birthday parties growing up."

"You must be really good," Layne said.

"I haven't played like that in a while."

"Why'd you stop?"

"Hey, guys," I said. They jumped.

"Sorry, didn't mean to scare you," I said. "Great party," I said to Layne.

"Thanks," he said.

I looked at Laney. "I didn't know you played the piano that much."

"You never asked," she said.

"Do you like Chopin?" I asked.

"Fuck Chopin," she said.

"Why 'fuck Chopin?' "

"He's too moody for me."

"Not very rock and roll, is it?"

"Who do you like?" Layne asked.

"Beethoven," she said.

"He's not moody at all," I said.

"There's something simple about his music. Well, that I could understand, anyway."

"Didn't he pee his pants?" Layne asked.

Laney laughed. "That was a movie."

"Doesn't mean it didn't happen," I said. I heard a glass break behind me, inside the house. The music got louder.

"I'll go make sure everything is ok and leave you two be," I said. I made eye contact with Laney until she broke it.

"Don't worry about it, man," Layne said, "We'll take care of everything tomorrow. We always do."

"Cool," I said, still looking at Laney.

"Hey, I think the guys are going to set up some instruments later on if you want to jam a bit."

"We'll see, man. We'll see," I said. I walked away from them. The stab of jealousy hit me again. I found Jeff inside, sitting by the fireplace alone with a bottle of whiskey.

"What have we got here?" I said.

"My medicine," he said.

"I want some medicine."

Jeff handed me the bottle and I took a long pull off it.

There was a thick cast-iron metal arm with a big black kettle attached to it against the wall. It looked like it could swing into the fireplace. I pushed it, just to see if it moved. It did, and it hit the wall and sent down a small pour of crumbled rock next to Jeff.

"Shit," I said.

"This is why we can't have nice things," Jeff said.

I looked behind the kettle, and there was a deep round dent in the wall that gave me the impression this wasn't the first time the kettle hit the stone.

I took another pull off the bottle and handed it back to Jeff.

"Have a seat buddy," he said.

I sat down next to Jeff. "Where'd the ladies go?"

"They went to the bathroom," he said and took a drink. "Well, I think it's time to come clean. I really thought I'd have them both to myself, but Max was asking about you."

"What'd you say?"

"I told her you were gay, but I don't think she believed me."

"You're a good man."

"I'm a goodman," he said.

Rachel and Max came back and sat with us.

"Rachel, Max, this is Paul," Jeff said.

They said, "Hi," and sat down.

"What's your tattoo say?" Max asked and moved over next to me and lifted up my sleeve and traced over my arm with her fingers.

Her perfume was clean and her hair smelled like cold fruit. I didn't mind sitting this close to her.

"I've got a tattoo," she said.

"Yeah?"

She stood up and lifted up the side of her shirt and pulled down her pants on one side below her hip. A long cherry blossom. Thin lines and light color, pink and brown. It wrapped up and over her shoulder, and ran down her thigh the other way.

"That's really good work," I said.

She leaned over and bit my ear, and then stood up.

"Let's all go get high," she said.

Rachel was sitting on Jeff's lap, playing with his hair. "Ok," she said and hopped off him.

The girls walked ahead of us.

I looked at Jeff. "This was unexpected."

"It doesn't hurt when you've got the number one song on the local indie station," he said and smiled.

"What?"

"Rachel showed me earlier. They went home and looked us up."

"That's great, man. Let's go tell Laney."

We walked out onto the terrace and saw Laney being led back into the house by Layne.

"Ah, we'll tell her later," Jeff said and slapped me on the back.

Rachel had good pot. We hadn't smoked that quality since a few weeks back when we bought a couple of dime bags off some kids in a park outside of a coffee shop in Colorado Springs. I'm still unsure if that was wrong. Selling drugs to kids—that's wrong, I get that—but, buying from them? Fuck it. It was good stuff and Rachel's was too.

The specifics of the rest of the night were hazy. We smoked. We drank. We stared at the desert. Some instruments eventually showed up. People jammed a bit. I had a vague impression of Jeff and I trying to play the entire score to *The Wizard of Oz*. At some point, Max led me away after Jeff and Rachel disappeared. She had another tattoo. It was a lotus flower in full bloom.

The next morning I heard feet walking around my head, stepping on plastic cups and pushing aside bottles. I opened my eyes. Sunlight. Burning. I shut them tight.

"Wake up," a voice said.

I put my hands over my eyes. Max was next to me on the floor. I saw feet hanging over the edge of a bed. A brown bandage on the right foot. Something stunk. Bad.

"Wake up." It was Gooch.

I squinted at him, my hands trying to block out the light.

"When'd you get here?" I said.

"A few minutes ago," he said and started rocking Jeff, waking him up.

Jeff moaned.

"Where's Laney?" Gooch asked.

I sat up and looked for my shirt. "Fuck if I know."

Gooch left. Jeff sat up. "What the fuck?"

"Yeah, man. Not cool," I said.

We shuffled down the hall. We heard Gooch's voice in a room.

Then we heard Laney. "Gooch!"

We went in the room. She was sitting up holding a sheet against her body. Her hair hung on her shoulders. Layne rolled over. Still asleep.

"We have to go," Gooch said.

"What time is it?" Laney said.

"7:30."

"Fucking load-in isn't for twelve hours. San Diego is five hours away," she said.

"Yeah, but our radio appearance is at 1."

She let out a deep breath and closed her eyes. She shook her head. "Fuck."

CHAPTER 6

Gooch drove. He drove fast. Laney and Jeff were curled up in the back seat under blankets and I sat in the front with sunglasses on and tried to sleep. Gooch didn't say anything to us after we hobbled out to the van, the sun already setting the desert on fire.

Dunk was wedged in between the driver and passenger's seats. He sat there on his little rock. My head pounded. I managed to doze off, but kept waking up when we braked or turned. When I was a kid I used to stay at my grandparents' house when my mom went out. My grandfather watched westerns and I'd fall asleep on the reclining chair and wake up to gunshots. A tire blew out on a semi in front of us and we all jumped up. I was disoriented. Gooch switched lanes to get around the truck, its hazards on, slowing down.

"Relax," he said. He seemed angry, but I knew him well enough to know he was getting joy out of this. Not saying anything was his way of saying, "I told you so." We fucked up. We knew this. He knew this. He fucking knew it last night and was waiting for this chance to be a dick. He thought of this as an opportunity to prove his point. If it was Jeff or Laney or me, yeah we'd be pissed too, but we'd also shrug it off as part of the gig. We all got each other's back. At least that's the way I thought, and assumed he did too, but what did I know about how anyone else thought anymore. My head hurt.

I looked out the window. Desert. Fucking desert for miles.

We stopped for gas in El Centro. There was a Motel 6 as we pulled off. And a McDonald's. Before I joined Qualia I almost forgot how much everything was the same. It doesn't matter where you are in America. It's all the same from the highways. The same stores and restaurants. Once in awhile you'll get a clever name for a gas station somewhere, but when it comes down to it, they all have the same shit. The same soda and candy and magazines.

A couple of old-timers I was on a gig with a few years ago were telling me about how the roadside, before the major new interstates and turnpikes were built, used to be full of all sorts of odd shops and themed gas stations. Things were gaudy and designed to get your attention—you had to stop. Then there was an explosion of muffler men in the 60s, giant fiberglass cowboys and dinosaurs. They said it's all bullshit now, a shadow of what it used to be, though some of the old stuff is still around. I'm not sure how much is truth and how much is nostalgia, but driving past a giant rusted-out cowboy boot next to an abandoned shack, and seeing the traditions and customs of a native culture dwindled down to a souvenir shop in Arizona, tells its own story. It's fucking depressing.

We stopped. Gooch ran into a Mexican restaurant and brought back burritos and bottles of water for everyone.

"Wake up," he said. "You have to eat."

"Thanks," I mumbled.

We unwrapped the burritos and ate them. I thought I was going to throw up and leaned back in the chair and took slow deep breaths to calm myself. I looked out the window. The town was gone. More desert. I wondered why anyone would live out here. I closed my eyes and when I woke up again we were pulling into a parking lot behind the radio station. It was 12:30.

Gooch lied for us to the DJ. Told her that the GPS tried taking us to Tijuana. We had to set up and be mic'd and ready to go in 20 minutes.

There's really only one thing to know about loading gear and setting up—it sucks. With a hangover and little sleep, it really fucking sucks. We set up quick, but fucked up somewhere and the engineer had to come in to make sure the cords that should be in the output jacks weren't in the input or aux jacks.

It's been said that there's only two types of people that wear sunglasses inside: rock stars and assholes. At least we looked the part.

The DJ seemed like a nice lady but was constantly flipping through papers and looking at screens on her computer. She hit a button every once in a while, and never made eye contact with us. Or anyone. We were going to play a stripped-down set. Gooch on percussion, Laney on acoustic. The studio was small and they put us all in a corner to give our amps space. They didn't want the sounds to bleed into the other mics. Too much bass in the guitar mic would fuck up the guitar sound, and vice versa.

Laney sat across from me, her headphones holding back her hair, pressing against the side of her sunglasses. She took her glasses off and stared into space, eyes puffy and red. There was a tangle of cords separating us. Had we gotten here earlier things would have been set up much smoother, but as it was we were hooked up and ready to go, even if it wasn't pretty.

I clipped my sunglasses into the V of my shirt. The DJ came on in our ears.

"We're on in two minutes," she said. "I'm going to lead in with 'Black Swan' and then open up with some questions. Where you're from, how long you're on tour, that kind of thing. Cool? One more thing, the control boards in front of you, the one that says 'level' controls the volume of what you'll hear in your headphones. The engineer will set you up. If you need more or less of anything, let him know. We'll have about a minute to get the levels right."

The engineer came on in our ears.

"Drums."

Gooch pounded on his drums. One at a time.

"Guitar." Laney strummed.

"Bass." I played a lazy and slow bar of "If I Only Had a Brain" before he called for Jeff.

"Can I have some reverb?" Jeff asked.

No answer.

Show time.

"KWBJ The Badger, San Diego's non-stop rock station. I'm Andrea and you just heard 'Black Swan' by Qualia. They're live in studio and you can see them tonight at The Badger's Next Big Thing, Tuesdays at Nick's on 39. Be sure to catch them now before they hook up with Spectacular Death Extras. So guys, thanks for coming in. Why don't you introduce yourselves and tell us where you're from?"

Jeff went first.

"Thanks, Andrea. We're from Philadelphia. I'm Jeff and I sing." His voice was gravel.

"I'm Laney, and I pluck strings."

"I'm Gooch, and I hit things."

"I'm Paul, and I don't like to rhyme."

"Well, it seems someone is a little cranky today. But, that's to be expected, you guys have been on the road for, what, nine weeks now?" Andrea said.

"Yeah," Jeff said, "We started out with an eight-week run as support for Lunchbox and Thermos and been on our own since. We'll be doing a few gigs with Spectacular Death Extras in a couple of days starting in San Francisco."

"Are you excited? They have really blown up the past few weeks."

"Oh, yeah. We're looking forward to that."

"Any stories from the road you'd like to share?"

"Is the FCC listening?" Jeff said and laughed.

"Always," said Andrea and laughed too. "Let's talk about your name. What's it mean?"

"Uh," Jeff said, "I think it's an old German name. From Gottfried or something like that."

"I think she means our band name, Jeff," Laney said.

"Oh," he said. "Well, ironically enough, that's also an old German name from Gottfried."

"Your name, Qualia, is that right? How do you pronounce it?" Andrea said.

"It's like koala bear and onomatopoeia," Jeff said.

"Minus the bear," said Laney.

"And most of onomatopoeia," I said.

"Minus the bear, that's a good band name," Jeff said.

"Oh, I like that," Laney said. "We are now Minus the Bear."

"Well, that's certainly easier to pronounce, and unfortunately, already a band," Andrea said.

"Damn," Jeff said, "Always a bridesmaid."

"So, for those of us with your EP, and going to your show tonight, how do we say your name?"

"Kwahl-ee-ah," Jeff sounded out.

"What does that mean?" she asked.

"It basically means how we all perceive the same things differently. For example, if we all had headaches, how is Paul's experience with the same headache different from mine or Laney's?"

"I think we do all have headaches now," Andrea said. "Well, now that's settled, these guys are going to play a song or two and I promise to do my best to get some dirt from the road out of them."

Andrea cut to a station ID.

"Is there any way to get some tea before we play?" Jeff asked.

"You're on in ten seconds," she said.

When we went live again we played an acoustic version of "Maybe." Jeff sang down a register and it worked well with the ambience. We didn't sound great, but we were tight given the circumstances.

We talked to Andrea a little about the difference between the east coast and the west coast. We talked about Philadelphia. And about cheesesteaks and *Rocky*. That's default Philadelphia conversation. Fuck being the birthplace of the nation—it's all cheesesteaks and *Rocky*. We're all experts on those things because we're from the city. Fact is Laney's never seen *Rocky*, and I don't think any of us except Gooch had eaten a cheesesteak in the past decade. Jeff told Andrea that Laney and he were vegetarians.

"Do you ever cheat on the road?" Andrea said.

"We eat fish sometimes," said Jeff.

"A pescatarian, then."

"That sounds really pretentious," Laney laughed.

"I'll eat meat once in a while. But I have a rule," Jeff said. "I'll eat it only if it would eat me."

"What?" said Andrea.

"I would have lion meat. Or rattlesnake, or bear."

"What about a dog? Like, what if you were dead and it started eating you?" Laney asked.

"It needs to want to eat me when I'm alive, not because it's starving," Jeff said.

"This is very complex stuff guys," Andrea said. "We've got time for one more. Thanks so much for coming in. Make sure to catch them tonight at Nick's. You can buy their EP online or tonight at the show. If you decide to try and eat Jeff, you've been warned. Here's Qualia with a live version of 'Half Full.' "

We left the radio station. We had over five hours before load-in that night. Gooch helped me lift the heavy gear into the back of the van as I arranged everything.

"Thanks for getting us," I said.

"One of us has to take this seriously," he said. He went to ask Laney where we were staying. I had the feeling it was going to be a long day.

We found a motel and crashed hard for a few hours. When we woke up we all felt a bit better and went out for some coffee on the way to the venue. The other bands were there. Pre-sales were good. The promoter said he heard us on the radio earlier and slipped us an extra round of drink tickets. People talked to us and asked if they could buy our EP and t-shirts, so we set up the merch and arranged things with the promoter to have someone from the venue man the table before and while we played. At local gigs or for small, quick tours, a band usually has one of their girlfriends or friends keep an eye on things. We'd have to do with paying a barback $20 and whatever he decided to skim off the top, which might be nothing—he seemed eager to not hump bottles and dirty glasses all over the place for a couple of hours.

I decided to take it easy and drive tonight and tomorrow. To try and ease the tension with Gooch. Laney had the same idea. Jeff was a few beers in before we hit the stage. I assumed he was going to chill tonight too, but he hit me up for my drink tickets before we went on. He seemed ok. There's a level of functionality that usually plateaus for guys who can handle their shit—before the steep drop. He seemed to be resting on that edge for now.

"Hair of the dog," he said and raised his glass.

"You're insane," I said.

"I'm fine."

"We're on in ten minutes."

"Last one. I promise."

"All right. I'll see you up there."

I went to tune up. Gooch was talking with the sound guy and Laney. We hopped on stage to run a line check.

"Where's your boy?" Gooch said.

I looked around. I couldn't find Jeff.

"Laney," I said across the stage, "have you seen Jeff?"

She looked up from her pedals and out into the bar. "Weren't you just with him?" she said.

"I was," I said. I went to test the mic and asked for some reverb.

Gooch stood up and looked out into the crowd.

"He's at the back bar," Gooch said. "What the fuck? We're on. Now."

The sound guy came on in the monitors. "All set?" he said.

"Fuck this," said Gooch and he started pounding out the drum intro to one of our songs. The lights dimmed and the audience filled in and cheered. I looked at Laney. Gooch kept playing, harder and harder. The audience started a rhythmic clap. A spotlight shot into the crowd. Jeff was working his way towards us.

He jumped on the stage and stared at Gooch and started bouncing in place to the rhythm of the song, his back to the audience. When the beat came back around he turned and grabbed the mic and let out a scream. Laney and I let a chord ring out as Gooch played a drum fill that brought us into the verse.

We played fast and loud. Jeff bounced around the stage. He stretched his vocals and sang up a register on some choruses, and on other songs he ground out the syllables and melodies like a cigarette under his foot. Someone from the crowd handed him their beer and he took it and swallowed it. The audience roared. We were sweating like madmen up there. Jeff took his shirt off and thrashed around the stage even more. For our final song his voice sounded like a bow rake dragged across concrete. He thanked the audience and jumped off the stage and went back to the bar, people putting their hands out for high-fives and slapping him on the back.

Laney, Gooch, and I went to the merch table and sold a ton of shit. People wanted us to sign our EP for them, and a crowd formed around Jeff. He talked, and shook hands, and signed their CDs and t-shirts. The house lights turned on and people started to leave. Laney packed up the merch and got our cut from the promoter while Gooch and I loaded up the van.

"So," I said, "what's this year of celibacy thing I hear?"

"What?" Gooch said.

"Laney told me you were giving up sex for a year."

He didn't respond.

"All right, all right," I said. "We don't have to talk about it. Just trying to break the ice."

"Do you know how much airfare is back to Philly?" he said.

"No."

"Well, I do. Another night like that and I'm fucking out of here."

"What, a night of a great show and a packed-out house?"

"You know what I mean."

I sat down on an amp.

"Gooch," I said, "we fucked up. You saved us. Thank you, and sorry. We're in this together, man."

"Together? Look at him, he was drunk on stage and sounded like shit."

"It wasn't that bad."

Gooch stopped wrapping cords and looked at me.

"Ok," I said, "he didn't sound great, but it worked. Given the circumstances."

"The circumstances he created by drinking too much. I thought you and Laney would have done a better job keeping an eye on him."

"We're adults, Gooch. I'm not babysitting anyone."

"Hey guys," Laney said, walking over to us, wheeling the merch crate.

"We have to go to the bank tomorrow," she said, and waved a thick brown envelope in the air.

"Ooh, how much did we make?" I asked.

"A lot."

"More than last night?"

She smiled and nodded her head up and down.

"Gooch," she said and tucked the envelope into her backpack. "Thanks."

Gooch looked at her. "For?"

"I fucked up last night. I forgot to put the radio interview in my phone calendar. I'll double check the rest of the calendar tomorrow."

I could see Gooch deflate a little.

"It's ok," he mumbled.

"No. It's not, it was my fault," she said. "I should have been on the ball. But that boy from Pilkington was so cute." She smiled.

"Were his arms rock hard?" I asked.

"Shut up," Gooch said. I could see a hint of a smile.

"For the record," he said, "I'm only giving up one-night stands."

"Thank god," I said. "I thought all this bed sharing wasn't going to lead anywhere."

He lifted his hardware bag. "Let's get this shit packed away."

"That's what he said?" Laney said.

Gooch snorted and went to the van.

"You're a savior," I said to Laney.

"Just trying to clean up my mess," she said.

I helped Gooch pack our gear. Told him we'd be back out in a few minutes and left him playing with Dunk. Laney was at the bar. Jeff was not.

"Where's Jeff?" I asked.

"One of the bartenders said he went outside with the manager," she said.

"Which one was the manager?"

"She had a ponytail and a black and pink shirt, I think."

"The one with fake boobs and too much make-up?"

"Sure," she said, "if that's how you remember her."

"What's up? Is something wrong?"

"No, I'm just cranky."

"Should I have described her as the cute one like the boy from Pilkington," I said before I could stop myself.

She didn't say anything.

"That was stupid," I said. "I guess I'm cranky too. It's bad enough Gooch is on our asses and keeps it bottled up. If you have something to say, just say it."

She shook her head. "Forget it. I'm just tired," she said.

I looked at her. I looked at her lips.

The staff was stacking chairs on tables and sweeping the floor. It was late. I've been on this other side of the night for most of my adult life. Things beat at a different pulse. Whether it's the booze or drugs, or being awake and alive when most of the world is asleep, there's a feeling that emerges—anything is possible. I wanted to kiss her.

A door slammed.

Jeff walked in with the manager.

I stood there with Laney and could sense the feeling evaporate.

Jeff walked up to us and had a big grin on his face. His hair was tousled and he smelled like alcohol, smoke, and perfume.

"Where'd you go, sailor?" I said.

"Oh, nowhere. Just outside to have a cigarette with Missy," he said.

"By the dumpsters?"

"Well, yeah. The dumpsters are out there. I didn't smoke *in* the dumpsters."

"Let's get you to a shower," Laney said.

"Ok," he said. He went to the bar and talked to Missy and she pulled a six-pack out of the cooler and gave it to him. She smiled at him and walked around the bar and gave him a hug goodbye.

"Let's go," Laney said.

Gooch was in the driver's seat when we went outside.

"Want me to drive?" I said.

"Nah," he said, "I like driving. It keeps me awake."

Jeff sat in the backseat. He opened a bottle and started drinking.

Gooch turned around and looked at him.

"Aren't there open container laws in California?" he said.

Jeff didn't say anything and took a long pull off the bottle.

Gooch shook his head. "What's the address, Laney?"

She pulled out her phone and handed it up front to Gooch. He punched in the address to the nearest Motel 6. It was twenty minutes away. Gooch made it there in twelve.

Jeff finished off the six-pack on the balcony. Gooch fed Dunk and got ready for bed. When Jeff came in, he kicked his shoes off. Laney and I looked over at him and at his foot.

"Dude, what the fuck?" I said.

"When's the last time you changed that bandage?" Laney said. The bandage was rust colored.

"Uh," he said, "when did you put it on?"

"Brother, I think your foot is rotting," I said.

He sat down in a chair and pulled the bandage off. It was like taking the lid off a hot trash can full of decomposing root vegetables and shit. We covered our noses and turned our heads.

His wound was green and pus filled, and we made him run his foot under the shower. Laney went out to the van and got the first aid supplies. We told Jeff to sit on the balcony to let his foot air out.

Gooch was in bed with his eyes closed. We were all fortunate enough to be heavy sleepers. When it was time for bed, it was time for bed. Playing, and all that comes with it—the setting up, the meet and greet, the driving—it's fucking exhausting, and after last night, I was ready for a long sleep.

I sat down on my side of the bed.

Laney was in the bathroom. I could hear water running from the sink. I looked at the carpet and the sheets—at the curtains and lamps and artwork on the walls.

The valve on the faucet turned off.

Silence.

I took a deep breath and closed my eyes and listened. I exhaled slowly and started drifting.

A door handle turning.

Hinges.

"Oh my god," Laney said.

I opened my eyes.

"What?" I said.

She went to Jeff's shoes. "I'm throwing these out."

"Thank you," said Gooch.

I turned to him and he was still laying there, straight, eyes closed.

Laney went outside and I could hear her talking to Jeff.

She came back in and got into bed.

"Is he staying out there?" I asked.

"Yeah," she said. "He wouldn't wake up."

"Ok."

I went to the bathroom and brushed my teeth. I laid in bed next to Gooch and shut the light off. Laney was already asleep and Gooch was breathing slow and even. I closed my eyes.

I woke up in the middle of the night. Jeff was standing next to me in between the two beds. He was taking his dick out and standing over the night table. It was dark in the room. Light from the motel sign and parking lot glowed through the open balcony door.

"Dude, what are you doing?" I whispered.

A small arc of piss hit the floor.

I punched him in the leg. "Jeff," I said.

He stopped.

He opened his eyes and stumbled away to the bathroom.

Just before dawn, he shook me awake, sitting across from me. Whispering.

"Did I wake you up last night?" he said.

"You woke me up now," I said.

"Sorry."

"You were going to piss all over the floor."

He looked at the floor and rubbed it with his hand.

"It's dry."

"Close call."

"Thanks." He put his head in his hands. "I don't feel very well."

"Go drink some water and go back to sleep. We play the Whisky tonight."

"I am the Lizard King," he said and stood up. "I can do anything."

I went back to sleep.

I found Jeff in the bathtub a couple of hours later.

CHAPTER 7

He was breathing. I called his name and he moaned.

"Dude, get up. I have to pee."

He didn't open his eyes. "Just go."

"You all right?" I said.

"My chest is thumping. The room is spinning."

I poured a glass of water and held it to his mouth. "Down the hatch, buddy."

I woke Laney and we managed to get him to bed. He was weak and we had to support him.

Gooch sat up. "What's wrong with him?"

"Hangover," I said.

"Looking like that?" Gooch said. "That's a bad hangover."

We got cleaned up and Gooch went out to get us coffee and take Dunk for a walk.

I sat down next to Jeff. "Feeling better bud? We're getting on the road soon."

"No," he groaned.

There was a knock on our door. It was Gooch standing there with his arms full.

"Take this," he said.

He had a small red spot on his forehead.

I took the tray of coffee and bag of water bottles. He rubbed his head with his free hand. "Man, that hurt," he said.

"What happened?" I asked.

"I knocked on the door with my head and hit the peephole."

I laughed. "Why'd you do that? You could have knocked with your foot."

"I wanted to be like Dunk." He looked at Jeff. "Is he all right?"

"I don't know."

"I got him some water with vitamins in it. It's supposed to revive you. We'll stop for food when we get gas."

We got Jeff out to the car. He seemed better after he ate and we made him drink two bottles of orange juice. We were almost to LA when he started complaining about everything spinning again and his chest hurting.

"I think I'm going to throw up," he said.

We pulled over and helped him out of the van. He kneeled down and put his head between his knees.

"Do you think we should take him to a hospital?" Laney said.

"Do you think it's alcohol poisoning?" Gooch asked.

"It doesn't seem like it," I said. "A girl I knew had that and she looked blue and wouldn't wake up."

"Well, whatever it is, it isn't good," Gooch said. "We've got a show in six hours."

Laney went and put her hand against Jeff's forehead. "Seems a little warm," she said. Jeff didn't say anything. He stood up slowly and crawled into the back seat to lie down. Laney looked up where the nearest hospital was.

She punched the address in the GPS and we were there in a half hour.

He was admitted to the emergency room. We described his symptoms and the drinking and drugs he'd done the past couple of days. Laney told the doctor about his foot. We stayed in the waiting room for two hours before a nurse came out to tell us what was going on.

"We ran some tests on him," she said. "He is severely dehydrated and his foot was starting to get infected. We're giving him IV fluids and some antibiotics."

"Can we go see him?" Laney asked.

We were led back to his bed. He was in a gown and he had an IV in his arm.

"Should I wear this on stage tonight?" he said and lifted the gown a little.

"Are you even ok for tonight?" Laney asked.

"Doc said I just need to take it easy today and I'll be fine," he said. "I already feel way better." He made a fist with his free arm and raised it. "Goddamn, do I feel better."

"Well, you look better, that's for sure," I said.

Gooch was leaning against the wall, behind us.

"Gooch," Jeff said, "I've been thinking." Gooch looked up at him. "I was pissed at you last night. I thought about yelling at you, but I think starting the set that way actually worked out. Good job."

"Yeah," Gooch said. "We'll sort it out later."

Gooch said he was going to check on Dunk and left the room.

"Dude," Laney said, "Are you trying to piss him off?"

"Fuck that guy, Laney," Jeff said. "We're lucky the crowd ate it up. That was not cool starting the set without me. I'm the goddamn front man."

"Maybe you should have been on stage then."

"*Et tu,* Laney? *Et tu?*" Jeff said. He looked at me.

"Hey man, I'm just glad you're feeling better," I said.

"But you agree with them," he said.

"Kind of, yeah. I don't think Gooch should have taken it upon himself to start the set, but it was time for us to go on and you weren't there," I said.

"I was on a phone call," he said.

"You were at the bar drinking," Laney said.

"And then I went outside to take the phone call and came back in when I knew we were on. You know what, forget it," he said and waved his hand. "Come back and get me in an hour. They're giving me another bag and want me to rest. I'd like to be alone."

"All right," Laney said. "Let's go," she said to me.

"Later," I said.

We walked down the hall towards the exit.

"I can't fucking believe him," Laney said. "He was fucking dying and now he's acting like that."

"Maybe he just needs some rest," I offered.

"Quit sticking up for him, Paul."

"I'm not sticking up for him."

"Let's just find a motel. I don't want to drive far tonight."

We went to the van and found a cheap motel off of Santa Monica Boulevard, not far from the gig. We had a light day tomorrow—just a small in-store performance at a record shop in San Luis Obispo and then on to San Francisco the day after that. I wanted to enjoy the strip. Walk around and soak it in. We had a couple of hours before load-in and I told Laney I'd meet her and Gooch back at the motel.

Growing up, I'd always read stories of West Hollywood and rock and roll in magazines and band biographies. I walked past some of the notorious motels. I found the Alta Cienega where Jim Morrison lived. The lesbian strip club across the street was still open. Jim used to go there when he wasn't at The Phone Booth. Just down the road should have been the Tropicana, where anything went. Everyone stayed there. Elvis Costello, Nick Lowe, Zeppelin, Janis, Cash, Tom Waits. Fuck, it was rock history. The Beach Boys, Marianne Faithfull, the Red Hot Chili Peppers, Guns N' Roses, Lou Reed, the New York Dolls, Nico, the Runaways, the Ramones. Goddamn. I was getting excited and thinking about seeing if there was a vacancy—to sleep inside the same walls that once held damn near every important rock star of the twentieth century. At the very least, I wanted to grab something to eat at Duke's Coffee Shop underneath the Tropicana. When I got to where the motel should have been it wasn't there. There was a newish looking Ramada Inn. And a fucking Starbucks.

I walked up to Sunset Boulevard and found the Whisky. It wasn't open yet, but it was good to see the building. Next door was Duke's Coffee Shop. They must have relocated when the Tropicana was torn down. I ran my hands along the outside of the Whisky and touched the doors. I walked down the street. There was the Viper Room. The only thing I knew about it was that Johnny Depp owned it once and River Phoenix died of a drug overdose right out front. It was sunny and hot out. There was no one on the sidewalk. The door to the liquor store next to the Viper Room opened, and a guy wearing sunglasses, a leather jacket on top of a tank top, and a small afro walked out carrying a brown paper bag. He crossed the street, walking towards me. When he got closer he lifted his sunglasses and squinted at me.

"Yo, Paul. Is that you, motherfucker?" he said and smiled.

"Drix?" I said, taken aback.

"What the fuck, man?" he said. We shook hands and pulled each other in for a hug, slapping each other hard on the back. Drix was my best friend in high school even though he was a grade below me and a year younger. We called him Drix because he looked like Jimi Hendrix, and did a lot of drugs. Even though he was a drummer, the name stuck.

"What are you doing out here?" he said.

"On tour. We're playing the Whisky tonight," I said.

"Dude, I'm fucking there."

Drix and I lost touch a few years ago after he moved out of Philly. We used to jam in different bands and ditch class and smoke weed in the woods when I brought an acoustic guitar in. I remember the day I decided to do music for my life. It was after school, fall of my senior year, and I was hanging with Drix. We were outside smoking cigarettes, waiting for the bus and talking about music.

"Yo," he said. "Let's be rock stars."

"Ok," I said. It was simple to say and felt right. We booked the rehearsal studio and called some of our buddies. I think we ended up getting high and playing "Hey Joe" for two hours.

We went into Duke's. I ordered a sandwich and a coffee. He ordered a coffee and took a bottle of Jameson out of the brown paper bag and poured it in his cup. He dumped a few ounces in my cup too. He offered me a pill. I declined. He swallowed two.

"Damn, man. It's good to see you. I forgot you lived out here," I said.

"It's cool," he said. "I haven't really been in touch with cats back home too much. Working my ass off the past couple of years, hustling out here."

"When was the last time you were in Philly?"

"I passed through a few times for a gig with different bands, but mostly been doing studio work."

"Yeah? You got something lined up now?"

"I just got this gig with these square motherfuckers. All straight-edge and shit. No drinking. Drugs. Man, I don't think they're even going to let girls backstage. They fired their last drummer, and I did some session work with that band that had a hit in the spring with the banjos. The Stewford Brothers or some shit. Yo, dig this, those motherfuckers aren't even brothers. Can you believe that?"

I laughed and shook my head. He was the same dude as he always was.

"Anyway, I made bank. Made sure to get some royalties. Those cats were all like, 'the bridge should go big,' and I was all like, 'the whole song is big, we gotta bring that shit down so when you come back in with the chorus everyone freaks the fuck out.' Fucking amateurs. I got a producing credit on that track. I knew it was gonna be a hit."

"Is that the one that goes 'bang, bang' and has claps and then stops in the chorus?"

"Yeah. The claps were my idea."

"Ah, man. Fuck you then," I said. "That song was annoying. It was stuck in my head for weeks."

Drix laughed. "Sorry, homie." He swallowed his coffee and raised his cup for the waitress to give him a refill. When she left, he poured another few ounces of Jameson into his cup.

"So, yeah, man. This dude calls me up last week," Drix said, talking and waving his hands. "He's friends with that other band's manager and he's all like, 'this band is getting huge and they just fired their drummer and they're going on tour. Are you available?' So I was like, 'depends on how much it pays and for how long.' He tells me it pays like six hundy a night for a week, plus an upfront bonus for rehearsal, and I might be able to join the band under a new contract if the tour goes well. He says they're gonna be huge again, and they just got signed like two weeks ago to a major, and the label is throwing dough at them. Telling them to finish this tour and then regroup to record a full length in the label's studio and they might get Rick motherfucking Rubin. Then it's back on the road again. Talking about opening up for U2 or some shit."

"That's insane, man," I say. "How do you feel about it?"

"Well, I said, 'yes,' so I guess I feel ok with it. But that's just the beginning of it. I go up to San Francisco to start rehearsals and look over the contract for the tour and I walk in and I'm smoking a cigarette and this dude runs up to me all frantic like telling me to put it out. Dig this, man, he's their new manager, the dude that called me, and he's all like 'didn't you read the email I sent you,' and I'm all like, 'fuck no,' I mean when would I have? I just got off the train and went right to the studio. So he tells me about the band being all straight-edge, even though they don't promote the image for business reasons, and that 'there is to be no drugs, drinking, or smoking.' He said that like Mr. Larkin. Remember that cat?"

"Yeah, he rode my ass all the way until graduation," I said.

"This dude actually said, 'there is to be,' all proper and shit. So he brings over the contract, and I'm all like, 'well, fuck, I'm here and I don't want to turn down the dough.' I figure I'll try it out and see how it goes. It might be good to sober up for a week. So I learned the songs and they're pretty cool dudes, but like after practice they wanted to hang out and watch *How I Met Your Mother* reruns and eat sodium-free saltines and drink lemonade and shit. Man, I had to get out of there, so I came back down here where I knew I wouldn't run into any of them and fucking get it out of my system before we hit the road."

"Goddamn. That's wild brother," I said. "Well, congratulations." I raised my cup to him. We clinked mugs and had a drink.

I added, "We'll be heading up to San Fran in a couple of days too. Maybe we could catch your set. What's the name of the band?"

"Far out man. Yeah. They're called Spectacular Death Extras, or some shit."

CHAPTER 8

We walked around the strip past the old haunts of rock royalty. The Roxy. The Troubadour. It seemed sterile now, but I chalked that up to the afternoon. Drix wanted to show me some of the old dives that were still here. I called Laney and told her that I ran into an old friend. To let me know when they were leaving and I'd meet them at the venue.

We went to an old bar called Little Pete's. It was off the strip behind a used car lot. It was five in the afternoon and the place was half full.

Drix walked in and sat down next to a guy with long gray hair pulled back in a ponytail. He was smoking a cigarette and drinking a beer.

"Yo, Little Pete," Drix said. "This is my friend and new tour mate, Paul."

Little Pete turned to me, cigarette hanging from his mouth, and put his hand out. "Pleasure to meet you," he said.

"Paul and I go way back, Little Pete. We're like brothers and shit," Drix said.

We ordered a couple of beers and Little Pete was telling us stories about the strip in the 70s and 80s. His wife was bartending and she kept our glasses full. Some shots showed up. Little Pete finished a story about hanging out with Elvis Costello—that he was drunk and practically kidnapped him. Costello wanted a reuben and hounded him until he would take him to get one. That's all he wanted, like he was possessed. Little Pete said Costello let the Russian dressing fall all over the place, never used a napkin once. He got up to use the bathroom and never came back and stuck Little Pete with the bill.

"Two sandwiches and six beers," Little Pete said. "Still owes me."

"Ain't that some shit," Drix said. "Yo, dig this, Little Pete used to roadie for Van Halen right when they got big."

Little Pete said he met them at Gazzarri's and they became friends. He told me stories of sex and drugs and far out shit that seemed made up if not for the fact that everything I've ever read about the famed clubs, motels and hotels said the same things, more or less.

"Mel," he said to his wife. "Hand me the Roth picture."

His wife took down a picture, one of about a dozen taped to the mirror behind the bar, and handed it to him. He slid the picture over to me. He was young and standing arm in arm with a shirtless David Lee Roth and three topless women with enormous breasts.

"That's crazy, man," I said. "What's your old lady think about this picture?"

He laughed loud and pointed to the picture.

"That one there is my old lady," he said.

Laney texted me. I had to be at the Whisky in fifteen minutes. I stood up and was a little drunk. I went to the bathroom and walked past a guy who looked like Lenny Kravitz sitting in a booth with some dude in a suit.

Drix said he'd catch up with me. I told him I'd put him on the guest list. The rest of the guys were at the venue when I got there.

"Man, do I have some news for you guys," I said.

I told them about Drix, and gave them the quick rundown of how he got the gig drumming for Spectacular Death Extras. Laney and Gooch didn't seem too responsive, but Jeff was curious.

"You don't think we all have to be straight-edge, do you?" he said. "We're not in the same bus or anything."

"I don't know, man. We'll feel it out. If they don't want to party with us, then fuck 'em," I said.

"You smell like alcohol," Laney said to me.

"I only had a little. I'll be fine," I said back.

"Well, we can't afford another trip to the hospital."

"I had a couple of drinks with an old friend. No big deal."

Laney wouldn't look at me.

"Let's get this stuff unloaded," she said.

We put our gear backstage. Gooch, Laney, and Jeff went to check out our dressing room and meet the other bands. I went outside to look at the marquee. There was our name up there, the same as it was for Otis Redding and Van Morrison. I smiled, thinking I'd be taking the same stage in a few hours. It'd be easier to name who didn't play the Whisky than to think about all the great acts that had played here. I went to our dressing room to find the guys. It was a small room painted black like the rest of the place. I was half expecting to find autographs all over the walls, but nothing. All black.

Gooch was warming up on a practice pad and Laney was running scales on her guitar. Jeff was sitting by himself reading a magazine.

"How you feeling?" I asked him.

"Like a million bucks," he said.

"More like 3,147 bucks," said Laney.

"What?" I said.

"That's how much the emergency room cost," she said.

"Fuck, man. Don't you have insurance?" I said to Jeff.

"Nope," he said without looking up.

I knew we raked in the dough the past two nights—but that was a big hit. Laney said we had just about a grand left and it was spoken for already in motels and gas over the next two weeks. We were just starting to pull ahead and then this happened. She said she wasn't sure if we'd have enough money to pay for the merch we ordered on her credit card. We were getting a shipment of t-shirts and CDs in Sacramento to stock up for playing with Spectacular Death Extras.

"We'll pay it off when we get back," Jeff said.

"We shouldn't have to," she said.

"I said I was sorry, Laney."

She didn't say anything.

The other bands were in their dressing rooms and Gooch and I went around to meet them and see about sharing gear onstage. Space Shovel was going on right before us and didn't want to use any of the other bands' gear or let us use any of theirs. We'd all like to play through our own rigs whenever possible, but logistically, it just makes sense to share a drum kit or bass amp. Christ, we even offered to set ours up for them to use.

A guy with a shaved head and full beard said, "We ain't sharing gear, bro," and closed the door.

"Let it go," Gooch said and headed down the hall.

"All right," I said, "he didn't have to be a dick about it."

"Yeah, but we need a good set tonight to make some of that money back. Let's just focus on that."

"Why was the bill so much?"

"IV bags, bed, antibiotics. A bunch of other shit."

"They didn't offer a cash discount?"

"That was the cash discount."

"Fuck," I said.

We found Jeff sitting at the bar with a glass of water. Gooch said he'd meet us upstairs in our dressing room. I looked down at Jeff's feet. He was wearing sandals.

"You're not wearing those on stage, are you?" I said.

"I don't have any other shoes," he said.

"Sandals and jeans," I said, and shook my head. "It won't be long before you start covering Dave Matthews Band and Oasis at college bars."

"Kill me first," he said and laughed.

The crowd was starting to come in.

"Ahhh, I want a drink," Jeff said.

"Dude, Laney and Gooch would flip out," I said.

"Yeah, yeah, yeah."

"Besides, you're on antibiotics."

"That's just a myth."

"What, that you're on them? I don't remember that one."

"It's true. Zeus was trying to bang some broad, so he told his wife she couldn't drink while she was on antibiotics. Off to the bar he went."

"Why was she was on antibiotics?"

"Fuck if I know. Man, did she get pissed about it later on."

"Well, I think there's a reason, beyond Zeus, you're not supposed to drink while on them."

"I know, I know," he sighed. "I don't want to wait until after the show to smoke. Shit makes me too paranoid on stage."

"You holding?"

He nodded his head and smiled.

"Rachel set us up the other night," he said.

"Nice." I looked around this room. "What do you think?"

"It's smaller than I expected. I might not have to ask the audience to move up."

"You're not a little pumped to share the same stage as a shit ton of rock legends?"

"A little," he said, "but it's not like they're here. I'm sure the stage has been redone."

"Killjoy," I said and eyed up the stage and balcony. This room made so many bands. They worked their asses off, but fuck, a lot of it happened right here.

"What is up, motherfucker?" a voice said as a fist punched me in the arm.

I turned around. Drix's pupils were dilated. He sniffed.

We hugged again and I introduced him to Jeff.

"Yo, you got a great voice, man," Drix said. "I made Little Pete play that shit through the speakers. We were all groovin' in there, man."

"Thanks," Jeff said.

"Right on," Drix said, looking around the room.

The bartender came over to us and Drix shook his hand.

"Yo, Nikita. This is my boy Paul and his singer Jeff. They're playing tonight. Set us up with three shots?"

"You got it," Nikita said. "Just a heads up, Space Shovel is playing again tonight."

"Again? Those motherfuckers were just here like two weeks ago."

"They bring a crowd," the bartender said and shrugged his shoulders. He poured three shots. "They're on me," he said and moved away to another customer.

"That's my boy, Nikita," Drix said to us. "He moved here from Russia. His dad was a male ballet dancer or some shit."

"A ballerino?" Jeff asked.

"I don't think that's what you call a male ballet dancer," I said.

"Nah, man. They're not ballerinos," Drix said and laughed. "They're called dancers. Look that shit up." He said "dancers" funny. "Cheers motherfuckers," he said and picked up his glass. "Looks like we're tour mates."

We did the shots.

"So much for Zeus," I said to Jeff.

"It's just one to loosen up," he said.

"What about Zeus?" Drix asked.

"Jeff is on antibiotics," I said.

"For my foot," Jeff said.

Drix looked down. "Sandals?" He looked at Jeff, "You're not gonna wear those on stage, are you?"

"I've no choice," Jeff said.

"That's a real shame, brother." Drix moved his jaw around. "But, Paul is right man. You don't want to fuck with antibiotics. People keep fucking with them and there's super-viruses and shit out there now."

Drix dug into his pocket and pulled out a little bag and cupped it in his hand.

"You guys wanna drop? This shit don't fuck with antibiotics and will probably start to kick in right before you go on. It's pretty low grade. Nice and even."

I was feeling good and figured no one had to drive that night. And also, fuck it. We went outside to have a cigarette. We each placed a tab on our tongues and let it dissolve. We finished our cigarettes and went back inside.

We watched the opening acts. Gooch and Laney stayed upstairs. She said she had some business to take care of before we got to San Francisco. Gooch wanted to work out a drum part for a song he was writing. There's an old joke about drummers writing songs—that's how you know it's time for a new drummer. I didn't say it to him given our conversation last night. I went back down to find Jeff and Drix. The acid was kicking in and I felt light and disconnected, but at the same time heavy and in tune.

Space Shovel came on. It took them a half hour to get set up after the other band took all their gear off the stage.

"Can you believe these guys?" I said to Drix. "They didn't want to share gear."

Drix shook his head. "Those dudes are fucking pricks," he said.

"Do you know them?" Jeff asked.

"I was on a bill with them last month with these cats I sit in with from time to time."

"What happened?"

"Their drum kit broke," he said and smiled.

"All by itself?" I asked.

"They were being assholes and their drummer threatened me." Drix shook his head again. "I don't believe in violence, man."

He pulled a stool away from the bar and sat down. "So dig this, we were sharing the bass rig and kit. My bass player uses a fuzz pedal and the dude from Space Shovel was giving him shit saying it's gonna crap out his speakers. My boy told him he wouldn't use it, but did anyway. You could see the other dude getting all pissed down at the bar. Just fucking glaring. About a third of the way through the set, I was jamming man, really fucking grooving, and I broke a stick. It's not like I did that shit on purpose, but I was in the middle of the fucking song, so I played with it until I could pause to ditch it and grab a new one. I was real careful to not stab any of the drum heads, but right after the song, the drummer runs on-stage and starts rubbing the drum heads and was all like, 'what the fuck man? I just put these heads on.' And I'm all like, 'relax, bro, it's all good.' The singer turns around and tells him to get the fuck off the stage, he's ruining our set. So dude is all like, 'you owe me for new heads,' and I'm all, 'whatever bro, they're fine.' Meanwhile, the audience is standing there, and some dude yells, 'get the fuck off the stage,' and the crowd cheers and the bass player starts the next song and I start the song too with the guitar player. Our singer grabs the dude and chucks him into the audience off the stage."

"Where's Patrick Swayze when you need him?" Jeff asked.

"I don't even know, man. Probably at the roadhouse or making pottery or some shit."

"Did you fuck up the drum heads?" I asked.

"Not yet. My singer hopped up on the rim of the kick drum to jump off for the end of our last song. He landed too hard, or the shell was cracked 'cause he bust right through it. And if that shit wasn't bad enough, the bass player dived into the kit like it was fucking Seattle circa '89. When the dust cleared and everyone was getting back up, the drummer and the other members of Space Shovel came on stage and started throwing down and the bouncers came over and broke shit up, but the drummer was coming at me and I'm on the floor after the bass player landed on me, so I picked up the broken stick and pointed it at him. A bouncer grabbed him and he's still looking at me and cursing and calling me names. So, I put the stick through his snare drum. I mean, fuck him. I didn't do anything."

"They still let them play here?" I asked.

"You heard Nikita. They bring a crowd. It's all that matters in this game."

Space Shovel started their set. They were loud. They were fast. I didn't want them to be, but damn, they were good and it seemed like half the audience was here for them—singing along to their songs. Everyone joined in on the chorus to an upbeat techno-ish song called "Date Rake"—"*Thought you liked me, guess you didn't. I should have said, 'No-woh-woh-woh-woh-woh-yeah.'*" Not the classiest song, but it was catchy. The guy with the shaved head was their drummer. He wasn't great, but he kept shit locked. All of a sudden everyone was green and then blue and then back to normal.

"Yo, how's this shit peak?" I asked.

"Just some visuals. You'll feel it in your bones up there. Just relax, man. You're good. Ain't nothing to worry about." His voice trailed and I was on stage tuning my bass.

Laney kept looking at me. Jeff was setting up the lights on the keyboard stands.

"I fucking love these lights," he said. "Good idea, Laney."

"Are you guys high?" she asked.

"Only a little," Jeff said. "Can't fuck with the antibiotics."

I looked at Gooch. He was tuning his drum kit.

"Hi, Gooch," I said. He looked at me. His head looked like a turtle. I laughed. "Which one are you?"

"What?" he said.

"Ah, you know," I said and adjusted the EQ on my amp. "You know," I said again.

We started our set. My body pulsed with the bass drum. I closed my eyes and I saw supernovas. When I opened my eyes, we were still in outer space—the stage lights swirled around the room, blue and red and yellow. Gooch counted off the next song. My hands and fingers fell into place. Jeff and Gooch were ambient, in time—Laney's guitar line floated through me. My bass line was playing a game of cat and mouse with her melody. The next song was fast and I felt it shooting out of my pores, this beautiful thing we were creating. I looked at Jeff. He was wearing clown shoes. I laughed and shook my head.

"Thanks for listening to us," Jeff said. "We're Qualia. We've got a couple more for you."

The audience cheered.

Jeff turned his back to the audience and nodded to Laney and me. We huddled up.

Laney was glowing. Jeff put his arms around us.

"What's up boss?" I asked.

"People are strange," he said.

"Yeah, man. I can dig it."

"Let's stick to the set," Laney said.

"It'll be fine. A cappella."

"I got you," I said. "Let's do it."

"Laney?" Jeff said

"Whatever you want," she said and pulled out of the group.

Jeff went to the mic. The audience was talking. Jeff stood there and closed his eyes. He took a deep breath. The audience quieted down. I walked up to the edge of the stage next to Jeff. The light man turned down the stage lights. Just a single light around me and Jeff. I looked out. I felt like I was on the ledge at the Grand Canyon—wide open. I thought of the monk. Jeff sang. He sang slow and drug the words out. It was a ballad, long and painful and beautiful. I felt alone with him up there and yet attached to everything. I joined in at the chorus, playing up an octave on the bass, creating a chord pad before walking back down the neck and laying the groove. When we were done the audience yelled and cheered.

"Thanks," Jeff said.

We played our last song. I got my hands ready on the keyboard and bass. I looked at Laney and then back down to the keyboard. Gooch led us into the song with a fill. Each beat and note throbbed. Gooch's hi-hat tisked behind me, swinging one-two-three-four-five-six. Laney strummed the acoustic and when the break happened and there was silence, the whole world stopped. Gooch clicked us back in for the outro and my body melted into the sound.

"Killer set, man," Drix said backstage.

Jeff came over. "Thanks for the shoes," he said.

"No worries," Drix said. I looked down and Jeff was wearing a red pair of canvas shoes that were only a little too big on him.

"It's all they had at the gas station. Function over style, brother. Didn't want to see you up there in fucking sandals," Drix said.

"Good man," I said.

"One day," Jeff said. "One day, we'll all be sandalmen."

"Yo, listen," Drix said, "I'm gonna peace out before I run into Space Shovel. I'll meet you up in San Francisco in two days."

"Cool, man," I said. "I'll be in touch."

We shook hands and hugged again.

"Fucking wild," he said and laughed.

It took me a while to pack up. Everything felt substantial. I moved with purpose. Laney went to the merch table with Jeff. Gooch wasn't talking to anybody and broke down his kit. We stored everything backstage in the hall that led to the parking lot behind the venue. On the way out to the floor we ran into the drummer and singer of Space Shovel.

"Good show," I said to them. Figured it wouldn't hurt to be polite.

They were stone. "You guys friends with Drix?" the singer said.

"Yeah," I said.

"Cool," said the singer. "Nice set," he said to Gooch.

They walked away.

"Those guys are fucking weird," I said.

"I don't like them," Gooch said. "What did you and Jeff take?"

"Just some acid. Pretty mellow stuff. Already peaked, but man, your drums were fucking inside me the whole show. Ever play while tripping?"

"No," he said, "I like to be clear up there."

"I can dig it," I said.

We went to the merch table. Laney and Jeff were talking to people and signing CDs and shirts.

"Hey," I said to Laney. "How's it going?"

"Fine," she said. She greeted the next fan.

"Good show tonight," I said.

"Yeah, it was fun." She didn't look at me.

A guy in a t-shirt with wolves on it came up to Jeff. "Fucking right on, man. I loved that song you did by yourself. Is that on your CD?" he said.

Jeff laughed. "Thanks. Yeah, it's a hidden track."

"Where can I find it?"

"It's hidden, man," I said.

"It's not on our EP," Laney said. "They're just fucking with you."

"Aw, damn. That song was, like, trippy or something."

He bought the CD and shook our hands.

"Who doesn't know that song?" Jeff said.

"That dude was high as shit," I said.

Laney looked at us and raised her eyebrows.

Over the next hour the place cleared out.

We didn't sell a ton of stuff, but every little bit helped. Laney went to get our cut of the door from the promoter. We packed up the merch and waited for her to come back before loading up the van and going to the motel. I had started to come down fast the past half hour and was considering swinging by Little Pete's for a nightcap.

Laney came back. "Let's get out of here," she said.

"What's up?" I asked.

"I'm tired and we only made our advance," she said.

"What? Nothing from the door?" Jeff said.

"Apparently, Space Shovel not only brings a crowd, but they pilfer the rest. They promised to put on a free show out in the desert if everybody said they were here for them. At least that's what someone from the opener told me."

"That doesn't even seem possible. Nobody was here for us or the other bands?"

Laney sighed. "The doorman was probably in on it."

"This is horseshit," I said. "Where are those motherfuckers?"

I looked around the room.

I went to the bar and found Nikita. He said he thought he saw Space Shovel leave a while ago. I told him about the scam at the door. He shook his head. Agreed that it was a shitty thing to do, but he had no say in the matter. Laney came over to me and put her hand on my arm.

"Let's just go," Laney said. "We've got a long week ahead of us. We'll make it back."

We went backstage to load up our gear.

Gooch's drums were gone.

CHAPTER 9

Gooch kicked the wall. "What the fuck," he yelled. "What the fucking fuck." We went outside and checked the dumpsters and alley. Nothing. Laney went to talk to the promoter and the bar manager. Nothing. There weren't any cameras backstage. Just over the bar. There was no proof it was Space Shovel.

"I'm calling the fucking cops," Gooch said.

"They're not going to do anything," Jeff said. "It's our word against theirs."

Gooch kicked the wall again. His foot broke through the drywall. "Jeff, they stole my fucking kit. I'm calling the cops."

The cops said they'd send someone around to file a report. It was closing time. Nikita stayed with us. An hour passed. The cops never showed up.

"Listen guys, I'm sorry, but I have to go," Nikita said. "Swing back tomorrow and we'll try to sort you out. Maybe I can call Space Shovel and see if they saw anything."

"We have to be in San Luis Obispo tomorrow," Laney said.

"With what drum kit?" Gooch said.

Nikita told us to call the bar tomorrow and check in. I thanked him and we left the venue.

"We'll play stripped down tomorrow. You still have your shakers," Laney said.

Gooch shook his head. "This is fucked up. I didn't even know those guys." Gooch looked at me.

"We'll replace it in San Francisco. We'll get there early," Laney said.

"Do you know how much that kit cost?"

She frowned. "We'll figure it out."

"I'm sure Drix will let you use his kit for the tour. We should have money for a new one after that."

"It seems like this is his fault," Gooch said. "They asked if we were friends with him, and then the next thing we know my fucking drums are gone."

Jeff looked at me. He didn't say anything. Fuck. Gooch was right. It was Drix's fault—sort of.

"He wasn't even there," I said to Gooch.

"You know what I mean," he said.

"I'll talk to him when we meet up in San Francisco. We'll work it out."

"You can't call him before then?"

I shook my head. "I didn't get his number."

I said I'd try to reach him at Little Pete's tomorrow, but that was the best I could do. I tried to reassure Gooch that everything would be fine. At last, back at the motel, he calmed down enough to accept that his kit was gone and we had to deal with it. I understood his frustration—I'd be pissed too if someone stole my gear. I was just relieved he was coming to terms with it. Mostly because I felt guilty as shit.

Laney worked out with Gooch what songs we would play tomorrow. Despite his anger, he was having a small amount of fun organizing the math of the songs—what he would do for certain parts, what percussion instrument he could use. He got a chance to rewrite the songs. They say music is a great release, that being creative is a good way to vent. Amen to that. It's not like Gooch had cancer or a tumor, but getting ripped off was still a pretty shit thing to have to go through in the middle of the night out on the road, on the other side of the continent.

I went outside to have a cigarette with Jeff.

"So, I guess it wouldn't be the best time to tell them the story Drix told us?" Jeff said.

"No. I think we should keep that to ourselves."

"Agreed."

"I've got some dough saved up. Not a lot, but let me chip in to help get him another kit. It shouldn't be all the band's money. We still have to make it back."

"Let's see where we are in a week," he said and smiled.

"What's funny," I asked.

"Nothing," he said. "I've got a surprise in San Francisco."

"I hate surprises," I said.

"You'll like this one."

Jeff took out a roach from his cigarette pack. "Might as well finish this off. I could use a little help getting to sleep."

He lit it and took a pull and then handed it to me.

We went back upstairs. Gooch and Laney were in their beds. I brushed my teeth. I looked in the mirror—my toothbrush was sticking out of my mouth. I wondered if Sting brushed his teeth when he was on tour.

I got into bed and curled up to Gooch. "Goodnight Gooch," I whispered. "I love you." I laughed. He sighed. "I love you too, Paul. Goodnight." I giggled to myself and rolled over to my side of the bed and fell asleep.

The next day we woke up and left LA.

I called Little Pete's. No answer. They probably didn't open until the afternoon. Or they never picked up their phone.

We made our way up the coast to San Luis Obispo. I drove and Jeff sat in the passenger seat. Gooch sat in the back with Laney. He was playing a game on his phone. Laney was responding to emails and updating our itinerary and playing road and band manager. I had to hand it to her. Organizing a twelve-week tour isn't easy, on top of all the promotional shit that goes with it. Sending out press kits and securing the dates so we're not driving fifteen hours overnight. I guess the first half of the tour was a little easier when we opened up for Lunchbox and Thermos. Their manager did most of the work for that one. But there are all the little details that need to be thought out. This isn't backpacking across Europe—you can't just put up your sail and see where it takes you.

The Pacific lay out to our left as we twisted around cliffs and hills. We stopped for lunch in Santa Barbara. We didn't get to southern California when we toured with Lunchbox and Thermos. We stayed north, hit Portland and then turned around. I was glad to be able to see this part of the country. There wasn't much time to walk around since we had to be at the record shop by three to set up. Gooch ordered a side salad for Dunk and fed him little strips of carrots and a leaf of lettuce. Laney told Jeff and me what songs we were going to play. We got back in the van.

Gooch and Laney sat in the back again. We were out on the highway. The ocean was blue and clear. The sky was wide. The hills were green and brown and dotted with trees and shrubs that looked like they would bite the wind or catch on fire if it got hot enough. Jeff flipped through the satellite radio stations and settled on one that played David Bowie songs in foreign languages.

"You know," Jeff said, "I don't like Bowie or other languages that much, but when they're together, it's pretty good."

"You don't like Bowie?" I said.

"Or Pixies," Laney said from the back.

I looked up at the rearview mirror and back at the road. It was nice to hear her talking to us again about non-band stuff.

"Really?" I said. "But we kind of sound like them. A little anyway."

"Only Laney's guitar does," he said. "Sometimes."

"Why don't you like them?" I said.

"I never said I didn't like them," he said and turned in his seat to look at Laney.

"Not exactly," she said. "But you did say they gave permission to other bands to sound like shit."

"Well, I mean, ok," he said. "I did say that. But that's not saying I didn't like them. It's like someone looking at a Picasso and thinking they could do it because it looks easy, without ever having painted before."

"I guess that makes sense. Sort of," I said. "So, you do like them?"

"Not really," he said and laughed.

"Or *The Godfather,*" Laney said.

"I've never even seen *The Godfather,*" I said and looked at Laney in the rearview mirror. Her eyes narrowed and she opened her mouth.

"What the fuck is wrong with you two?" she said.

"Gooch," I said, "what's your take?"

"Yes, and yes," he said.

"What's that mean?"

"I like Pixies and have seen *The Godfather.*" He put on headphones.

I looked at Jeff out of the corner of my eye.

I looked at the GPS.

"The Forever Lost says we'll be there in an hour and a half."

A song I recognized as "Life on Mars" came on. It was simple and slow. Nylon guitar, an even baritone voice. I was trying to piece together the words based on what lyrics I did know, and what words seemed like Spanish. That lasted a second since my Spanish was shit.

"Turn this up," Laney said.

"You know it?" I said.

"Yeah. Seu Jorge. He's Brazilian."

"Is that a language?"

"No," she said. "It's in Portuguese."

The words became melodic white noise. "*Para uma life on Mars,*" he sang. We drove on.

PART 2

CHAPTER 10

When we got to San Luis Obispo we checked in with Boo-Boo Records. We parked around back and brought our gear inside to the vinyl room where they had a small riser for in-store performances. We didn't need much space. We set up the keyboard and my bass amp. Laney was going to play acoustic through the house system, which was decent enough for this type of stripped-down performance. Gooch had his shakers.

We had a couple of hours to kill before we played. Jeff said he wanted to go to the bookstore next door and get a tea and read.

"Do you want me to get you a sweater and a cat?" I asked.

"That would be nice," he said. "I'm feeling a good relax today. I could use a nice relax."

I knew what he meant. The residuals of tripping last night put my head in a very mellow spot. I felt peacefully insane. When a string is plucked it vibrates to create sound. The string is visibly moving. If the note rings without interference, the sound keeps going even though the string looks like it has stopped. But it is still moving. The vibrations grow smaller and tighter as the sound diminishes—an invisible buzzing. That's what I felt like—like I was vibrating.

Gooch got Dunk out of the van and carried the bowl like a football against his side. We left the record shop. "I'm going to walk around," I said. "Anybody want to come along?"

"I think I'm going to chill out today too," Gooch said. "I saw a park when we drove through, over there somewhere." He pointed down the road. "I've got some calls to make. Maybe read a little."

"I didn't know you could read," Laney said.

"Sometimes I can read good," Gooch said. "But I have to say the words out loud."

"If you use your finger you can go faster," I said.

"That's what she said," Gooch said.

"Why would she say that, Gooch?" Laney asked.

Gooch clenched his jaw and lowered his eyes. He put his free hand to his face and stroked his chin.

"Uh," he said. "Vagina? Things?" His eyes shot up and darted back and forth between us. "Boob."

We laughed at him.

"Ok," Laney said. "Don't hurt yourself."

"I'll see you guys later," Gooch said. He stuck his hand in Dunk's tank and petted his shell. "Say goodbye to Uncle Paul and Aunt Laney." Gooch looked up at us. "He's being shy." He stood there.

"I think I saw him wave," I said.

"Yeah, he definitely blinked like he was trying to say something," Laney said.

"He's growing up so fast," I said.

"Where does the time go?" Gooch said and sighed. "Well, I'll see you guys later." He shook our hands and walked away, Dunk under his arm.

"Where to?" Laney said.

I was glad Laney wanted to come with me, given the brief episodes of tension the past couple of days. It would be nice to hang out outside of the van or a venue for a change.

"I think there was an old mission somewhere around here," I said.

"I think it's the law in California for a mission to always be around somewhere," she said.

We walked through the streets. The old part looked new. National chain stores and smaller independent shops filled the buildings, and the streets and walls were given a facelift. New brick, plaster, paint. It wasn't bad. The shape was still the same as what it probably was two hundred years ago. A quiet influence seemed to pervade everything. We found the old mission.

We went our own way once inside. I've always preferred to explore museums and tourist sites on my own. To take in the art or scene at my own pace and not have my perception altered by someone else's opinion. It's good to hear other opinions after, but I find it better to approach art with a clean slate—to let it come to me unfiltered. I walked around and read the plaques and signs. The patron saint of the mission, and who the town was named after, was from France. He was royalty and renounced his title when he was taken hostage. He was a young man who died from exhaustion or a fever in the thirteenth century while doing his work.

I saw Laney at the other end of the church taking pictures. I waved to her and pointed to the door. She waved back and nodded her head. I walked outside into the courtyard. I felt like I was in Spain. A few years ago I got a gig with a cruise line playing in their house band. It was an ok job, but the benefits far outweighed the pay. We weren't supposed to fraternize with the clientele, but after everybody on the staff got tired of drinking with and fucking each other, it was only natural our eyes turned outward. I made decent enough dough, but I could see myself getting stuck in that rut of looking for the next cruise like a junkie until I was forty and had nothing to show for it. It was fun, but it wasn't the career I wanted. When it was over and we docked in Barcelona, I ended up staying in Spain for almost three months, traveling around and looking for work. I got a few jobs, but nothing substantial and I returned home. Being here in California reminded me of then. I remember feeling young and strong and untouchable.

I walked to the end of the courtyard and sat on a wall looking down into the trees surrounding a small stream. It was quiet and I felt calm, and still, like I could disappear.

"You all right there, Dawson's Creek?"

I jumped. It was Laney. "Goddamnit," I said, "you scared me."

"Sorry," she said. "I was going to wait for you to turn around, but... " She brought her hand to her mouth like it was a microphone and sang, "I don't want to wait," in a high tight voice.

I laughed and shook my head.

"I like this place," she said.

"Me too. I don't think I could live here, though."

"How come?"

"I need culture and excitement in my life. I'm a man of the world, Laney."

She sighed. And made like she was going to say something, than stopped.

"What's up?" I said.

She sighed again. "I didn't like you last night."

"You like me now?"

She shook her head and smiled a little. "It's one thing to party after the show. I don't want to have to worry about you remembering your shit up there too."

"We played fine," I said.

"That's not the point."

I looked at her. I could tell this mattered to her. "Ok. I get it. It won't happen again," I said.

"Just like that?"

"This isn't my band. I don't want to fuck up all of your work. I got carried away last night being at the Whisky and running into Drix."

She nodded.

"I get it, Laney," I said. "I want this to work, too. I'm not in it for some summer jaunt across the country. I think the four of us have good chemistry up there. We sound good."

"We do," she said. "By the way, this is your band too."

"How so?"

"It's not just for the tour. I want you . . . me and Jeff want you to stick around when we get back."

I smiled. "Cool."

We stayed there, taking in the scene. The peacefulness of everything. It seemed so far removed from what we usually see. The dankness of clubs in the middle of the night. The smell of stale beer and sweat. A breeze passed through.

"I do like it here," Laney said.

"I guess it's not too bad," I said.

"It wouldn't be the worst place to come back to after it's all done."

"Yeah, but I feel like I'd get lazy and fat if I had to live here."

"Get?" she said and poked my side.

"Easy there, sasquatch," I said.

"What's that supposed to mean?"

"Your legs are hairy. Like a sasquatch."

"You have no idea how liberating it is to say fuck it to shaving my legs." She raised an eyebrow. "Besides, why are you looking at my legs?"

"I'm a pervert, Laney. A big, fat pervert."

"Don't be so hard on yourself. You're not a pervert." She laughed.

"Shut up," I said and turned around. I slid off the wall and lost my balance when my feet hit the ground.

"Watch it," she said.

"Sorry," I said, standing there, close to her. Our bodies were touching. Her eyes were green and brown. I never noticed that before. I could feel her heat. I didn't move, she didn't move. I could feel my hand around her waist. I could feel myself pulling her in. I didn't.

"What do you want to do?" she said, quiet.

Her lips parted. I swallowed.

"Come here," I said.

CHAPTER 11

A bunch of kids were walking into the record shop when we came back. We could see Jeff on a couch in the bookstore, through the front window. It was almost time to play our set. Laney and I went in and sat down on opposite sides of Jeff.

"What are you reading?" I asked.

"*Moby Dick; or, The Whale,*" he said.

"Two titles?" Laney said. "Is that good for marketing?"

"Only if people buy it twice by mistake," Jeff said.

"Did he find Moby Dick yet?" I asked.

"They find him?" Jeff said.

"I have no idea," I said.

"So far it's about seamen."

"That's gross," said Laney.

Jeff looked at her. "Men of the sea, Laney," he said. "Not, semen." He gestured with his hand, moving away from his crotch.

"Ohhhh," she said. "Did you see the little crowd we've got next door?"

"Really?" Jeff said.

"A bunch of kids just walked in the store," I said.

"How many?" Jeff asked.

"Fifteen, twenty?" Laney said.

"Cool," Jeff said. "I was afraid we wouldn't be playing to anybody."

Laney booked this gig for us before we gained momentum with Lunchbox and Thermos. All of our solo dates were booked prior to our small surge in popularity. It felt cool that twenty kids in this town were coming out at five on a Thursday to a record shop.

"Let's go get set up," Laney said and stood up.

Jeff was deep into his book. "You ready, Bozo?" I said.

He looked up. "Bozo?"

"Your shoes," I said. I looked at his shoes and they weren't as big as I thought they were last night, but they were bright red.

"I like my shoes," he said and turned his ankle. "They make me feel fancy."

"Yeah, you're fancy all right." I stood up.

"I think I'm going to buy this," Jeff said and waved his book.

"Can we name the next album two titles?" I asked.

"If it's good enough for Herman, it's good enough for us," Jeff said.

"What are we going to call it?" Laney said.

Jeff turned the book. "*Songs; or, The Whale.* Oh, what about just *Or, The Whale?*"

"*Gooch; or, The Whale,*" Laney said.

"I'm taking the whale," Jeff said.

"Ah, give the guy a break," I said.

"He'll be getting a break," Jeff said.

"What's that supposed to mean?" Laney said.

"Remember that phone call I took that everyone was so pissed off about?" Jeff looked at each of us. "I was going to save the good news until tomorrow, but I guess we could use the morale boost now."

"What is it?" Laney said.

"I think it'd be better to tell everyone at once," Jeff said. "Let me go pay for this and we'll head over."

Jeff went to pay for his book. Laney and I stood there.

"Hi," she said and bumped into me with her hip.

"Hi, back," I said.

"Do you come here often?" she said.

"It's the damnedest thing, but actually, no."

"I guess it's your lucky day."

"I'm the lucky one?"

"Uh, yeah," she said.

"How come you're not the lucky one?"

"Trust me," she said. "You're the lucky one." She pinched my ass and moved away.

"Watch it lady."

Jeff came back and looked at us in turn. "What's up?"

"Nothing," I said.

"You guys are fucking weird," he said.

"You're the one buying dick in the middle of the day," I said.

"I'm a dickman."

Laney shook her head. "All right boys," she said. "Let's go and cheer Gooch up."

We waited until a quarter after five to start our set. Gooch wasn't there and didn't respond to our texts. We figured he got lost or thought we were on later or his phone was dead. The crowd was getting antsy. It'd be different at a real venue. They can have a drink and hang out. They're there for the evening anyway if a band has to go on a little later than scheduled. It's still not professional, but it's less awkward. You're not sitting in the front of the room with a bunch of people looking at you, three feet away.

Jeff picked up Gooch's shakers and we muddled through the songs. We didn't play bad. It was a very mellow set and we invited some of the kids to play along with us, using Gooch's shakers. Once we were playing, the crowd warmed up. We opened up the floor for questions if there were any. We played a very warm and subtle version of our last song. Jeff sang well while Laney played acoustic. I'd never heard him sing so well. He was usually good, but today, on that song, he was exceptional.

"Do you think something happened to Gooch?" Laney said.

"What could happen to him in this town?" I said.

"Text him again," Jeff said. "We need to get a move on it. We can make it to San Fran tonight, easy. And then get a head start on sorting out his drums situation. We aren't going to use fucking shakers tomorrow night."

Laney took out her phone and sent off another message. Jeff helped me carry my amp out to the van and Laney carried our guitars. I opened up the hatch and there was a folded piece of paper just inside. My gut dropped and I did a quick scan for Gooch's bag. It wasn't there. I grabbed the paper and opened it up.

I skimmed the letter.

"What's it say?" Laney asked.

Jeff took out a cigarette and lit it.

I read out loud.

I'm sorry for leaving you guys in the middle of the tour, but losing my drums was the last straw. There's too much partying and drinking and drugs and all of us aren't taking this seriously. I thought about leaving last week, but didn't want to leave my drums. Now they're gone. Good luck. You're a good band and the songs are good, but until everyone treats each night as important and goes after every opportunity I can't see you living up to your full potential and getting to the next level. I don't want to be a part of that. Sorry for dragging you into this Paul, and sorry for leaving you Laney. – Gooch

We stood there silent for a moment.

I felt empty. I felt that it was over.

"What the fuck are we gonna do?" I said. I kicked the bumper. "Fuck."

"We could hire someone for the week," Laney said.

"With what money?" I said.

Jeff started chuckling to himself.

"What's funny?" Laney said. "We're fucked."

He choked on the cigarette smoke and put his hand up, coughing and laughing. He took a deep breath. "Whew," he said. "Oh man, this is too funny."

"I don't see what's funny about this," I said.

"Relax. I still have good news, and good news. Which do you want first?" He took a drag off his cigarette and threw it on the ground. "Ok, I'll start with the good news." He sat down on the bed of the van, under the hatch. "The phone call I got two days ago was from Sony's A&R man." He smiled. "New York is now a showcase gig. If we don't fuck up, we'll most likely end up signed."

He crossed his arms and looked at Laney and then me.

"Really?" Laney said. "How come they called you?"

"Remember my friend Mark, who recorded our first EP?"

"Yeah."

"He was doing some work for the label. He had our new EP on while he was setting up. The label guy was passing through the studio and asked who that was, and got my number from Mark and checked us out online. And now we've got a goddamned showcase. Fucking luck of the draw."

"Why didn't you tell us?" Laney asked.

"You guys were being all bitchy about me getting dehydrated. I figured I'd wait. And then I figured I'd wait until San Fran on the eve of the bigger leg of the tour. I thought it'd be dramatic."

"We still don't have a drummer," I said.

"Not yet. But we will," Jeff said.

"How," Laney said. She had her hands in her pockets and was looking at Jeff. Her face was still. I couldn't tell if she was happy or annoyed or angry.

"While Paul was busy rubbing against the walls of the Whisky looking for guidance, I had a good long talk about all of this, the tour, Gooch, the showcase in New York, with someone that can help us out."

"Who?" I asked.

"Your boy, and most likely our new drummer, Drix."

"You're kidding?"

"I tried telling you, but you were really fucked out," he said and laughed.

"What about tomorrow?" Laney asked.

"I'll call him now," Jeff said.

"You have his number?" I asked.

"Yeah," he said.

"Why didn't you tell us that when we were trying to reach him this morning?"

"I wanted to see how this would all play," he said. "We couldn't use his drums today anyway."

I didn't like feeling manipulated, but that wasn't exactly manipulation. More like I didn't like things being kept from me, or the band. I didn't say anything. I could see how the theater of keeping this secret could have been a nice touch, but this information could have been used to keep the band together—not to let it fall apart and reunite with different members in the middle of a goddamned tour.

We left San Luis Obispo and headed north towards San Francisco. Jeff called Drix and left a message. We put my amp and our guitars in the van. There was a lot of empty space and I wasn't in the mood to be a packmaster that evening. Being ditched by Gooch stung. It was a shitty thing to do even if I could half agree with his reasons. Part of me was pissed off and anxious about what would happen, and part of me was looking forward to playing with my old friend again. I remembered all those jams in the woods and each other's basements. That was over ten years ago. I had a small panic attack and Pink Floyd's song "Time" crept in my head. I was suddenly aware of myself, my age, the past ten years slogging it out in clubs, giving lessons, sitting in with bands for fifty bucks a night, trying to catch a break. It all amounted to riding in a used rental van, driving up the coast to start a six-night support run for a band that didn't have an album out yet. We had no drummer. We were broke. These weren't my songs. I was a barely paid hired gun holding down a bartending gig back home to make ends meet.

Jeff was right—it was the luck of the draw. None of us controlled any of this. They made an EP and by sheer luck someone heard it—fuck all the promotion, the touring, the gigs, the handshakes every night—the guy heard something they recorded six months ago. All the legwork of the past few months helped the band's internet visibility and proved we weren't a bunch of assholes in a garage with a laptop and microphone. But it still amounted to this moment of random fucking chance in the face of all the hard work.

I knew a couple of guys back home that toured Europe or Asia every year for a few months. They had a small hit in the 90s. No one listened to them in the States anymore. When they came home the singer picked up jobs working for a contractor doing maintenance on buildings over the winter. Last year their bass player was working at Burger King. My heart started beating faster. I didn't want to be forty and working in a fucking Burger King between tours.

I wound down my window and turned up the radio. I looked for that Bowie station, but when I put it on it sounded like someone was playing the Wallflowers' version of "Heroes" with a sitar and tabla. I turned the radio back down and pushed the scan button and let the sounds become white noise. I closed my eyes and tried to relax. Taking deep breaths.

"You all right?" Jeff asked.

"Yeah," I said. "I'm cool."

I took a cigarette out of Jeff's pack on the center console and lit it. I took long drags and watched the cherry move down the burn rings on the paper. I smoked it right down to the filter and chucked it out the window.

An hour outside of the city Jeff's phone buzzed.

"Get that for me," he said. "Both hands on the road, that's what I've always said."

"It's eyes, dipshit," I said.

"Fuck me," he said. "I've been looking at the speedometer the whole time."

He looked over at me. "We're lucky to have made it this far."

"Watch out," I yelled. He jumped and jerked the wheel as his head snapped to the road. The road was clear.

"Fuck you," he said. "You almost gave me a heart attack."

It felt good to yell and get a reaction.

"Take it easy," Laney said from the back. "You're making me lose my game."

I turned around and her face was intense, looking at her phone. Her fingers tapped the screen. I picked up Jeff's phone and looked forward. It was a text from Drix. "Right on," the message read.

I felt a small sense of relief run through my body. A little later another message came through with an address and a time for practice. A flicker of anticipation, of "shit's gonna be ok," started to grow in me. Maybe this is how it was supposed to be, if anything is ever supposed to be anything.

"We've got practice at two tomorrow," I said.

"See," Jeff said, and smiled. "Nothing to worry about. This is exactly how a little band called the Beatles got Ringo. Ever hear of them?"

"No," I said. "Who are they?"

"Well laddie," Jeff said in a terrible English accent, "if you wouldn't mind bumming me a fag, I'll tell you."

Before I could take a cigarette out for him, he yelled, "Bum me a fag, would you? C'mon now, guv'ner. Don't be coy." He laughed to himself.

It was still early, by gigging standards at least, when we pulled up to a motel down near the airport. Jeff had calmed down after making up an elaborate fictitious story about the Beatles that involved a kangaroo, marmalade, and lots of German hookers. The hookers' part, from what I've read, wasn't exactly that inaccurate. We got out of the van and stretched our legs.

"Do we have to get a room with two beds?" Jeff asked.

"Where do you want me to sleep?" I asked.

"There's only three of us now," he said. "We can take turns on the floor or chair. It'll save us a little bit of money until we get paid."

"Ok," Laney said. "But you're on the floor first."

"Whoa," Jeff said. "I didn't actually mean I had to take turns."

"Dibs," I said.

"Dibs," Laney said.

"What's this? A fucking conspiracy," Jeff said.

"It was your idea," Laney said. "And you didn't call dibs."

"You didn't call dibs," I said.

"I'm calling dibs for the rest of the week," he said.

"You can't do that," I said.

"Yeah, I can."

I raised my finger, pointing to the sky. "Dibs shall only be called on the day of said event."

Jeff shook his head. "This is horseshit."

"Better luck tomorrow," I said and slapped him on the side of the arm.

"Just remember the rules," he said.

"Call it tomorrow," Laney said.

"Oh, I will," he said. "But I'm talking the 'Fleetwood Mac Rules.' "

"What are those?" I asked.

"Never fuck the chick in the band," he said.

"Gross," Laney said.

I didn't look at her. I grabbed Jeff and said, "No worries. I've grown quite fond of sleeping next to a man these past few weeks. Tomorrow night." I tried to kiss him on his cheek but he pushed me away.

"What's with boys and gay stuff?" Laney said.

I shrugged my shoulders. "The book of Kurt says, 'What else can I say? Everyone is gay.' "

"Let's go check in," she said.

Jeff lit a cigarette. "Let me know which room. I'll be up in a minute."

We grabbed our bags and walked around to the motel entrance. Laney looked at me out of the corner of her eyes. Her lips curved up.

"No funny stuff," she said.

"I'm not that kind of guy," I said.

"Right," she said, dragging the word out.

CHAPTER 12

We smoked a joint out of the window and found a cable channel that only played infomercials. We made bets after we established some rules—how soon would they throw in a second or third item free? How much would the price drop? Was there an extra gift? Did we have to act fast? How much were similar, more expensive products? When all was said and done, I had a nice little pile of M&M's in front of me.

It was pushing three in the morning when we were tired enough to fall asleep. Jeff's foot was healing and didn't stink anymore. We made him clean it again and put a new bandage on anyway.

"The foot goes next time it gets bad," I said.

"I am strong like bear," he said.

"What is that?" Laney said.

"Bears are healthy and strong?" Jeff said and laid out a blanket on the floor.

"Except for the sick ones," I said.

"Well, yeah, except for the sick ones," he said from the floor.

Laney and I looked at each other from opposite sides of the bed and stifled our smiles. She hit the lights. We stayed on our respective edges of the bed when we got in.

"Don't break up the band, Yoko," Jeff said in a sleepy and worse British accent than before.

"Dude, she wasn't even in the band," Laney said.

"Tell that to John," Jeff said.

"Is hand stuff ok?" I asked.

"Don't be a grossman," Jeff said. "Wait, is it tomorrow yet?"

"I guess."

"Dibs, motherfuckers."

Fuck. I didn't want to sleep on the floor, but in the half second it took me to decide that I wasn't going to call the bed, Laney called it.

"Bastards," I mumbled.

Jeff was breathing heavy, and I closed my eyes. I felt Laney's hand reach across the bed and squeeze mine. I squeezed back and she withdrew her hand and rolled over.

In the morning I woke up and I had a raging hard-on. Aside from not wanting to breathe in each other's faces all night, Gooch and I slept back to back to avoid any nocturnal swordplay.

Jeff got up.

"My neck fucking is killing me," he said.

"We could get an air mattress," I said.

"Have you ever slept on an air mattress?"

"Yeah."

"Then you know how much of an asshole you sound like," he said.

"Touché."

"I'm going to hop in," he said and pointed to the bathroom.

I turned towards Laney.

She rolled over and stretched. She moved close to me.

"Morning," I said.

"Morning," she said. We kissed.

"Your breath stinks," she said. "Did you brush your teeth?"

"Last night."

"With shit?"

"I was out of toothpaste. Besides, your mouth isn't bursting with roses and sunshine, either."

"It's not that bad," she said.

I clenched my teeth and breathed in. "It's pretty bad," I said.

She cupped her hand over her mouth and breathed.

"Oh, fuck," she said.

I pulled her close to me. "Just don't breathe."

She slid her hand down my body.

"What's this?" she said and kissed me again.

I put my hand between her legs and used my fingers. There's a saying that musicians are good with their fingers.

It's true.

We were breathing heavy when the shower shut off.

"That was quick," she said and sighed.

"Did he even use soap?" I said.

"To be continued," she said before pulling away from me. She got out of bed and sat at the little desk and checked her phone that was plugged into the outlet.

When Jeff came out I grabbed my bag and went in the bathroom.

We left the motel and drove into the city. We had a few hours until practice with Drix. We headed north up to the marina. Laney said she wanted to see the Golden Gate Bridge. The drive along the waterfront was a bitch and I cut over to explore the city. I ended up on a wide street that the Forever Lost said would take us straight to the top.

"I think City Lights is around here somewhere," Jeff said.

"Want to find it and stop?"

"Eh, I'm over the beats."

"Jeff was a huge nerd in high school," Laney said from the back. "He wore this sweater like every day and he used to recite poetry."

"That's enough, Laney," Jeff said.

"I want to hear about the poetry reciting," I said. "Did he read Shakespeare?"

"He used to say this one because he could tell America to go fuck herself. He thought he was hot shit," Laney said.

"What poem?" I said.

"Yeah, what was that poem?" she said to Jeff.

Jeff shook his head. "It was 'Howl' by Ginsberg."

"Recite it for us," she said.

"Yeah, I want to hear it," I said.

Jeff was quiet. He turned off the radio. He looked down.

He closed his eyes and sat there, unmoving.

"I'm not going to recite it unless I have some bass," he said in a low, even whisper.

"On it, boss," I said and began imitating a walking bass line. "Ba-doom, doom, doom, doom."

Jeff opened his eyes and started reciting a poem in a deep voice. He snapped his fingers after each line and shook his head. Somewhere after a few stanzas, and after he told America to go fuck herself, he started the lyrics to "Wicked Game" by Chris Isaak.

"That's all I've got," he said.

"Man, you must have had all the ladies," I said.

Laney laughed.

"What?" I said.

"Jeff didn't get laid till after high school," she said.

"What's this?" Jeff said. "The fucking 'revisit the adolescence hour of Jeff'?"

I put my hand on Jeff's shoulder.

"It's ok buddy," I said.

Jeff turned to Laney. "Wanna talk about all the flannel you used to wear?"

"Flannel is cool," she said.

"Not when you wore it," he said.

"How was it not cool when I wore it?"

"When it was the pattern for your pants . . . that matched your shirt."

"Fuck, I forgot about those."

"Were you one of those kids that hung out at the mall?" I asked.

"The mall would have been great," she said.

"She wasn't allowed out," Jeff said.

"I was allowed out," she said.

"After your parents dropped you off, and met the other people's parents, and exchanged numbers."

"I guess they were a little over-protective."

"Remember the talent show senior year?" Jeff asked.

"That was the worst."

"Did you guys play?" I asked.

"It was our first gig," Jeff said.

"It was bad," Laney said.

"What did you play?" I asked.

Jeff laughed. "We played 'Come On Eileen.' It's a pretty dirty song, but since no one actually knows the lyrics except for the chorus, we decided to make up some of our own and make it even dirtier."

"It was acoustic and real sensitive. It was the first song I learned on the guitar," Laney said. "And my parents were there to hear every innuendo and grunt."

Jeff let out a big laugh. "I forgot about the grunting."

"Did you win?" I asked.

"Fuck no," Jeff said. "We almost got suspended."

"Jeff made a big plea about the First Amendment and artistic freedom," Laney said, "and how we have to sing the national anthem, which is really about being proud of bombing and murdering people."

"It was glorious," Jeff said.

"Did you wear your sweater?" I asked.

"You bet your ass I did."

There was a park up ahead and I pulled into the lot. We got out and walked up to see the bay. The sky was clear and the water was gray and blue. A bit of green. The breeze was steady.

"Well," I said, "there's your bridge, Laney."

"Isn't it something?" Jeff said.

"It's very orange," Laney said.

We stood there admiring it. There were some sailboats cruising around the bay and some clouds hung low, obscuring the top of the bridge. An old man carrying a light jacket came up to us and started talking about the bridge. He was informative at first but then started to talk shit about the Golden Gate Bridge before expounding on the superiority of the Bay Bridge. Jeff egged him on.

"What's so special about the Bay Bridge?" Jeff said. "It's not in any movies or TV shows."

"It's longer, and the level of engineering that went into it makes this one child's play," the old man said.

"It's not always about length," Jeff said.

"Which one is wider?" Laney said.

"The Bay Bridge," said the old man, swinging his arm and pointing away to nothing.

"But this one's orange," Jeff said.

"Ah," the old man said and waved the comment away and shook his head. He walked away mumbling. I guess it doesn't matter what you do in this world. Whether it's a song, or a book, or a bridge, there's always going to be someone who thinks it's shit and something else is better.

We walked around for a bit before heading back to the van to go to practice. We drove south. Jeff wanted to find the steepest hill.

"I think they all are," I said.

"We should find it and go down it," he said.

Laney took out her phone and after a minute started giving me directions. We drove up and down some steep hills and I could feel the strain on the brakes. Cabs flew past us and screeched at the stop signs and lights.

"How are any of these not the steepest?" I asked.

"Don't be a sissy," Laney said. "Keep driving."

Jeff egged me on from the passenger seat until we found it—or at least the hill that Laney told us some guy on the internet said was the steepest in the area.

We arrived at Vallejo and Romolo. I backed the van up so we were facing down, like at the top of a roller coaster.

"Guys," I said, "we might die."

Jeff and Laney put on their seatbelts. I gripped the wheel tight and eased off the brakes and started down the hill with some gas. It wasn't a long street, but it was steep, and then it got steeper—and then the bottom dropped out. The sudden momentum shifted all our gear and my foot pushed on the pedal harder than I wanted and we took off. I was certain the van was going to flip over, back to front. I managed to press on the brakes and felt the pads grind through the pedal. It wasn't enough. We were going too fast.

"Fuck, fuck, fuck," I said. We blew into the intersection at the bottom and I jerked the wheel to the right and prayed there wouldn't be any cars. The wheels on the right side of the van lifted off the ground and the gear slid in the back. We crossed over into the third lane of traffic and were facing the wrong way. Cars were coming towards us, or they were still, and we were moving—I couldn't tell. I stepped on the gas and made a quick left turn and pulled over in a bus lane. I killed the engine. My hands were shaking.

"Holy shit," I said.

"Fuck, dude," Laney said. "Fuck." Her face was white.

Jeff sat there, staring forward. He was grabbing the handle on the door. He let go and took a cigarette out of the pack on the console. He lit it. He looked out his window.

"There's City Lights," he said.

He got out of the van and stood there, looking at the building. He threw his cigarette on the ground and moved away, up the street a few feet.

I got out of the van and walked around to the sidewalk just in time to see him throw up all over a white fire hydrant.

CHAPTER 13

We drove slow and got to the rehearsal studio just at two. We rang the bell and after a minute the door flew open, and Drix jumped out with jazz hands.

"Yo, yo, yo, motherfuckers," he said. He looked at his watch. "You bitches and Laney are three minutes late. Chop, chop. Let's get inside."

"Hey, man," I said and gave him a hug. "Traffic was a bitch."

"Man, traffic's always a bitch. Let's run the set a few times," he said and motioned with his head to come in. I looked at Laney. She raised her eyebrows and smiled a little. I wasn't exactly sure how she felt about Drix since he gave me drugs, and Gooch blamed him for his drum kit. But his giving us shit for punctuality was a good start.

We set up and got in tune. Drix said he listened to the EP and the other tracks Laney sent him and had all the tempos and changes marked down.

"When did you learn to write charts?" I asked.

"It's do or die out here, brother," he said. "I'm not gonna lose out on a gig because I can't read."

"Good shit," I said.

"Let's run the EP and the other songs straight through so we can get a feel and make shit jive, and then let's run a set," Drix said.

Drix had the tempos programmed into his phone and he counted each song off. I was getting excited playing with him. It felt right and like old times. He knew the songs and was practiced. He began to mention a tricky transition in one of the songs and was working it out as he was talking. I don't know why drummers do that. They'll talk to you while hitting their drums, which aren't exactly quiet. "Never mind," he said as he played the part perfectly, "I got it." We ran the set, and we sounded good—a little different than with Gooch, but different in a good way. We made a perfect reproduction of the recordings. Hopefully, after a few gigs we would have chemistry and a live sound going for us. Usually takes a couple of swings on stage to find out where we can go with each other in a room full of people.

It was late afternoon when we finished rehearsal. We paid for the room with our dwindling funds and went outside.

"I can't believe those motherfuckers stole his drums," Drix said.

"Yeah, he was pretty mad. It's fucked up," I said.

"Let me see what I can do. I got some contacts at Yamaha and Zildjian. Worked out a couple of small endorsement deals after that hit last spring."

"That's cool. They giving you free stuff?"

"They sent me a case of sticks and a couple of cymbals. Nothing crazy yet, but I'm working on it."

"So you're doing pretty well out here, eh?" Jeff said.

"Yeah, man. Took a page out of Samuel L. Jackson's book. That motherfucker always had the next six jobs lined up. He was always working. Still is. Only way to make a living doing this," Drix said. "Just gotta keep at it and hope a big break comes one day."

"What's the big break for you?" I said.

"Ideally I'd like to morph into Questlove, but that shit's unlikely. So it's either break through with a new band," he said and looked at us, "or a gig with one of those legacy motherfuckers like McCartney or Springsteen. "

Jeff laughed. "Bruce Springsteen?"

"Yeah man. I'm not saying I dig his music like that, though some of his shit is real good. I'm talking about that level of playing. Once you start jamming with those dudes you start making bank and you meet all sorts of other people and all sorts of doors open. That's the big show for me as a session musician."

"Let me know when you jam with Paul McCartney," I said. "That dude is sick."

"Paul is dead, Paul," Jeff said.

Laney cleared her throat. She was leaning against the van. "What's Spectacular Death Extras think about you pulling double duty with us?" she said.

"I haven't told them yet. Haven't even seen them. I got a text from their manager earlier," Drix said.

"I hope they're cool with it," Laney said.

"No worries, lady. I checked my contract. All I got to do is show up for gigs and promotional things, hit the drums, and be straight around them. It's like working two jobs. Just so happens the one job is exactly before the other."

"Since we're talking business," Laney said, "we split the door money four ways after thirty percent goes into the band fund. I know this is last-minute so I crunched some numbers and figured we could give you a cut of merch sales, like a hazard pay or something."

Drix laughed and shook his head. "No way, dudes. No fucking way am I taking a dime of your dough. Those cats are paying me."

"You have to take something," Jeff said.

"Man, you guys are funny. I'm happy to do this." He put his arm around me. "Haven't seen this motherfucker in a decade. Last time we jammed together he had this ponytail and leather pants. Skinny little dude looked like he was trying out for Mötley Crüe or some shit."

Laney and Jeff looked at me and laughed. "Oh, this is going to be fun," Jeff said. "Tell us more."

"I think that's it for today," I said. "Right, Drix?"

"Not by a fucking long shot, brother," he said.

I shook my head and closed my eyes. "Can I at least have a last meal?" I said.

"Yes, food. I'm fucking starving," Jeff said. "I left my breakfast on a fire hydrant."

"Why'd you do that?" Drix said.

"It's a long story," Jeff said. "We'll tell you on the way."

"Right on. Yo, there's some good burrito joints not far from here in the mission district. You guys down?"

"Fuck, yeah," Jeff said. He looked at me and Laney.

"I'm down," I said.

"Can we buy you a burrito?" Laney asked.

"Fine," he said with mock exasperation.

"Thanks, Drix," Laney said. He nodded at her.

Jeff gave him a pat on the back. "You're a goddamn hero," he said.

"Yeah, yeah, yeah," Drix said and gave Jeff a pat back. "Let's get some grub. I gotta meet up with those dudes in a little bit."

We walked down the street past different Mexican shops. There was a cartoon picture in one of the windows of a giant prawn advertising a "Super Prawn Burrito."

"I want that," Jeff said.

"Gross," Laney said.

"Yeah, bro. I don't know," Drix said.

"Super prawn burrito," Jeff said.

We kept walking and Jeff kept saying, "super prawn burrito," like it was his mantra. We stopped at a place and looked at a menu on the window to make sure the vegetarian options were good. Jeff reached his arm over in between all of us and ran down the list with his finger.

"They don't have it," he said.

"All right," I said. "We'll go back. But it's your ass, my friend."

We walked back and checked out the menu. It was fine. We went in and walked to the counter. Jeff was bouncing around on the balls of his feet, bumping into us.

"Are you hyperglycemic?" I said.

"It's *hypo*glycemic," Drix said. "Hyper means too much. Hypo means this motherfucker needs to get some shit in his body."

"Excuse me nerds," Jeff said, pushing past us. "I'm fucking hungry-glycemic. One super prawn burrito," Jeff said to the man at the counter.

We ordered and sat down. Jeff's burrito was about the size of a football.

"Holy shit," Laney said. Within a minute Jeff was a quarter of the way done.

"That's a lot of prawns," I said and looked closer. "It's like all prawns. Is it good?"

Jeff shook his head up and down with the burrito in his mouth as he took another bite.

"Fuck," he said, with his mouth full, "I needed this. Bad." He took a long drink of soda.

"This is too much food, man," Drix said. Our burritos weren't as big as Jeff's, but they were way more than one person could eat. We ate about half. Jeff kept eating.

"You going for it?" Laney said.

"If I put it down I'll never finish," Jeff said. He took a deep breath and went back at it. We began chanting "eat it" and hitting our fists on the table. When he took the last bite, we cheered. He sat back and chewed and took another deep breath and closed his eyes.

"That was a whole school of prawns, brother," Drix said.

"They put up a good fight," Jeff said. "But I wasn't going to leave a man behind." He rubbed his stomach.

"Feel better?" I said.

"You have no idea," he said. "I need a cigarette."

We left the Mexican place and walked back to the studio where we were parked.

"I have to go meet up with those dudes. I'll see you guys later," Drix said.

"Cool," I said. "Tonight is going to be good."

"Yeah, man," he said. "Thanks for the burrito."

Drix got in his car and wound down his window. "One more thing," he said and looked at all of us. "No more joyriding you crazy motherfuckers."

We had some time before load in and went back to the motel to relax before heading out to the venue.

"You been taking your antibiotics?" Laney asked Jeff.

"Almost done," he said.

"Almost done?" she said. "They're supposed to last a week."

"The doc said they were for three days. He said they were the good shit."

Jeff stretched out across the bed and closed his eyes.

"I've never heard of that," Laney said. "Where's the bottle?"

"In my bag," Jeff said.

Laney went to Jeff's bag and opened it up. She shuffled around and took out a small orange plastic bottle. She held it up and read. "Take one, three times a day until the bottle is empty. Quantity, twenty-one." She looked at Jeff. "That's a week. How many have you been taking?"

"Three," Jeff said.

"How many times a day?" I asked.

"Three times," he mumbled.

Laney shook her head. "Dude," she said. "The doctor didn't tell you they were for three days."

"He definitely said, 'three,' and 'day.' He said a lot of things."

"I guess if you're feeling better," Laney said.

"Strong like bear," Jeff said.

"Does it list any side effects?" I asked.

Laney rotated the bottle. “No,” she said and took out her phone and looked up the side effects of his antibiotics. She laughed. “Look at this.” She gave me her phone.

“Diarrhea, rash, itching,” I said, “and my favorite, taste perversion.”

“My mouth isn’t perverted,” Jeff said.

“Except for prawns,” I said.

“Yeah, that was perverse,” Laney said.

“You’re perverse,” Jeff said. “I’m going to take a nap, if you don’t mind.”

“Not at all,” I said. “I’m going to slip outside to make a phone call.” I looked at Laney when I stood up. I went outside and sat in the van.

She came out after a few minutes. “He’s asleep.”

I drove the van to the far end of the parking lot and turned off the engine, but kept the radio on.

Laney crawled into the back seat and pulled her shirt over her head and looked at me with her head lowered.

“Goddamn,” I said and followed her.

We came back to the motel with a tea for Jeff and two coffees. We woke him up. He groaned. “I don’t want to go to school today.”

“Sorry, sweetie,” I said. “You’ve got a big test to take.”

He rolled off the bed and went into the bathroom.

“Hey,” I said to Laney.

She smiled. “Hey, back.”

“How do you think tonight will be?”

“Good,” she said. “I like Drix. He’s a good drummer and I like his attitude.”

“Me too.”

“Do you think he’s going to stay with us till New York?”

"I don't know if Jeff asked him outright."

"We're going to need to know."

"Worst case we hire Gooch for the night if it comes down to it," I said.

"Do you think he'd do it?"

"I don't know. I still want to do something about his drum kit. If things go well, financially, we could use that as an incentive."

"Let's see how this goes with Drix. We'll still be shit out of luck until New York if he stays with Spectacular Death Extras."

I nodded. "Fucking drummers."

Jeff came out of the bathroom holding his stomach. "I wouldn't go in there."

The smell followed him. "Dude," Laney said. "Light a match."

I handed him his tea. "Let's get out of here. We should be there soon."

"Jeff," Laney said. "Me and Paul were talking. Is Drix staying with us after this week?"

"Uh," he said. "He knows our situation."

"Did he say anything about it?"

"I'm working on it," Jeff said.

Laney stood up and looked at me. She picked up the keys to the van. "I'll drive," she said.

"Shotgun," I said.

We drove to the venue and brought our gear in. It was a new club called Vaquero Caballero. Everything was painted black and red, and the wall had stencils of burros and Mexican cowboys with monocles riding horses. A giant V and C logo was painted across the wall in Victorian looking letters. There was a stencil of a mustachioed man wearing a poncho and pointing a gun in the air that made me think of Gooch.

The promoter told us to park and load in behind the building. It was 6:30. The first band was going on at 8:30. We went inside and the stage was to the left, and the green room was to the right. I could hear people talking behind the door. I knocked and we went in.

There were three young dudes wearing bowties and vests and jeans, with their hair just so, sitting on a couch. And there was Drix sitting off to the side, sunglasses on, flipping through a magazine, the small halo of his afro occupying the corner. He nodded to me when I came in.

"Hey guys," I said. "I'm Paul."

They stood up and shook my hand. Laney and Jeff introduced themselves. All the guys looked the same. Ryan and Sean were brothers, they sang and played guitar, and their cousin, Mason, played bass.

"Congratulations," I said.

"For?" Ryan said.

"Drix told us you guys just got a deal with a major."

"Oh, yeah. Thanks."

"Which one?" Jeff asked.

Sean spoke up, "We'd rather not say."

Then Mason, "We're trying to keep things a secret until we meet up with a big act in Vegas next week."

"Who're you hooking up with?" Jeff said.

"We'd rather not say," Ryan said.

Jeff looked around the room, and then leaned in.

He whispered, "It's Tom Jones, isn't it?"

"No," Ryan said.

"So, Drix told us he's drumming for you as well," Sean said.

"Yeah," Jeff said. "Our drummer got sick and had to go home."

"In the middle of the tour?"

"Yeah," Jeff said.

Ryan and Sean looked at each other.

"We were thinking," Ryan said. "Just so the audience doesn't get confused, we're going to have you guys open up before the local acts go on."

"The 8:30 slot?" I said. "Before the opening act?"

"Why would the audience get confused?" Jeff said.

"Same drummer. They might confuse us," Ryan said.

Jeff looked at him up and down. "I don't think you have to worry about that."

"Don't your fans know what you sound and look like?" I said.

Sean stepped forward and put his hands in the air, in front of his chest. "Listen guys, I'm going to be honest. It seems unprofessional to us that your drummer quit in the middle of the tour. And it seems weird to us that you're using our drummer, who we have under contract, to play to our fans."

"They won't all be your fans," Jeff said.

"Most of them will be," Ryan said and stared at Jeff.

"This is bullshit," Jeff said. "We're not going on first. Why don't you go on first so there isn't any confusion."

Laney stepped in between Jeff and Ryan. "Easy guys. Relax."

She took out her phone and held it up. "I have our agreement, right here in an email. The one we cleared with your manager three months ago. Where is he?"

"He's on his way," Mason said and then looked at his bandmates who looked down at the ground, avoiding his eyes.

"Let's just cool off and wait for him, and we'll sort this out," Laney said.

We left the green room and went outside.

"Can you fucking believe those guys?" Jeff said.

"I didn't know straight-edge also meant asshole," I said.

"Maybe it's not that big of a deal," Laney said.

"It's the principle," I said. "We're the second biggest act on the bill. We go on before them. Not before the local act."

"Between us and them, we've got the room," Jeff said. "They're making a play at something, and I think they want us to go on before them because we're better than them. We'd be a harder act to follow."

"They're pretty good," I said.

"That song on the internet is pretty good," Jeff said. "We haven't heard them live."

"I'll sort it out," Laney said.

We unloaded our gear and stored it backstage. We went back out to the parking lot and Jeff and I had a cigarette. Drix came out.

"Yo," he said. "Sorry about that guys."

"Yeah, man," I said. "What was up with them?"

"I told them that I was helping you out and they got all weird. Started talking about their upcoming gigs with Green Day."

"They're opening for fucking Green Day?" Jeff said.

"Shit. Don't say anything," Drix said. "They told me just before you got here."

Jeff shook his head. “What does that have to do with trying to muscle us into a shitty spot on the line-up?”

“I don’t even know, man. I told you those dudes were weird. Motherfuckers in this game get a little bit of a leg up and they start acting all kinds of strange. Truth is, opening for Green Day isn’t that big of a deal. I mean, in terms of playing to a shitload of people it is, but it doesn’t make you Green Day, you know what I mean? I hope they don’t act this way around those dudes.”

“You know Green Day?” Jeff asked.

“I had a gig with a band that opened for Foxboro Hot Tubs,” Drix said. “We hit it off and I did some studio shit with Mike and Billy. Just jamming mostly. Tré was in Germany or some shit.”

“Did you tell them,” Jeff said and nodded to the venue, “That you know them?”

“Fuck, no. Those dudes are leeches in there.”

“Leeches who are signed and are opening up for Green Day,” said Laney.

“Ah, fuck Green Day,” Jeff said. “Billy made a Christmas album for Starbucks. Let’s just make the most out of playing with these kids. We’re with them now.”

“What’s their song up to now?” I asked.

Laney took out her phone and looked it up. “Fuck.”

“What’s it at?” I said.

“Almost five million.”

“You’ve got to be fucking kidding me. How’d that happen?”

Laney thumbed away at her phone. “Seems like that British comedian with the long hair tweeted about it two days ago.”

"The one that was in that movie with the other dude?" Jeff said.

A car pulled into the parking lot. Drix tapped me on the arm. "That's their manager," he said.

"Let me handle this," Laney said.

Their manager parked his car and got out. He slammed his door and walked fast. He was wearing jeans and a blazer. And a lot of bracelets.

"Hi, Luke," Laney said, putting her hand out to him.

"Luke?" he said. He sounded raspy, like a whispering Cookie Monster. "My name's Graham."

"What happened to Luke?" Laney said.

"Luke was replaced six weeks ago. The band decided to put on their big boy pants and lose some dead weight."

"Oh," Laney said. "We didn't know."

"Don't worry," Graham said. "I figured if you showed up, you'd be on the tour with us, if you didn't I'd find somebody else. But you're here, so there's that." He cleared his throat. "How's the tour been so far?" he said with a hint of sarcasm.

"Great," said Jeff.

"Well, thanks for having us," Laney said and forced a smile.

"Listen," he said, shaking his head and ignoring Laney. "I talked to those guys on the way over." He looked at Drix and then back at us. "Between you and me, it's a shit move to bump you in the line-up, but we're all on the same bill and that's as good as it's going to get."

"What about the agreement we made?" Laney said.

"That was months ago, with Luke. Now you don't have a drummer and are using ours."

"What's that have to do with the line-up?" Jeff said.

"It's about branding," Graham said.

"Branding?" Jeff said. "You're kidding, right?"

"No," Graham said, face fucking stone. "Branding. It's always about that."

"What about the music? They are a band," Jeff said.

"Fuck the music. It's the image that sells first," Graham said and shook his head again. "There's only one question you need an answer to." He leveled his eyes at us. "There's a shitload of other bands with drummers just itching to get on this bill. Do you want on this fucking tour or not?"

"Yeah," Laney said. "We want to play."

Jeff looked at her.

"Good," Graham said. "You'll open. You're on at eight-thirty. Keep the set to thirty minutes or less."

Jeff made to say something, but Graham cut him off, and stared. "Also," he said, "No drinking backstage. Not a fucking drop." He turned away and went inside, his jewelry clanging at each step.

"Isn't he a goddamn peach," I said.

"What the fuck," Jeff said and took out another cigarette.

"I told you, man," Drix said and looked away. "Motherfuckers get a little bit of a leg up."

"They'll get a leg up," Laney said. "When my foot goes up their asses."

We all looked at Laney.

"That's the spirit," I said.

"I'm tired of people going back on their word," she said. "First the Whisky, then Gooch, and now these fucktards in suits."

"Fucktards?" Jeff said.

"Yes," Laney said.

She took a deep breath.

"What was up with dude's voice?" I said.

"That's how he sounds," Drix said. "Probably from yelling at motherfuckers all the time."

"I liked it," Jeff said and imitated him. "I see skies of blue, assholes too." He trailed off and took another drag of his cigarette.

"A few more years of cigs and whiskey, and you'll get there," I said to Jeff.

Jeff frowned at his cigarette and flicked it on the ground.

"Yo. Sorry to bring shit up now, but since we're talking about dude," Drix said. "He wants me to stay on after the tour and go to Vegas with them."

CHAPTER 14

Drix told us that he had till the end of the day tomorrow to decide and get his affairs in order. They said they liked his playing during rehearsals and that he could join as a semi-permanent member if things went well, with a better contract.

I felt uneasy again. Without even playing a gig with Drix, we had our eyes on the horizon for another drummer. We told him he had to do what he thought was best for him. I could understand that sentiment more, and probably meant it more, than Jeff and Laney. Even if this was my band now, it was still a hustle for me. I latched onto the best thing that came my way. Drix and I weren't that different. We kept at it and kept our chops up, made connections. I had the fleeting thought of moving out to LA and trying my hand as a session musician if New York fell through. Maybe Drix could set me up with the right people. I didn't like thinking about leaving Qualia, and had no intention of doing so. But, if New York fell through...

I looked at Laney sitting on the couch in the green room. She was warming up. She looked up and smiled and then back down at her guitar. I took out my bass and warmed up too.

The guys from Spectacular Death Extras were in sound check. When you're the headliner at bigger venues you get a proper sound check, which is a way more thorough line check. The sound man writes down or saves the settings for each instrument and mic. Takes notes as to what happens where during the set—reverb on the drums for a song, delay on the vocals for the intro—things like that. That's the reason the headliner almost always sounds better than the opening acts. It's not a mistake. When a band is consistent enough with ticket sales and can sell out 1,000 seat venues, they'll usually have their own people making sure the sound is as good as the venue allows. But a lot of the smaller big venues use their own guys. I knew that when Spectacular Death Extras opened up for Green Day, they'd probably be using Green Day's people. Of course, those people wouldn't make Spectacular Death Extras sound better than Green Day—just the opposite. Maybe the drums would be a little quiet, maybe the vocals would have a little too much mid-frequency. They wouldn't sound bad, but when Green Day hit the stage, the audience would subconsciously know they sounded better. It was a constant battle. Even when you caught a break, there'd be another new and annoying obstacle. The only way to overcome all that shit was to play well.

Laney, Jeff, and I sorted out a super power set list. Thirty minutes of balls-out rock and theater. If Spectacular Death Extras were going to bump us, we were going to give the audience a hell of a ride. Make those motherfuckers come to work, and fucking play and get their suit vests dirty.

When Drix came back from sound check, we ran through the set list with him. He said it looked ok and took out his phone to program the tempos to the songs in order. We were on in about an hour. The doors opened in twenty minutes. We set up our gear and I went and chatted up the sound man. Turns out he was an Irish guy from Lancaster, Pennsylvania and used to run sound at the Chameleon Club and Tellus360 before coming out west to get into engineering. We talked about Pennsylvania, and how it's basically Philadelphia and Pittsburgh, and everything else in between might as well be Kentucky. I slipped him twenty bucks and got his address. Told him I'd send him some Tastykakes when I got back, and went to run a line check. He made us run through a song to get the levels right.

We stayed out on the floor while Drix hung out with Spectacular Death Extras backstage. Jeff went to the bar and ordered a shot and drank it. I looked at him.

"I'm not backstage," he said and shrugged and then made a sour face.

"You all right?" I said.

"My stomach's been rumbling since I woke up," he said.

"We told you not to get the prawns," Laney said.

"It's probably the antibiotics," Jeff said. "It's just a healthy diarrhea."

"Just don't shit yourself on stage," Laney said.

"Not so fast," I said. "This could work to our benefit."

"I'm not shitting on the stage," Jeff said and laughed. He grabbed his stomach. "Fuck. Laughing is no good."

"We're on in a few minutes," Laney said. "Can you make it?"

"I think so," Jeff said.

The room was filling up. It was almost at full capacity. Can't count on that every night, but at least for the first show of the tour we had a room. We went onstage and got our instruments ready to go. We tuned up while the house music was blasting through the PA. Drix came onstage and sat down. He put an earbud in, connected to his phone. The house music stopped and Drix counted off the first song. Jeff turned around, his eyes wide.

"Fuck," he said and ran off the stage. Drix kept playing the groove. I motioned to Laney and we moved closer towards the drums.

"Just lay into the drums, low and steady. We did this with Gooch. It'll work," I said to Drix.

"Dig," he said. He was wearing sunglasses still. I wondered if he was on something. He gave the floor tom a roll with his sticks.

My pocket buzzed. I slipped my phone out.

Still shitting. Ready to wipe. One minute.

I told Laney and Drix. We hung out for as long as we could, swaying to the drums. A minute-long intro is too fucking much. We were nearing two—it'd be a grace of the music gods if we didn't lose the audience. I took a deep breath.

The crowd moved forward. I looked at Laney and we began the intro after a few more passes of Drix on drums.

I saw a body moving through the crowd, making its way to the side of the stage. It was Jeff. He ran onstage and stood in front of Drix. He was sweating. He looked grey. He counted off and then turned and grabbed the mic, just as before, when Laney and I hit our chords and notes. Drix followed and kept up. He was a goddamn professional. Gooch was a good fucking drummer, no doubt about that. Drix was a fucking machine.

We stuck to the set that we outlined and most of the audience listened. Some people were talking in the back, but those people would probably talk during the rest of the bands too. Jeff bounced around the stage, a sweaty madman. No time for banter in between the songs. He thanked the venue once and told the audience our name. Jeff didn't wait for Drix and counted off our last song a little faster than usual.

We blasted through the song. It felt weird, but it worked. And then it was over. Jeff thanked the audience and ran off the stage. The crowd clapped and cheered. We played for twenty-eight minutes and gave them every fucking second of it. The other bands would have to top that.

Laney and I moved our gear backstage. The next band, Fire Police, was a new wave punk band from San Francisco. They hopped on stage and positioned their amps and set their kit up in front of Drix's since he was headlining.

We went to the merch table and there was a small line. We talked to some people and sold out of EPs. We were running low on everything else. Laney said the shipment should be at the next venue up in Sacramento. Jeff came over to the table as the next band was running a line check.

"How do you feel?" I asked.

"Not good," he said. "Every time I sit down it's a prawn faucet."

"That's disgusting, man."

"Make sure to drink a lot of water," Laney said. "You can't get dehydrated again."

Fire Police went on. They looked homeless and they must've been hanging out on the floor the whole time, because I didn't see them backstage once. I had a passing suspicion that Graham told them they weren't allowed backstage. I had nothing to base that on, but he seemed like the type of guy to boss around a bunch of kids he didn't like. To their credit, they had a couple of good songs, but their execution was a little sloppy. A dropped drumstick, a missed transition, too much talking in between the songs—all the things a young band does while cutting their teeth. They weren't awful, but this was what Spectacular Death Extras wanted. They were going to sound great compared to these guys. Jeff went to the bathroom again during the set. Laney got him a glass and a pitcher of water from the bar. I really wanted a drink, but didn't want to rock the boat just in case Graham was watching.

The band finished and the room was packed out. I stood there with Jeff and Laney as Spectacular Death Extras took the stage. The audience cheered for them. I nudged Jeff in the side and nodded to the stage.

"Drix is wearing a fucking vest?" I said.

"He can't fuck up the image," Jeff said.

They started their first song. Their bass player was good. That's the first thing I noticed. The second thing was they were dead without Drix.

The songs were catchy enough. Pop rock music. Ryan and Sean were sloppy and sounded like a shitty Weezer. Drix and Mason propelled the songs, kept the groove going. They still sounded better than the punk band.

When they played their single that was getting all the views and airtime, the audience went apeshit. I'll give them credit. They wrote a pretty damn good song. But Jeff was right. We were better than them.

When they finished their set, they thanked Fire Police for joining them. They didn't mention us. We stood at our merch table while the audience left. We filled a few pages of contacts and sold the last of the shirts and stickers. We'd have to get to the venue early tomorrow to sort out the new shipment. Jeff was rocking back and forth.

"I gotta go," he said.

"We got this," I said.

He left the table and went to the bathroom. Again.

Spectacular Death Extras wandered out to their merch table with Drix. They had some members from their street team running the table for them. There was a surge towards them when they came out. People wanting autographs and to meet them. While I admired the do-it-yourself aesthetic to Qualia, I couldn't help but wonder if we should step up our game. Get more involved—maybe even get a legit manager, instead of having Laney run everything. She was doing fine. The band was doing fine. But Spectacular Death Extras, with their average music, were further ahead in the game than us. And when I saw Graham come out from backstage with an envelope, I knew it was because of him. I didn't like the guy, but I knew he knew when and where and how high they should jump.

"Here's your cut," Graham said and put the envelope on the table.

Laney picked it up and counted it. She looked at him.

"Something wrong?" he said.

"We agreed to twenty percent."

"That's what you got, minus my handling fee." He stared at her. "It could be more."

She stared back.

He leaned over the table. "Or, we could work out another kind of handling fee." He looked at her body.

"Back the fuck up," I said and moved.

Laney grabbed my arm.

Graham laughed. "Lighten up. I'm just kidding." He winked at Laney and went to the next table where his band was.

"How much did he undercut us?" I asked.

"About three hundred dollars. We still made seven."

I shook my head. "I guess it's not that bad. But I don't like that motherfucker one bit."

"Me either," she said. "Tomorrow will be better. We'll have more merch to sell."

I took a deep breath. "Just five more days."

Jeff came over to the table. "My ass hasn't been this sore since cub scouts," he said. "I think it's all gone."

"Have they all returned to sea?" I said.

"I hope so. I don't think I can handle another dump." He looked at the envelope in Laney's hand. "That our cut?"

"Yeah," she said.

"Cool," he said.

I looked at Laney. She wasn't going to tell Jeff.

The last of the crowd left and the building curfew was in a half hour. Spectacular Death Extras went onstage to break down their gear. Drix walked past us and gave us a nod.

"Nice vest, Sinatra," I said to him.

He pointed his finger at me and shook his head. I couldn't imagine what he was thinking. I'm sure he was aware, even more so than us, how much of an asshole Graham was.

Graham walked past the table, and then doubled back.

"Oh, one more thing. I damn near forgot." He pulled a paper out of his pocket and handed it to Laney. "There's been a change of plans. We're heading to LA tomorrow."

CHAPTER 15

"What the fuck are we going to do?" Laney said. We were back at our motel. Drix was staying with Spectacular Death Extras since he was on their dime. I sent him a text and was still waiting for a reply.

"Can we have the club ship the merch to LA?" Jeff asked.

"We'll be gone before it gets there," she said.

"That's if they even send it out," I said. "I'm sure the club is pissed that Graham pulled the bands from the line-up."

Jeff cracked open a beer. We had stopped at a gas station on the way back to the motel and grabbed a couple of six-packs and a case of water. We told Jeff he had to drink one bottle of water every hour before bed.

Laney shook her head. "We'll have to get the merch shipped to another gig." She took a pull off her beer. "This is gross."

Jeff shrugged. "It's all they had in pounders."

"You could have not gotten pounders," she said.

"I like counting my beer in pounds," he said and took a long drink. "That's three."

"Let me see that list again," I said.

Laney handed me the new dates. "We're fucking backtracking," I said. We were now going back to LA, San Diego, Phoenix, and Flagstaff before ending in Las Vegas, where they scheduled a warm-up gig before playing with Green Day the day after.

"None of our people are going to come out a week after we just played," I said.

"I don't want to say it," Laney said. "But Ryan was right. We will be playing to mostly their fans. Merch or no, the exposure is going to be good."

Jeff threw his empty beer can at her. It flew slow across the room and landed on her foot. He spoke in a high, mocking voice, "Oooohhh, Ryan was right." He pinched his nipples when he said it and began prancing around the room singing, "Oooohhh, Ryan was right."

"Shut up," Laney said. "I'm just trying to see a bright side to this."

Jeff grabbed another beer and sat down. "What happened to putting a foot up their asses?"

Laney clenched her jaw and then took another pull on her beer.

"Speaking of asses," he said and grabbed his stomach again.

"Dude," Laney said. "That's unnatural."

"There might be one more on deck," Jeff said, "but I think it's passing." He took a deep breath.

"I was waiting for you to shit yourself onstage," I said.

"You don't even know," he said. "It was close."

"You did a good job. I could really sense the urgency."

"I could smell the urgency," Laney said.

Jeff spit out his beer. "That snuck out," he said. "Sorry about the crop dust. I thought I might have shit myself."

My phone buzzed. It was Drix.

Fucking kill me, he wrote. *No booze or nothing. These motherfuckers are lights out already.*

I took a picture of a beer can and sent it back.

What motel you at? he replied. *Meet up at my place tomorrow. You guys can crash. Let me know when you get in. Load-in is at 7.*

I told Jeff and Laney. They were fine with that. We needed to talk to Drix anyway about his intentions. We had to be in Omaha two days after we finished with Spectacular Death Extras. We were supposed to end with them in Spokane, and that would have still been a bitch of a haul. Laney scheduled a day off to just drive since we would have already played the Northwest with Lunchbox and Thermos. Still, Vegas to Omaha wasn't going to be any less of a pain in the ass.

Laney took out her phone and searched the internet for drummers looking for work. We watched a couple of demo videos from some dude in Denver and one girl in Omaha. She sent out an email to both of them. This was definitely not ideal, but if we gave any decent drummer a few days heads up they should have the tunes under their sticks in no time.

I was getting that creeping, sinking feeling again. Of losing control. So much of this had nothing to do with individual effort. I could bust my ass and be the best bass player in the world, but there were too many variables. I thought again of life as a session musician. It wouldn't be that bad and would sure beat bartending.

Jeff held up his pack of smokes.

"Nah, I'm good," I said.

"Suit yourself," he said and left the room.

Laney went to the window.

"What's up, lady?" I said.

"Nothing." She turned around and walked over to me. "Making sure he was out there."

I was sitting on the edge of the bed. She wiggled her way in between my legs and put her hands on either side of my face and kissed me. I ran my hands down her back and grabbed her ass.

"Are we going to keep sneaking around?" I said.

"Isn't that half the fun?" she said.

"It's some of it. Not all of it."

She pulled me closer and her legs were rubbing against me. She broke away and sat back down. "I don't think Jeff would care," she said.

"But he might?"

"Maybe."

"You guys . . ."

She laughed. "No. That's gross. He's like my brother."

"So he might want to kick my ass?"

"I don't think he could kick anyone's ass."

Jeff came back in the room. "Ah, flavor country," he said.

He grabbed another beer and sat down next to me.

"You might want to take it easy," Laney said. "We have to get up early and drive tomorrow. Six hours."

"Make Gooch drive," he said and lay down.

"Have you heard from him?" I asked Laney.

"No. You?" she said.

I shook my head.

"Well," Jeff said. "If we have to sleep, we should get to sleep."

He sat back up and took a joint out of his cigarette pocket. He held it up to us.

"How much did Rachel give you?" I said.

"More than I should be crossing state lines with," he said.

"I guess it would be rude of me to decline. Need to lessen that load in case we get busted. Laney?"

"Maybe a little," she said. "I'll drive first tomorrow."

"You are the best," I said.

"The best," Jeff said. We raised our beer cans to her and sang, "For she's a jolly good fellow."

"Shouldn't it be fella?" she said.

"She's right. It should be 'fella,' " Jeff said. We sang again. And then went to the bathroom to smoke up.

We were huddled in the bathroom, passing the joint around. This motel was a bit nicer than we were used to. Some of the places are dumps and you can pretty much do whatever you want. We felt it would be better to use caution. I felt like a teenager trying to smoke without my friend's parents catching us. We exhaled into a damp towel and Jeff emptied the roll of toilet paper and stuffed some tissues in one end in the absence of a dryer sheet. We kept the joint inside the tube to keep the smoke from escaping. Whatever did escape was pulled away into the exhaust vent.

"You know," Laney said, "We could have just gone outside to the van."

"Would MacGyver have just gone to the van?" I said.

"No way," Jeff said.

"Damn right," I said. "Now hand me that paper clip and blow dryer."

"What do you need the blow dryer for?" Jeff asked, excited.

"To stick in my belt loop like it's a gun," I said. "Like a lawman."

"You two are idiots," Laney said.

In the morning we texted Drix again. He sent us his address and Laney called the shipping company and got our merch shipped to San Diego. She checked the venue's listing to make sure everything was legit first, as far as us playing there. We doubted Graham would pull another last-minute change this late in the game. It made sense to head towards Vegas since that's where they had to be in six days. He did a lot of things that made sense. He was just a dick about it.

When Laney got off the phone with the shipping company she said it was going to cost us an extra hundred bucks for next day shipping, and re-fulfilling the order, whatever the fuck that meant. We were losing money on merch as of now.

We showered and got in the van. Jeff laid down in the backseat. LA was about six hours away.

"Let me know when you want to switch," I said to Laney.

"Ok. I slept pretty well last night," she said. "I'm good for a while."

We were heading south. We were playing a bigger venue than the Whisky that night. I didn't really care. I was excited to play to a big crowd, but going back to LA seemed anti-climactic. At least we would save some dough staying with Drix. We left early enough and were making good time. We'd be at Drix's by three.

There were hills to my right and plains to my left. It was a boring drive. The California aqueduct snaked along the road. I pointed it out to Jeff and Laney.

"I saw a show about that," he said. "If we go pee in it, it will end up in LA."

"I don't think it works that way," I said.

"It's true. It starts all the way up past San Francisco."

"Do you think the prawns are following you?"

"No need. They won the battle."

"You fought bravely, young Jeffrey," I said. "How do you feel today? Stomach, foot, head?"

"Pretty great," he said. "Just need a little nap and I'll be good."

"Take that nap," I said. "I'm driving next."

"Cool. Before I forget, can we stop at a grocery store before Drix's?"

"Yeah. Maybe we can make food instead of eating out tonight."

"I haven't touched a knife or a vegetable since we left," Laney said. "Is Drix a vegetarian?"

"He wasn't in high school," I said.

"I'll think of something," she said.

"Make that butternut squash lasagna," Jeff said from the back, half asleep.

"Dude, it's the summer, in California. There's no squash."

"'Merica," Jeff said. "We can get anything."

"Go to sleep," she said.

Jeff hummed a few bars of "God Bless America" softly before drifting off.

Laney and I played a game, naming songs, A-Z, from bands. We started with the Beatles. No Q, U, V, or Z.

That was easy. Zeppelin was a little more difficult. No E, J, Q, U, V, or Z. I swore there wasn't a P, but she got "Poor Tom." We did a few other bands and then named the best desert island bands of each decade. The rule was we had to pick bands that broke through and had a legacy, and that released an album in that decade. We started with the 50s and split on Buddy Holly and Chuck Berry. The 60s were tough. It was a toss-up between the Beatles, The Doors, and Hendrix for me. I settled on the Beatles.

"That's original," she said.

"You picked the Stones," I said.

"At least the Stones were cool. The 60s sucked."

"Bite your tongue."

I picked Zeppelin for the 70s and Tom Waits for the 80s. She went for Queen and Queen.

"You can't pick them for both," I said.

"Sure I can. I was going to pick R.E.M., but Queen was better."

"Everyone was better than R.E.M.," I said. "Also, isn't Queen a 60s band?"

"Nope."

"They formed in the late 60s as Smile," I said.

"In 1968, without Freddie Mercury. He joined in 1970 and that's when they changed their name. They played their first show in June. Don't tell me my Queen."

She grinned.

"All right, all right," I said. "You can have them. But pick a new band for the 90s."

I picked Jeff Buckley.

"Oh, that's a good one," she said. "I pick Radiohead."

"Now who's being original?" I said.

"They're a great band," she said.

"They've got a great bass player, that's for sure. Ok, 2000s."

"Yours is Creed," she said.

"They sold more records than Nirvana, sooo…"

"No they didn't. Did they?"

I smiled.

"I can't tell if you're serious," she said.

"You'll never know."

"So what would yours be?" she asked. "For real?"

"This is tough," I said. "The 2000s had no identity. They tried, but the most original big band was System of a Down, but they were kind of just one thing. Probably won't leave a legacy. I think I'm stealing your Radiohead."

"No identity? What about Arcade Fire? Or the Flaming Lips? Yoshimi was '02."

"Settle down with the Arcade Fire. They're decent, sure. But c'mon. They're no Murder by Death."

"What?"

"Arcade's just another bullshit mainstream band pretending they're still in a garage," I said. "Nobody *really* likes them. It's just cool to say."

"You wouldn't trade places with them?"

"In a fucking heartbeat," I laughed. "Who's your 2000s? If you say the Strokes I'm driving us off a cliff."

"I'm going Queens of the Stone Age."

"Ah, fuck. I forgot about them," I said. "Can I change mine?"

"Nope," she said.

"What about a band without 'Queen' in the name?"

"I get two? Rufus Wainwright. All day."

"Really? There's a lot of orchestration and piano music on your list. Wouldn't have guessed it."

"Why?"

"You don't play like that. I know the two aren't related, but, just an observation."

"Tom Waits and Jeff Buckley aren't exactly bass music," she said.

"I'm a sensitive guy, Laney," I said. "So, do we pick for the 2010s?"

"They're not over."

"I think it's all shit."

"You're getting old."

"Some things we can't change," I said and shook my head. "I pick Leonard Cohen. R.I.P."

"That's a weird pick."

"Your face is a weird pick. Leonard was a goddamned poet," I said. "*You Want It Darker* was fantastic."

"Do you think 'sensitive' means 'solemn' and 'depressive?' " she said with mock concern and put her hand on my arm.

"Funny."

"I think I'm going to wait until the decade's over," she said.

"You owe me an answer in a few years."

"Deal."

We stopped for gas and woke Jeff up in case he needed the bathroom. It was my turn to drive. Laney sat up front with me and Jeff stayed in the back. He took out *Moby Dick* and started to read it again.

Outside of LA we stopped at a supermarket. I couldn't remember the last time I was in a supermarket. Tons of convenience stores and drugstores, but no supermarkets. Jeff branched off, said he needed to grab a few items. I walked up the aisles with Laney. I felt weird. Like an explorer visiting civilization after being in the jungle. It felt domestic.

"What are you going to make?" I asked.

"Something easy that doesn't use a lot of dishes. I'm not sure what Drix has," she said. "He's got to have a pot and a pan."

"I'm starting to kind of like this vegetarian thing."

"Thinking about joining us?"

"Fuck no. It's just a nice change. If we weren't supposed to eat animals, why would they be made out of meat?"

"You're an ass."

She grabbed groceries for a vegetarian chili. Beans and vegetables and cheese.

"When did you learn to cook?" I asked her.

"When I was too poor to go out every night. Pretty much after we moved to Philly."

"I've always wanted to make bread."

"I'll teach you when we get back."

"Get back? Christ, I haven't actually thought about that. I almost want to stay on tour forever."

"Well, the last gig is in twelve days. And then we'll be home."

I had this vision of me and Laney back in Philadelphia. Unpacking groceries in her kitchen. Making food and listening to music. Going to bed afterwards.

"You all right?" she said.

"Just thinking," I said.

"You do that a lot."

"Think?"

"Zone out. You go into your weird little Paul place."

"I told you I'm a solemn depressive," I said and laughed.

She looked around and then kissed me. We went to pay for the groceries. Jeff was waiting at the front of the store with his bag.

"What'd you get?" I asked.

He opened up his bag. Flour, eggs, sugar, butter, and chocolate chips.

We parked out front of Drix's place. I didn't see his car. I wondered if he left it in San Francisco. He said he'd be home by three-thirty. It was just after three. A girl came out of Drix's apartment carrying a box. She was screaming about something.

"Maybe he is home," I said.

The girl threw the box on the sidewalk and plates and books and records spilled out. She went back in the house.

"Damn," Laney said.

"Whoa, I didn't know people actually did that," Jeff said from the back. "You think Drix is home?"

"Fuck if I know," I said. "I'm not going near crazy over there."

She came back out with a snare drum. She lifted it over her head and threw it down the steps. She went back inside and came back a second later, shuffling the bass drum through the door.

"What the fuck. Not his drums," I said and got out of the van and ran across the street.

"Hey," I yelled. I stepped over the box and snare drum on the sidewalk and ran up the steps to the porch just as she figured out to turn the drum sideways to get it through the door.

"Hey," I said again. I didn't know what else to say, but I couldn't let her destroy his gear.

"Who the fuck are you?" she said.

"I'm Paul," I said and smiled and stuck out my hand. She squinted and looked at me and then down at my hand and then back up. She had dark hair, olive skin, and green eyes as still as statues.

"You looking for Drix?" she said.

"Yeah, we were supposed to meet him here."

"He's not here. He's in San Francisco fucking some bitch."

"Uh," I said. "I think he's playing with a band."

"He's always playing with a band," she said. "But, he's also fucking some bitch behind my back."

I had no idea if Drix was screwing around on this girl or not, and wasn't sure what to say. I covered for him anyway.

"Drix was with me the past two days. He hasn't been out of my sight until we left San Francisco this morning. We must have just beat him here."

She stared at me. She was mean beautiful. The kind of girl that's on Italian advertisements. The kind of girl you want to fuck because she'd be in charge.

I heard a car pull up in front of the house and a record crunch under the tire. I broke her gaze and looked down to the street. It was Drix.

Thank god.

"Nadia," he said. "What are you doing, baby? We talked about this."

"Where were you?" she said.

"Damn girl, I told you I was hitting the road for a few days." He looked down at the sidewalk, at his stuff, and then back to us. "Paul, this is Nadia, Nadia, this is Paul."

"Hey man, I'll give you guys some space," I said. "Nadia, it was nice meeting you." Drix nodded. Nadia didn't say anything to me, and started in on Drix again.

I got back in the van.

"Jesus Christ," I said. "That chick is a typhoon."

"Is that his girlfriend?" Jeff asked. "If she isn't anymore, do you think he could set me up?" He laughed. He leaned over the front seat. "What did she smell like?"

"No idea," I said. She actually smelled really fucking good, but I didn't want to say that in front of Laney.

"Come on, man," Jeff said. "She had to smell like something."

"Dude," Laney said. "Why are guys attracted to train wrecks?"

"I'm a man, Laney," Jeff said. "We're attracted to danger. Just like how girls like assholes."

"Not all girls," Laney said.

"Right," Jeff said. "Gerard is a real prince."

"You dated a guy named Gerard?" I said.

Laney looked at Jeff. "Let's drop it."

"What?" he said. "That guy was a dick. Who almost fucked this whole tour up by trying to drag you to Saint-Tropez."

"Argentina," she said and looked forward. "We're here now."

"Well," I said, and started the van. "This concludes another episode of 'Things That Happened in Qualia Before Paul Joined.'" I drove down the street. "Let's give Drix a little time to sort his lady out."

I felt weird. I was processing that Laney had a boyfriend before the tour, and that maybe she still did have one. I felt jealous and conflicted. I didn't think I was the jealous type. I drove around and didn't say anything, trying to play it cool. I knew that eventually Laney and I would talk about it. She reached over and turned on the radio and shuffled through the stations until she found a local rock station.

"Why do rock stations play the same things all the time," Jeff said.

"Yeah," I said. "The same two or three songs by Pearl Jam, Weezer, Zeppelin, and Metallica."

"And whatever new song is out by Muse."

"Some of them play our song," Laney said.

"At night," Jeff said.

My pocket buzzed. It was Drix.

"It's safe to go back," I said.

We parked out front. There were broken fragments of a record in the street, but everything else was picked up. We brought in the groceries.

"Sorry about that guys," Drix said. "Thanks for saving my kit, man," he said to me.

"Don't mention it," I said.

"We brought food," Laney said and held up the bag.

"Right on," Drix said. "The kitchen is back there. I'm fucking starving. Those dudes woke up early as shit and ate without me, and then we hopped straight on the road and went to the radio station."

Drix had a small fridge in his living room. There was a couch with a chair and a small end table. The middle room had some gear stacked up against the wall. His place was clean, but spare. He opened the fridge and took out two beers. He tossed one to me and one to Jeff.

"Laney?" he said.

"No thanks," she said. "I'm gonna go get started." She went to the kitchen.

"I'm going to help," Jeff said and followed her. Drix took out another beer for himself and sat down on the couch. I sat in the chair and opened my beer.

He let out a long sigh after taking a swig.

"How'd the radio station go?" I asked.

"Dude," Drix said. "It was bad. Those dudes aren't too weird around themselves, but as soon as someone else enters their bubble besides Graham they turn into fucking mutants. Everything is canned and scripted. It's gross to see. You can see those motherfuckers transform like that chick in *X-Men.*"

"Did you know we were coming back to LA?"

He sighed and shook his head and took another pull from his beer.

"Just found out last night. Probably right before you guys did. I wouldn't have drove up to San Francisco otherwise if I knew we were coming back. Would've rented a car or rode with you guys or some shit. I asked Graham if there were any more surprises, and he said there wasn't, so..."

"Fuck that guy," I said. "Is he being as much a dick to you as he is to us?"

"No," Drix said. "He's still a prick, but he needs me more than I need him."

"They're dead without you," I said.

"I know."

Drix looked towards the kitchen. "Are they smoking without me back there?"

We went to the kitchen and Jeff was standing over a small pot. Stirring. Buttery, weed scented steam wafted up. Laney was sitting at the kitchen table looking at her phone.

"Yo, yo, yo, what's going on back here?" Drix said.

Jeff looked over and smiled. "Oh, just making the butter for my grandma's famous cookies."

"Fucking most excellent," Drix said.

"I figured if we can't drink or piss around them, we could at least be relaxed."

"My tolerance is for shit on those," I said.

"Most people's is if you actually want to do things," Jeff said. "The four of us could probably split a cookie and be nice and relaxed for the evening. Maybe top off after we play."

"I'm good," Laney said, staring at her phone and swiping her finger. "I'll wait till after we play and collect from Graham."

"Then it's a three-way," Jeff said. "One cookie. Three dudes."

"That's a four-way, dude," Drix said.

"Call it whatever you want guys, just as long as none of us makes eye contact," I said.

"Deal," Jeff said.

"Nah man," Drix said and laughed. "I'm gonna look long and hard into your soul."

"Holy shit," Laney said.

We looked over at her. She was smiling and looking at her phone.

"What's up?" Jeff asked.

She looked up and smiled wider.

"Pitchfork was at our show last night."

CHAPTER 16

A top editor for Pitchfork did a write-up of our show last night and posted it on the "Rising" section of their website—with the link and blurb on their homepage. Laney read us the article:

> *Last night there was a rock show. The bands: Spectacular Death Extras, Fire Police, and the highlight of the evening, Qualia.*

"The highlight, eh?" Jeff said.
"It gets better," Laney said.

> *The venue: Vaquero Caballero. A new space in San Francisco with great sound and plenty of room to dance or get intimate with the band. Don't let the decor throw you—it looks like Quentin Tarantino's hipster nephew was the designer—this place was built for live shows.*
>
> *I was on assignment to cover Spectacular Death Extras, who just signed with a major. If you don't*

know their song, look it up. It is good. Go. Do it now.

Qualia, a four-piece out of Philadelphia, has been putting in the hours and the miles all summer in support of their self-titled EP, and has been getting some major buzz. I went early to check them out and to say my mind was blown would not only be lazy writing, but an understatement.

Theater. Drama. Dynamics. The band started their set with a catchy rhythmic number that only really began when the singer ran on the stage with the immediacy and flair of Freddie Mercury and joined the band.

Jeff leaned against the counter and put his hands behind his head. "Read that line again," he said.

"Shut up," Laney said. "Let me finish."

The band performed with intensity and precision. The rhythm section was primal and fierce. Their bass player thrashed around his instrument like a toy while locking in with their sunglasses-wearing drummer, who I swear was a robot.

I put my fist out for Drix. He hit it and we nodded to each other.

Their lady guitar player picked lines she wrangled out of her guitar or let slither away under her fingers, laying on top of the rhythm section. Every great band has a great lead singer. Qualia is no exception. Their lead singer performed with the urgency of a time bomb and he was no less explosive.

We all laughed at that.

"Did he follow you to the bathroom after the show?" I asked.

"There's a little more," Laney said. She went on.

His voice was clean, and turned gritty when it needed to be. I may still be reeling and indulging, but I don't think it is far off the mark to say he sounded like a blend of Jeff Buckley, minus the whining, and Chris Cornell, minus the nasal grunge angst.

The band launched into each song and did not relent. They were there, and then they were gone. Keep your ears open for this band. Their EP is good (I have listened to it twice since last night), but their live show is a force that overshadowed the evening.

Laney read us the rest of the article, which reported on Spectacular Death Extras and Fire Police without much of a review.

"Well, goddamn," Jeff said. "Let's keep that up."

"Good shit, guys," Drix said.

I looked at Laney. And then at Jeff. I could tell we all were thinking the same thing. That Drix was part of that. Jeff turned to his butter. "Almost done," he said and began dumping flour and eggs into a bowl. Laney got up and started opening the cans we bought and poured them into a big pot.

Drix and I sat at the table and drank our beers. His phone buzzed and he took it out of his pocket.

"This chick," he said. He shook his head, and typed away.

"What's the deal with her?" I said.

"Man, I don't even know," he said. "One week we're on, one week we're off. Been like that for a year. I told her we needed to chill last week after I found out she was fucking the new Spanish bartender at the club where she works. I don't blame her since shit's been pretty stale lately and I'd be a liar if I said I didn't think about it either."

"How long you been going out?" I asked.

"A little over a year. Longest relationship I've been in, man. Besides with my drums," he said. "I told her we'd sort shit out when I got back, but she thinks I'm out there fucking chicks just because she was banging other people. All guilty conscience and shit."

"Where'd you meet her?"

"I was on a gig at the club where she works. It's some weird joint that claims it ain't a strip club even though the girls that dance on the stage show their tits for money in private rooms."

"That sounds like a strip club."

"They call it a cabaret, which could fucking mean anything."

"That's weird man. I didn't think strip clubs hired male bartenders," I said.

"I never said it was a dude," Drix said.

I raised my eyebrows and smiled a little.

"That was my first thought, brother," he said. "She wasn't into it and it made her jealous. Can you believe that shit? She got jealous."

"What are you going to do?"

"Finish the tour and pretend I'm Jay-Z. I got ninety-nine problems, know what I mean?"

We finished our beers and got another round. We had to be at the venue in two hours. Jeff finished baking the cookies and Laney told us to help ourselves with the chili, which was really fucking delicious.

We were sitting around Drix's living room after dinner, just relaxing. Drix was warming up on a practice pad, tapping away. We had to get to the venue soon.

"So," Laney said to Drix. "Which way are you leaning?"

"For?" he said.

"You have to tell Spectacular Death Extras your decision tonight."

He looked down. "Oh, yeah," he said. "I'm not sure yet. I mean, they are signed and it's the next step..."

Laney cut him off. "It's ok, dude. We get it. I would just rather set up another drummer sooner than later."

Jeff and I were sitting on the couch, listening, and looking at Drix and Laney.

"I don't want to let you motherfuckers down," Drix said and looked at me. "But this shit was kinda lined up already. You know?"

I nodded.

"It's cool," Laney said. "There's a couple of drummers that we found that we could get for the final gigs. They're not as good as you, but they'll do after some practice."

Jeff cleared his throat. "You don't think there's a chance you'll be in New York in a week for the showcase?" he said.

"Man, if I could be, I would," Drix said. "I want to help, but I've been out here a long time banging away, trying to make this shit happen."

"Ahh," Jeff said. "Just wishful thinking. We'll sort it out." Jeff took a big freezer bag full of cookies out of a grocery bag and tossed them across to Drix. "Here's a going away and thank you present to help get you through the rest of the tour."

"Dude," Drix said, weighing the bag in his hands. "This is a lot."

"You'll need a lot to be around Graham and those assholes," Jeff said.

"And to wear that vest," I said.

"Don't remind me, man," Drix said. "You know we still have five more gigs together, right?"

"Yeah, but it goes fast," Jeff said.

"Yeah, it does," Drix said. He stood up to put the cookies in his gig bag, along with his sticks and practice pad. He laughed. "Thanks for the inscription."

"What's it say?" I asked.

"'To Drix, Love, Gran Ma-Ma,'" Drix said and tucked them away in his bag.

"Nobody fucks with Gran Ma-Ma," Jeff said.

We got to the venue and parked around back. I was hoping we'd get to play at one of the other old joints, but this place was relatively new and looked like it could hold about a thousand people. Maybe more. None of the other bands were there yet. I saw Graham on my way to the bathroom talking to the venue's manager or promoter and making gestures with his hands, pointing up. I didn't want to go near him and went backstage after taking a piss.

"Graham is here," I said.

"Great," Laney said. "Let's bring our gear in."

We brought our amps and guitars in. Laney stayed inside to sort out the shipment that was due at the club tomorrow in San Diego. Jeff and I went back out to give Drix a hand with his kit. A van pulled in the lot and parked. I looked over. A guy got out of the front. He looked familiar. Three other guys got out of the side door of the van and walked around and stared at us. One of them had a shaved head and a big beard.

"What the fuck?" I said and put down the drum I was carrying.

"What's up?" Drix said, turning from his car.

"Is that fucking Space Shovel?" Jeff said.

I didn't respond and went over to their van.

"Yo," I said and nodded my head up as I walked towards them. They didn't say anything. The bald guy looked at me, and the guy I recognized as their singer clenched his jaw. The other two guys were looking at Drix, who was following right behind me.

"Hey dickhead, where's our fucking drums?" I said to their drummer, inches from his face.

"Fuck you," he said and pushed me.

I pulled my right fist to punch him. Drix grabbed my arm as their singer swung at my face. Drix pulled me away fast, and the hit rolled off my cheek after making contact. Jeff ran over and the other guys in Space Shovel came at us. Jeff ducked and caught the bass player in the balls with his fist. I heard a door slam and saw another van pull into the parking lot.

The singer kicked Jeff in the side and he fell.

Then I saw Graham. He jumped in the middle of the melee. "What the fuck is going on?" he yelled.

Everyone stopped. "Are you guys fucking fighting like a bunch of assholes? On my bill?"

I rubbed my face. "They started it," I said.

Graham took a deep breath and glared at me.

More doors opened and Ryan, Sean, and Mason came over.

"Hi, Graham," Ryan said and then looked at Jeff getting up off the ground and Space Shovel's bass player cupping his crotch and wincing.

"You're fucking late," Graham said, now staring at the guys in Space Shovel. "Load-in was ten minutes ago."

Nobody moved. Everybody stood around looking at each other and holding their wounds.

"Move," Graham said. We backed away to Drix's car and Spectacular Death Extras went to their van. Graham stayed there with Space Shovel. I could hear him yelling at them. I was glad for that. I looked at Drix.

"Why the fuck did you stop me?" I said.

"This ain't Philly, bro," he said. "We're not kids anymore. We can't just go around socking people."

"They stole Gooch's drums," I said.

"And busting your hand on that dude's head won't get them back."

I knew he was right. "But it would have made me feel better," I said.

"You all right?" he asked and looked at my face.

I touched my cheekbone. It hurt a little. It would have been worse if Drix didn't pull me away.

"It's not bad."

"Cool," Drix said. "Sorry, man. I don't want to see you fuck up for stupid shit. We cool?"

"Yeah, man," I said. "Always."

"Aww," Jeff said. He was leaning against the car smoking a cigarette. "You guys are so cute together."

"Shut up," I said and laughed. "How's your side?"

"It hurts, but I'll live," he said.

"Yo, dude," Drix said. "A cock punch? That's your move?"

"Right in the co-jones," Jeff said.

"You mean *cojones*?" I asked.

"I said what I meant," Jeff said. "My old sensei always said, 'A man can't stand, he can't fight.'" He took a long drag off his cigarette.

"You were in karate?" Drix asked.

"Not really," he said. "But my older cousin made me watch the *Karate Kid* movies with him every time I went to his house."

Drix put his hand on Jeff's shoulder. "I'm real sorry to hear that, man," he said and laughed.

"What's so funny?" Graham said, walking over to us.

"Nothing, man," Drix said. "Just trying to chill things out."

Graham looked at him and then us. "I don't want you guys anywhere near each other tonight," he said and motioned towards Space Shovel. "If anything goes wrong, no one gets paid. Got it?"

"Yes, sir," I said.

He leveled his eyes at us, then looked at Drix. "They told me you broke their drums a few weeks ago?"

"Nah, man," Drix said. "Wasn't me."

Graham shook his head. "I'm not fucking babysitting. Qualia's gear stays backstage, Space Shovel keeps theirs in the green room. I don't want any fucking problems," he said. He walked away mumbling to himself.

"Well, I guess that settles that," Jeff said.

"Yeah. No green room for us," I said. "We'll have to mingle with common folk out on the floor."

"Or backstage," Jeff said. "I still don't trust them."

"Or we could just roll after we play since we don't have any merch. Take us out of the equation," I said.

"That's a smart motherfucker, now," Drix said. "See man. It takes so little to do the right thing."

Jeff bowed to Drix. "Ah, yes. Master Drix very smart. Very smart."

"What is that voice?" I said to Jeff.

"Miyagi, Pauly-san," he said and then stood in the crane kick position, with his cigarette hanging out of his mouth.

Laney came out.

"Do you want a piece of this, Laney?" Jeff said, turning his head to her.

"A piece of what?" she said.

Jeff skipped around on one foot to face her head on, his arms hanging high above his head, his right knee up.

"You look like an idiot," she said.

Jeff jumped and kicked, barely leaving the ground, and his shoe flew off his kicking foot and hit Laney in the boob. "What the fuck?" she said and rubbed herself.

"Shit, sorry," Jeff said.

Laney picked up his shoe and threw it at him.

"Did you see who we're playing with?" she said. She looked at me. "What happened to your face?"

"I saw who we're playing with," I said.

We told her what happened and about Graham and our gear. Jeff embellished his part and said he did a split and punched two of them in the balls. We let him have that one.

We helped Drix with the last of his kit and put it onstage. Jeff and Laney went out to get a hot tea for Jeff from the gas station across the street. I stayed with Drix and helped him set up. Ryan, Sean, and Mason finished setting up their amps. Graham waved to them and they got off the stage.

"Does he tell them when to shit?" I said.

"You don't even know," Drix said. "He's got them locked down."

"He's gonna have you locked down soon, too," I said.

"Not like that, he won't," he said. "He knows my role. He's a real prick, but he's also a smart businessman."

"Just don't lose yourself in all the shit."

"Don't worry about me, brother. I got this."

The sound man came over to the stage. "Where's the rest of the band?"

"They just left," Drix said.

"Let's start with drums, then," he said.

Drix asked me to go to the green room and get a drum key out of his bag and tell Spectacular Death Extras it was time for sound check while he ran sound on his drums.

"It's little and silver. Looks like a 'T'," he said.

"I know what it looks like," I said. "But I'm not supposed to be in there."

"You'll be in and out, dude. No worries," he said.

I went to the green room and opened the door.

The only band in there was Space Shovel, sitting on the couch, surrounded by their gear. Their drums were stacked in the corner just inside the door. I saw Drix's bag, the one he stuck his practice pad in at his house, leaning against the wall. I went over to it. I didn't say anything to Space Shovel. I could feel their eyes on me. I opened Drix's bag and took out the cookies and set them on the floor and rummaged for the drum key.

"What are you doing in here?" one of them said. "You heard the man."

I didn't say anything and kept looking.

"We're talking to you," the same voice said.

I found the drum key in the bottom of the bag and stood up, and made for the door. A drumstick hit me in the back, and then fell on the floor. I turned around and stared at their singer and drummer.

"What?" the drummer said.

I shook my head and breathed deep. "Nothing, man," I said. "Nothing."

I left the room and gave the drum key to Drix, who was hitting his drums, with one stick, evenly and slowly.

"Thanks," he said. "Where're the other guys?"

"Beats me," I said. "I'll go take a look."

I hopped off stage and went outside.

There was a guy on a ladder adjusting the marquee. I looked up and he was putting the words "Sold Out" after the time. We had second billing on the sign.

I saw Jeff and Laney crossing the street and I nodded to them.

"Give me a cigarette," I said to Jeff.

"You all right?" he said.

"Yeah," I said. "I just ran into Space Shovel."

"You didn't try to fight them again, did you?" Laney said.

"No. But I really, really want to lay out the singer and drummer."

Jeff handed me a cigarette. "Easy there, champ," he said. "We'll be out of here soon."

I pointed up to the guy getting off the ladder. "Did you see the line-up? Did something change?"

"No," Laney said. "We're the bigger band. Nationally anyway."

"Than Space Shovel," I said.

"Well, yeah," she said.

"Second billing, on a sold-out show, at this venue," Jeff said and took out a cigarette for himself. "That's not too bad."

"Except we're not playing that slot in the line-up," I said.

Jeff squinted his eyes and let the cigarette hang out of his mouth.

"Ehhh, fuck the line-up," he said imitating Graham, but sounding like a bad Marlon Brando impersonation. "It's about the branding, kid." He slapped me, slowly and twice on the cheek.

"Oh, god," Laney said.

I looked at him. "Are you high?"

"I had a nibble," he said in the same voice and moved his hands with each syllable. "Just a nibble. You don't want to fuck with Gran Ma-Ma."

"I can't believe you ate a cookie," Laney said.

"I'm good," he said, squinting his eyes still. "I'm good."

I looked at Laney.

"Relax guys," Jeff said in his regular voice. "I just had a tiny bit. I know my shit. It'll pass quick. Just a nice little mellow before the show."

"I hope so," Laney said.

"Here, look," Jeff said. He took a cookie out of his pocket, wrapped in a plastic bag. He was right. There was only a quarter size bite taken out.

"That little bit got you fucked up?" I said.

"I wouldn't say 'fucked up,' 'fucked up,'" he said. "But, yeah. This is the good shit. I'm leveling out now. Took a nib after our scuffle."

"All right," I said.

"I'll be good," he said. And then as shitty Brando, "I never make a promise that I refuse to keep."

"You're a fucking idiot," Laney said and laughed.

We finished our cigarettes and went inside. Spectacular Death Extras was running a full sound check. There was a little bar off to the side. We went over and pulled down some stools and sat and listened while Jeff drank his tea. It felt weird to be in an empty big venue again. We'd been through this with Lunchbox and Thermos for a few weeks, but back then I was still adjusting to the band, and life on the road. Those weeks were a whirlwind.

In a little over a week from now we'd be in New York and auditioning for a label. I felt good about the Pitchfork write-up, and listening to Drix up on stage with his band I wished we could have him with us. I had the idea of texting Gooch to see if he would play the New York set with us. I wanted it to be as close to perfect as possible.

"Goddamn, he's good," I said to Laney and Jeff.

"Yeah," Laney said. "The girl in Omaha isn't bad either."

"Is she Drix good?" I said.

Laney didn't answer.

"Do you think we should get in touch with Gooch sooner than later?" I asked.

Jeff looked over.

"Let's see what happens with Omaha first," Laney said.

"Ok," I said.

Spectacular Death Extras finished their sound check and went backstage. The doors opened in an hour and we were on a half hour after that.

Graham came over to the bar.

"Nice write-up guys," he said.

We looked at him.

"Thanks," Jeff said, looking away and taking a sip of his tea.

"Listen, tonight is sold out and I was thinking about waiving my handling fee," Graham said.

Jeff looked at him and then Laney.

"It's a formality," he said, looking at Jeff. "One that needn't be if you had proper management."

"What's wrong with our management?" Laney asked.

"Nothing, if you want to stay small time," Graham said. "If you keep playing like you did last night, I know a guy."

"I thought the music didn't matter," Jeff said.

"Not for them it doesn't," he said, motioning towards the stage. "I didn't put them in suits and give them faggy haircuts for the hell of it."

"I think we're doing fine," I said.

"You have no drummer. No merch. And you're in a shitty van driving around like a bunch of fucking soccer moms."

"Who's your guy?" Jeff asked, and took out a cigarette and put it behind his ear.

Graham took a business card out of his jacket pocket and handed it to Jeff. He looked at Laney. "Just think about it. I'll throw your drummer in the deal. He's good, but he doesn't fit the image, if you know what I mean."

"I don't follow," I said and stared at him.

"Relax," he said. "You need to start thinking bigger. I'm going out to dinner and will make some calls. I've got some people in town. Play well tonight, and it's your move."

Jeff put the card in his pocket. "We'll talk it over."

Graham smiled. "Don't think too much. Say 'yes.' This isn't a standing offer."

He walked away and out of the building.

"That guy is a fucking shark," I said.

"So, Laney," Jeff said. "What's this handling fee he was talking about?"

Laney told him about the percentage Graham was taking.

"You didn't have some sort of agreement with him?" Jeff said. "Something he couldn't break?"

"I thought we did," she said.

Jeff shook his head. "Three hundred dollars."

"Which is nothing compared to three thousand," she said back.

"I got sick," he said.

"You got yourself sick."

Jeff narrowed his eyes. "Maybe he's right."

"About?"

"We should look for management."

"You're not seriously considering him?"

"Fuck, no," Jeff said. "But, before New York. Who's going to handle our contract?"

"The one we don't have yet?" she said.

"You don't think we'll get it?"

"No, I'm just not arguing hypotheticals."

"Ok," Jeff said. "Forget hypotheticals. We just got took for thirty percent—which should have been fifteen, max, if we had a legit manager. And that fifteen would have gone to him, the guy on our team. Not some jerk-off with finger rings."

"All right guys," I said, standing up. "Let's cool off for a few. This is Graham's game. The guy is poison."

Neither of them said anything. I looked at Laney and she avoided meeting my eyes.

"Come on," I said to Jeff. "Let's go outside for a smoke before we run a line check."

I looked over to the stage. Drix was bent over, tightening the hardware on his drums. "Yo, Drix," I yelled. "Smoke?"

He nodded and put his finger up.

Just off stage I saw Mason looking at his bass amp. He brought his hand to his mouth.

CHAPTER 17

Laney stayed inside and said she was going to email Omaha and set up a time to talk. Jeff, Drix, and I went outside.

Jeff held up his cigarette. "We really need to stop this when we get back."

"My boy uses those nicotine lozenges," Drix said.

"Do they work?" I asked.

"He hasn't smoked since."

"Cool," Jeff said. He let out a big sigh and looked at me. "You know I'm right, right?"

"Yeah," I said. "I was thinking the same thing."

"Right about what?" Drix said.

"We should probably get a legit manager," Jeff said.

"Oh, yeah," Drix said. "Laney is cool as shit, but yeah man, you're gonna def want representation if you got a label interested in you. Someone you can trust to handle the business side while you focus on rock and roll."

"Do you have a manager?" Jeff asked.

"Nah, man. I'm freelance. My contracts are always short term."

"Are you going to get one before you sign on with those guys? That's happening real soon," I said.

"It's different. I know this dude I'll pay to look over the new contract. That's about as much as I'll need—make sure I get future royalties and a fair cut of the dough from gigging. Then I'm just along for the ride on Captain Graham's ship. I'll let that motherfucker handle the big shit, as far as the band goes."

"What if they don't make it?" I asked. "Like if the album doesn't catch? Or the label doesn't give them support?"

"Then I'll cut my losses, and add another job to the résumé. Make some contacts at the label and studio. It's all part of the process man. That's why a lot of dudes don't stay in the game. You got to network like a motherfucker if you want to keep your head above water."

"I hear you," I said.

In truth, I was shit at networking. I made my contacts through friends of friends and never went much beyond the regular working musician. I had the creeping thought again of life after Qualia. Moving out to LA or New York and getting hooked up with some session guys. I probably wouldn't join a new, younger band on my own again. I didn't think anybody would want to see a thirty-year-old bass player on stage with a bunch of twenty-two-year-olds. It happens sometimes when the label sets up a group, but it looks weird. At that point, if I started looking too old, I'd rather be a hired hand who stayed in the background and out of focus. Most live performances on talk shows and SNL, or the Super Bowl, by a singer like Beyoncé or whatever new young sex object the label is pushing—the players in the band are pros. In it for the paycheck. It's a job. I could live that life. Pop up to New York or out to LA for a couple of days here, a couple of days there. Meet the right people and go on tour for a summer, playing festivals.

But I was getting ahead of myself.

Jeff told Drix about Graham's proposal. About him being aware of the Pitchfork write-up and throwing Drix in the mix.

"That doesn't surprise me," Drix said and shrugged.

"You don't feel betrayed?" Jeff said.

"By that dude? Man, if anybody dealing with him isn't expecting to have the rug pulled out from under them at any point, they're the fool."

"That's an unfortunate attitude to be forced to have," I said.

"There's always a sacrifice. That's why I'll have my guy read over the new contract before I sign it," Drix said. "Make sure my expectations and demands are met."

"What kind of demands?" I asked.

"Topless women riding mechanical bulls?" Jeff said.

"A mechanical bull?" I said and looked at Jeff.

"Yeah, man. I'm a drummer. Not a director for an 80s music video," Drix said.

"Which video was that?" Jeff said.

"Fuck if I know. I was like two or some shit."

Drix sighed and stretched. "All right. I'm gonna check in with those dudes. See if there's anything I need to know."

"Make sure you get all the wrinkles out of your vest," I said.

"Go fuck yourself," Drix sang to the tune of "Summer Wind" and went inside.

Jeff took the last drag off his cigarette and flicked it into the street. The sun was still up, but it was beginning to sink and shine acutely between the buildings. If we were driving it would have been blinding at the wrong angles. I felt tense and anxious. Restless. The past few days were up and down and it didn't seem that there would be any let-up until we settled into a groove with Omaha.

"I was just thinking," I said to Jeff. "Is Omaha going to meet us in Denver?"

"I thought Omaha would meet us in Omaha," he said.

"We have a gig in Denver the day before."

"Shit. We do?"

"Yeah, man. Don't you look at the schedule?"

"No."

"Well, we have a gig in Denver before Omaha. With no drummer."

"She'll have to meet us in Denver to practice before the gig, then. It'll be fine."

"Seems like a lot of work on her end."

Jeff put his arm around me. "Paul, it takes a lot of work to cross a river when the train sails off track."

"I don't think that's right."

"Don't you worry about that," he said in his shitty Brando voice again. He waved his hand out in front of us, towards the empty street. "Someday, this will all be yours, my boy."

I laughed. "What the fuck are you talking about? You're not still high?"

He let go of me. "Sober as a nun on Sunday. Just lightening the mood."

"All right," I said.

"Let's go make up with your girlfriend and figure out our next drummer."

"My girlfriend?"

"Please, dude," he said. "I've known Laney a long time. She's had a crush on you since Cincinnati. She might not have known it, but she did." He smiled at me. "Don't worry, I won't bust your balls. Just don't fuck in the van."

I didn't say anything. I stood there with a blank look on my face.

His face contorted. "Aww, man. You . . . ?" He shook his head and put his hands up. "I don't want to know. I don't want to fucking know."

We went inside the venue.

Jeff went to talk to Laney, who was chatting up the sound man. We had to run a line check since the doors were opening soon. Jeff pulled her away and they made their way back over to the bar area where there was a bartender setting up for the night. I went to the bathroom. I didn't want to be around them while they sorted things out, and especially since Jeff knew about us. Again, I felt conflicted and added another thing to the list that Laney and I would have to talk about once we had a minute alone. I could understand a lot of things—the transient nature of being on the road, and all that Buddha shit about the impermanence of everything. What I couldn't understand is why she wasn't upfront. That's all I needed. Maybe it wasn't. Maybe she needed things too. Fuck if I knew. I reminded myself that we'd only been hooking up for two days—I was getting ahead of myself again. It's easy to slip out of reality on the road. There's a slowed down pulse to everything and two days can seem like a goddamn eternity.

I came out of the bathroom and ran into Drix. His sunglasses were on his head, and his face was slack.

"Dude," he said and shook his head. "Not good, brother."

I'd never seen him look worried. "What's wrong?" I said.

"Not good, man," he said again. "Come with me."

I followed him backstage and towards the green room. He nodded towards the door.

"I went in to grab a new set of sticks and all those motherfuckers were all chilled out on the couches and shit," he said.

"So?" I said.

"The cookies are gone from my bag."

The goddamn cookies. I left them on the floor.

"Fuck."

He pushed open the door. Space Shovel and Spectacular Death Extras were lying around.

"Drix," Mason said, loud and slow. "My nigga. I can say that, right? We're in a band and we're gonna be famous and on the internet."

Drix looked at me. "See what I mean, man."

"What the fuck is he doing in here?" said the singer from Space Shovel. He didn't move, and didn't seem as wasted as the other guys, but he was definitely fucked out and he stared at me, his head rocking side to side, slowly.

Ryan made to get up and fell back down. Everyone laughed at him.

"Thanks for the cookies," Ryan said. "Your grand mom's the best." He said it like it was all one word.

"How much did they eat?" I said to Drix.

"No clue, man. I don't know where the bag is," he said. "Yo," he yelled at the room. "Where's my cookies motherfuckers?" Ryan, Sean, and Mason jumped. They looked like scared kittens in a basket, sitting in a row on the smaller couch.

"I'm sorry," Mason said.

Drix looked at him. "For?"

"I thought it could be our thing, and you would call me 'my Caucasian,'" Mason said.

"Shut the fuck up," said the singer from Space Shovel.

"Hey, that's my cousin," Ryan said. "That's my caucousin." He laughed at himself and so did Sean and Mason.

Space Shovel's bass player opened his eyes and chuckled to himself. He put his hand on the singer's leg and patted it. "It's all good," he said. "It's all good," he said to Ryan.

Nobody moved. They were rooted to the couches. Everybody was fucking baked and didn't know how to handle it. We were on in forty-five minutes. That gave them about an hour and a half and two hours and change respectively to get their shit together.

"Last time motherfuckers. Where's my cookies?" Drix said again.

"Graham has them," Sean said.

"Why does Graham have them?" Drix said.

Sean dug his phone out of his pocket and started to thumb away.

"Fred from Space Shovel said you gave us the cookies as a welcoming gift," he said. "Here, look." We moved over to the couch.

He held up his phone. It was a picture of him and Ryan and Mason eating the cookies and holding up the empty bag. "Drix gave us cookies," the text read under the image. And then a smiley face.

"A smiley face?" I said to him.

"It means I'm happy," he said, facing his phone away from us.

"It means you're a goddamn fag," Fred from Space Shovel said.

"Your mom's face is a fag," Mason said and laughed.

"How much did you eat?" Drix said.

"I don't know," Sean said. "All of them?"

I looked at Drix, and whistled out slowly. "Whoa," I said.

"I know, bro," he said. "I know."

We left the green room and went out on the floor.

"This isn't good," I said. "I can't believe they ate the whole bag and didn't realize they were pot cookies."

"If you don't know, you wouldn't know until it kicks in. I can't believe they went into my bag and took my shit," Drix said.

"About that," I said. "I might have left the cookies out by accident."

I told Drix about them giving me a hard time when I went in there.

"Still, they took my shit just to be dicks and now they fucked themselves. Those dudes are going to think they're dying in about an hour."

"You can't overdose on pot."

"Doesn't matter. Shit's gonna be real when they feel like it. Which those dudes, especially the brothers and cousin, definitely will."

Jeff and Laney walked over to us. I looked at Laney. She didn't say anything. I looked at Jeff and he gave me a slight, quick wink. I assumed that meant things were cool and he didn't tell her he knew.

"Line check?" Jeff said.

"Graham didn't come back yet, did he?" Drix asked.

"We didn't see him. I assumed he'd be back for our set in a little bit."

"The doors are opening up soon. We should go run a line check," Laney said.

"Cool," Drix said. He looked at me and then back at them. "We've got some news."

"Good or bad?" Jeff said.

"Depends on who you are, I guess."

Drix and I told them about the cookies.

"Holy shit," Jeff said. "Those guys aren't doing anything tonight."

"How many were in the bag," Laney asked.

"Twenty-six," Jeff said. "Twice a baker's dozen. You know, because you get baked."

"Those dudes definitely got baked. That's three cookies each and then some," Drix said.

"Damn. I don't even think I'd want to do a whole one at once," Jeff said. "Not with Rachel's pot anyway."

"What should we do?" Laney asked.

"Let's just ignore them," Jeff said.

Drix looked at me. I nodded and sighed.

"That ain't gonna be so easy," he said. "They sent a picture to Graham saying I gave them the cookies."

"Lie," Jeff said. "Blame it on Space Shovel."

"Yeah, he'll believe you over them," Laney said.

"Maybe he would if Space Shovel wasn't also high as shit. It wouldn't make sense to fuck yourself over too, know what I mean?" Drix said.

"Just plead ignorance. Like you have no idea what's going on," Jeff said.

That's what we decided to do. Just go about getting ready for our set and pretend we didn't know about them. We weren't supposed to go in the green room anyway. This put Drix in a precarious situation. He'd have more reason to be in contact with Spectacular Death Extras, but he said he'd just say he was avoiding Space Shovel and hanging out with us. Under the circumstances, it seemed to be the best solution. Laney suggested calling Graham and being upfront about everything before talking herself out of it. We needed the money. If we didn't play there wouldn't be any money.

"I still got a bad feeling about this," I said. "Those dudes aren't going to be able to play."

"Not our problem," Jeff said. "We're holding up our end of the bargain."

"Problem is there are two other ends, both of which aren't able to do shit," I said.

"Do you not want to play?" Jeff asked.

"I always want to play," I said. "Just expressing how fucked things are going to be when we get off that stage."

"We'll deal with it then," Jeff said.

"Laney?" I said.

"I say we go ahead and play. He's not here to manage the situation," she said with emphasis on "manage."

"All right, then," Drix said. "Let's go get those levels."

We ran a line check and then holed up backstage. The house music was on and loud. The doors opened and we watched the crowd fill in. In a half hour the place was damn near full of people talking and drinking. Still no sign of Graham. It was time to play.

We played our set like we did last night. Fast, tight, balls out. Minus the theatrics of Jeff running off stage to shit. The crowd was into us and I even saw some Qualia t-shirts in the crowd. That's always a tough call—wearing the t-shirt of the band you're going to see. It was cool anyway that some of the people came to our show a few days ago and came back to see us again. Maybe the other dates wouldn't be so bad. We finished up and broke down our gear and stored it back in our van since we were planning on peacing out soon. It didn't take long considering we were down to our amps, guitars, and keyboard.

Space Shovel should be on in twenty-minutes. They should have been ready to set their gear up as soon as we were done so they could run a quick line check and play. No sign of them. We walked off stage and into the crowd and hung out at the bar instead of backstage. Some of the people in the audience gave us nods and pats on the back. When we got to the bar there were a couple of dudes in suits nodding at us.

"Hey," said the taller of the two. "Good set guys."

"Lots of energy," the other said, putting his hand out to us. "Lots of energy."

They introduced themselves to us. The taller guy worked for BMI and the other for some promotional company. They gave us their business cards.

"Graham was pretty excited about you guys," BMI said. "So, tell me. Do you own the publishing rights to your music?"

"Very important," said promotional. "Very important."

"We copyrighted the songs on our EP," Laney said.

"Not the same thing," BMI said, shaking his head. "That tune of yours, the one with the quick drum intro, that's got TV written all over it. Could be a good breakout number."

"I can see you guys at some festivals next year," promotional said. "Smaller stage at first. Depends on marketing and label interest, but definitely small stage at Firefly, or Bonnaroo. Maybe Coachella. We're working on Burning Man for next year or the year after."

"Burning Man?" Drix said. "I thought that was some Into the Wild shit. A 'leave no trace' hippy event."

The shorter man laughed. "It's getting too big to not take advantage of. We're going to add, not subtract from it. Blow the doors off the event. The hippies can still have their raves—but we're talking big money here."

BMI put his hand on his friend's shoulder, and looked at us. "Let's not get ahead of ourselves. Just throwing some options out there for Graham's new band."

Laney, Jeff, Drix, and I looked at each other.

"Graham's new band?" Jeff said.

"What?" BMI said. "Are you not? He was very excited about you."

"Very excited," said promotional.

"They are not," a voice said from behind us.

We turned around. It was Graham. Glaring at us. I'd seen him angry, it was kind of his thing, but this was something else. He flashed a smile and pushed through us to his friends. He put his arms around them and led them away. He talked to them, making gestures with his hands, and at one point he turned towards us and said something at which the other two guys looked at us and shook their heads.

"I guess he found out," Jeff said.

"So much for being Graham's new band," Laney said.

Graham shook his friends' hands and made the "I'll call you" signal with his hands. I didn't think people did that in real life. He looked like a bigger douche than usual. His friends left. He came back over to us.

He looked at me, Laney, and Jeff. “You’re off the tour.”

Then to Drix. “You’re fired.”

PART 3

CHAPTER 18

The lights shut off in the building and the house music cut out. The emergency lighting came on, covering everything in harsh tones. Security ushered people outside, waving little flashlights, telling them the building lost power. They'd have to call tomorrow to get a partial refund. Some people gave an attitude, but most just were resigned to the fact that their evening there was over and chugged their drinks and left. We made our way backstage. Graham followed us.

"What the fuck did you give them?" he said to us.

"What are you talking about," Jeff said.

"Don't pull that shit," Graham said. "What did you give them?"

"Give who, what?" Drix said.

Graham took out his phone and tapped at it, all the while huffing and puffing. He shoved the screen in our faces. There was a video that started with an up-close image of someone's leg, and we heard the word "fag" and then laughter and then the video showed Drix and me standing in the doorway of the green room—Drix saying, "How much did you eat?" The rest was inaudible but showed me and Drix looking at each other and then leaving the green room. The video cut to an up-close image of Sean, his eyes half closed, a dumb smile on his face before swinging around to the other guys in the room. Graham put his phone away.

"So, I'm out with my friends, on your fucking behalf," Graham said, "and I get a text saying you gave them cookies. And then an hour later I get this video showing my talent and their support, who you already had a fight with, lying around backstage like it's a fucking opium den. So, don't give me that shit."

"They were mine," I said. "Space Shovel stole them from my bag and wrote on the bag. They must've given them to the talent and ate them too."

"How many?" he said.

"Fuck if I know," I said to him. "They're the ones that stole them and ate them all."

Graham dismissed what I said. "They were yours, so it's your fault. And now it's your fault your band is off this tour. It's been nothing but trouble since you joined."

"We still want our cut," Laney said.

"You mean the cut of nothing?" Graham said, waving his arm back to the now almost empty room. "Do you know how much fucking money I just lost on shutting this show down, and how much of an asshole I look like because of you?"

"Yes, we are aware of how much of an asshole you look like," Jeff said.

Graham lunged at Jeff. I cut him off and grabbed him in a bear hug, from the side, pinning down his arms. "Easy big fella," I said. He tried to squirm out of my grip, but I wasn't letting go.

"Get the fuck off of me," Graham said.

"Only if you promise to be a good boy," I said.

"Let him go, dude," Drix said.

Jeff and Laney were trying to stifle their laughter.

"Not until he promises," I said. "Promise," I said to Graham who tried to free himself again and sent us in a clumsy waltz. We almost fell and I let him go.

"You're fucking done," he said to us.

"We got that," Jeff said.

"Yo," Drix said. "Why don't you guys take off, let things cool out here. I'll meet you back at my place."

"You don't want help with your drums?" I said.

"Nah, man. I got it," he said. He looked at Graham. "I've got some business to handle."

Graham looked at him. "Really?"

"Hey man, I get it. But business is business," Drix said. He pulled a paper out of his back pocket and tapped it. "You and I have some words and shit to sort out, dig?"

Drix led Graham away, back over to the now abandoned bar except for the bartenders who were shutting down. I felt bad for them. This was their night to make dough and they didn't get a real chance to.

We left and walked towards the back exit. The door to the green room was shut. Jeff tapped me on the shoulder and nodded to the door.

"Let's say 'goodbye' to those guys," he said.

Laney shook her head. "I'll go start the van," she said.

"We'll be right out," Jeff said.

"We'll?" I said.

"Yeah. Come on," he said and put his hand on the doorknob and turned it.

The room was dark. Jeff turned the light on. Everybody looked up at us, squinting.

"Is it time?" the singer from Space Shovel said.

"Guys, I have real bad news," he said.

Ryan, Mason, and Sean looked over, their eyes red slits, their faces slack. They looked like ghosts.

"I'm real sorry to have to be the one to tell you this," Jeff said.

"What is it?" Ryan said and looked at Mason and Sean and then back at Jeff.

"You're dead. You guys died," Jeff said.

Sean started crying.

"How do you know?" Ryan said. "I don't feel dead." He held up his hand and looked at it.

"Have you ever been dead before?" Jeff asked.

"No."

"This is what it feels like."

"Is it time?" Space Shovel asked again.

"That was last time," Jeff said.

"That was last time," I said. I looked at Ryan. "Is it time?"

"You guys are freaking me out," he said. "Knock it off."

"You guys are freaking me out," Jeff said. "Knock it off."

"I'm sorry," Sean said. "I don't want to be dead."

"You're not dead," the drummer from Space Shovel said. "They're fucking with you."

"I am sorry," I said.

"I am sorry," Jeff said. He elbowed me and nodded to Space Shovel's drums stacked in the corner. "I'm just fucking with you guys. It's time to play. Graham told us to come here and help you set up. We just finished."

"We don't need help," the drummer from Space Shovel said, lying at a deep angle in the corner of the couch.

"We don't want to help," I said. "But Graham told us to, and he's the boss. Tell them Ryan."

Ryan looked away from his hand. "So we're not dead?"

"No," Jeff said. "Tell them."

Ryan looked at Sean and Mason. Sean was wiping his eyes. "We're not dead," Ryan said.

Jeff laughed. "Tell Space Shovel that Graham is the boss and asked us to help them set up."

"Graham is the boss," Ryan said.

Jeff opened the door and looked down the hall. He looked at me and nodded.

"Graham is right outside, by the stage," Jeff said. "Relax. He's paying us for helping. You're on in fifteen."

I grabbed the end of the drummer's hardware bag. I forgot how heavy that shit was. It was the size and weight of a body bag. I dragged it out of the room and down the hall. I kicked open the back door and saw Laney sitting in the van with the window down. She looked over at me and then the bag. "What's that?" she said.

"Remember Cincinnati?" I said to her.

"Yeah?" she said. And then she half smiled, "Dude."

"Unlock the hatch and get ready to go."

I hoisted the bag into the back and Jeff came waddling out with the bass drum and he threw that in the back too.

"Let's get out of here," I said.

"We're not leaving a man behind," Jeff said and ran back. I followed him. When I got to the room he had the snare drum and cymbals. I picked up both rack toms by the straps on their cases with one hand and the floor tom with the other. We ran back out to the van and threw the kit in the back. I didn't like how disorganized it looked, but I let it go. I jumped in the van. Jeff ran back in.

"Where the fuck is he going?"

Laney tapped her fingers on the steering wheel. "Come on," she said. "Come on."

Jeff ran back out and got in the back seat. Laney tore off out of the parking lot.

"What did you go back for?" I asked.

He was in the middle of lighting a cigarette and looked up at me and grinned and continued lighting his cigarette. He blew out the first drag. "I needed a light," he said.

I shook my head. "And that was worth going back?"

"Yes," he said and smiled again. "Laney," he said leaning over the front seat. "Let's find a pawn shop that's still open."

We drove around to a sketchy part of town. It wasn't south central or anything, but it looked a little rougher than where we were and we wound up the windows. There were a bunch of liquor stores and bodegas. The neighborhood wasn't too bad, I told myself, despite all the neon lights and Latinos in tank tops with neck tattoos. TV conditioned me to avoid this scene—it also conditioned me to the thought that this was where you could unload stolen gear without any questions. The sun hadn't completely set all the way and there weren't a ton of people out. I had the feeling that I wouldn't want to be here later on. We pulled up in front of a pawnshop. Jeff went in and told us to wait in the car. He'd handle the talking.

"Hey," I said to Laney. It seemed forever since we'd been alone.

"Hey," she said and smiled a quick smile at me, and looked away.

"It's ok," I said, surprising myself. "We don't have to talk about it."

"Talk about what?" she said, looking out the window.

I raised my eyebrows. "Nothing," I said.

Jeff knocked on the window and startled us. I wound down the window.

"It's all good," he said. "Dude's name is Lorca. Just let me do the talking."

We humped the drum kit inside the shop and the owner opened up the cases and inspected the drums. He was a big muscly son of a bitch in a buttoned-down Hawaiian shirt. He had teardrop tattoos around his eyes. I read somewhere that you get those in prison for every person you killed.

"Two hundred," he said with a thick accent.

"The hardware alone is worth five," Jeff said.

Lorca looked over at the bag. "Two twenty-five."

"That sounds fair," I said. Jeff and Lorca looked at me, and then back at each other.

They both started talking in Spanish and waving their hands around and pointing to the kit. Jeff pointed to something in one of the cases. Lorca went around behind the cases and opened a small safe. He counted off some bills and put them on the counter. Jeff took the bills and pointed down. Lorca opened the case and pulled out a polaroid camera. Jeff picked it up and looked at it. He pointed down again and said something in Spanish that sounded pretty aggressive, and held the camera up and laughed. They were talking too fast and I couldn't understand them. Not that I would have been able to anyway. Lorca looked up at me and said something to Jeff. Jeff turned around and they both laughed again. Lorca went back into the case and took out a small package and gave that to Jeff.

"Gracias," Jeff said. They said some more words in Spanish and then shook hands. Jeff walked back towards me and smiled. Something caught his eye and he stopped. He picked up a Viking helmet. He took it back to Lorca and he shook his head and waved his hands. "Veinte," Lorca said.

"Cinco," Jeff said.

"Diez."

Jeff said a bunch of other things and handed over what looked like seven bucks and two cigarettes. We left the store. Jeff was wearing the Viking helmet and carrying the polaroid camera and a little package of film.

"What the fuck was that all about?" I said.

"Just doing some business," he said. We got in the van and Laney started the engine and drove off.

"When the fuck did you learn Spanish?" I said to Jeff.

"In school, like everyone else. Didn't you have to take a language?"

"Yeah. But nobody learned it," I said.

"We had French and Spanish in grade school. In high school I picked Spanish because I liked burritos. Laney picked French because she's a snob," he said.

"All the girls picked French," she said.

"Oh, right," Jeff said. "The teacher was this Frenchman all the girls wanted to fuck."

"Score one for affluence," I said.

"How much did we get?" Laney asked.

"Three-fifty, a polaroid camera and film, and this awesome Viking helmet," Jeff said.

"What are you going to do with a Viking helmet?" Laney asked.

"The better question, Laney," Jeff said, "is 'what aren't we going to do with a Viking helmet?' "

We drove back to Drix's house. We parked out front and waited for him.

"Do you think this means Drix will come with us?" Laney said.

"We'll find out real soon," Jeff said and pointed out the window.

Drix was driving down the street. He made a U-turn and honked his horn and backed-in in front of us.

He got out of his car and was shaking his head and smiling. "You crazy motherfuckers."

CHAPTER 19

We brought our gear inside Drix's house for the night, and helped him with his drums. For not having a drummer I felt like we touched a lot of drums that day. We'd been lucky with leaving our gear in the van so far, but he said he wouldn't trust it overnight outside. Had his car broken into when he first moved here, and never left anything in there overnight.

"It's best not to tempt the karma police," Jeff said.

"Why would they be tempted?" Drix asked.

"No reason," Jeff said and looked at me and smiled.

We piled up our gear in Drix's living room. It was still early. He grabbed us each a beer. Jeff took the wrapped-up cookie out of his pocket, unwrapped it, took a little bit and put it back away.

"What's going on, Jeffrey Squirrelman?" I asked.

"Did you see what these did to those guys?" he said.

"Yeah, man," Drix said, nodding his head. "Can you spare one?"

"Sure thing," Jeff said and went in his bag and tossed a cookie across to Drix. Drix took a small bite.

"Which one of you got jokes?" Drix said, looking at us each in turn.

"What do you mean?" Laney said. She was leaning back in a chair. She took a sip of her beer.

"I'm squaring up shit with Graham, and we're just about done, and fucking place turned into *Night of the Living Dead.* Dudes came crawling and staggering out of the green room onto the floor talking some shit about a fire and we all have to get out. Motherfucker from Space Shovel sees a fire extinguisher and goes over to it and starts talking to the hose end of it, giving it directions to put the fire out."

We all laughed. I looked at Jeff, who shrugged his shoulders and turned his hands up. "Don't look at me," he said.

"What happened next?" I asked.

"First thing, we think maybe there is a fire, so the club manager who's standing around waiting for Graham, and already pissed as shit that he had to shut down for the night because of those motherfuckers, and now thinks his place is on fire, goes running backstage. I look around and think about bolting out the front. Fuck me if I'm gonna burn alive and die surrounded by those dudes. Then I look at my drums and am like 'damn, I can't save all of my kit' and decide that if I see flames I'll grab my snare and hi-hat and get the fuck out. The manager comes back out a second later and asks the zombies where the fire was, and they're fucking baked man. I mean really fucking baked—way more than I thought they were and I'm surprised they were even standing, all leaning against the bar now and kinda rocking back and forth and shit." Drix took a pull on his beer. "So dig this, these dudes have no idea what the fuck he is talking about. Ryan said some shit about a roadie telling them the place was on fire."

"A roadie?" I said and looked at Jeff. "I don't know why you keep looking at me," he said.

"Anyway, to make a long story short," Drix said, "we decide there isn't a fire and those cats were tripping. Graham and the club manager corral those dudes back into the green room and it's funny as shit to watch. Like trying to lead blind goats. I heard Graham say some shit about letting them chill out for a couple of hours until they come down off their high so they can load up their gear and peace out."

"Well, damn," I said. "That's a hell of an end to the evening there."

"Yeah, man," Drix said. "Hell of an evening, indeed."

"What happened with Graham?" Laney asked. She was quiet for most of the ride home and was sitting there during Drix's story, listening, surveying the room.

"Motherfucker owed me my cut," Drix said.

"The cut off nothing?" Laney said.

"Yeah, sorry about that," Drix said. "I had a contract with them."

"I thought you didn't read it?" I said.

"I didn't read the email about being all square around them, but you bet your ass I read my contract. Faxed that shit to my guy before we started rehearsals."

"You 'faaa-ksss-did'?" Jeff said. "What is that?"

"That's what my dude wants," Drix said. "We made some provisions and amendments, Graham agreed to them and signed off."

"What type of provisions?" Laney asked.

"Rain or shine, baby. Rain or shine," Drix said. "I didn't trust that dude from the moment I saw him. Motherfucker cut me a check right there at the venue."

"Damn. Good for you," I said.

"Yeah, good thinking," Laney said and leaned forward. "So . . ."

"Relax little sister," Drix said and waved his hand. Laney looked at him, confused. He laughed. "I'll go with you dudes to New York."

Jeff jumped up and landed on Drix.

"Fucking right on," Jeff said.

"My beer," Drix said, holding it up. "Don't spill my beer."

I nodded to Drix and smiled. He nodded back.

We sat around his living room bullshitting and laughing at how baked the other bands were, and how angry Graham was. Jeff told Drix again about the A&R guy from Sony. Drix went to his laptop to check him out.

"You don't believe me?" Jeff said.

"Man, it ain't even like that," Drix said. "This dude knows all kinds of shit about you and you don't anything about him. It's smart business."

"That's a good point," I said. "We didn't know anything about Graham, and look what happened."

"That was a last-minute change," Laney said.

"Yeah, that was some weird shit," Drix said, tapping away on his keyboard. "But look at it as a learning experience."

Laney didn't say anything.

"Got him," Drix said, and turned at an angle so we could all see his laptop. "Chester Darvey. Was in some band in the mid-90s, had a hit with that song 'Degenerated.' "

"I remember that," I said.

"I keep forgetting you're an old man," Jeff said in mock disgust.

I shook my head. "Dude, I'm like three years older than you."

Laney leaned over to get a better look at the screen. I could smell her. She still smelled nice after all the loading gear and playing.

"What else can you find out about this guy?" she said.

"Let's see," Drix said. "Motherfucker better be all over social media if he's in A&R."

Drix found his Facebook and Twitter pages. They were public, but didn't divulge much personal information. We did learn that he came from Sony's Legacy department, which dealt with re-issues and compilations from artists like Dylan, Miles, Roy Orbison, Alicia Keys, the Boss—artists that could move units. He just got the job this year at Columbia.

"So he's not Sony then?" Laney said.

"I guess not exactly," Drix said.

"He told you Sony?" Laney said to Jeff.

"Uh, yeah," he said. "I mean he's not exactly lying. Columbia is owned by Sony."

"I guess not," Laney said.

"Columbia is still a big deal. It's a major," I said.

"Fuck yeah," Jeff said. "I don't care if it's Sony, or Columbia, or Death Row."

"I don't think we'd be a good fit on Death Row," I said.

"Well," Drix said, "dude seems legit. Might not be a bad idea to shoot him an email to reconfirm and see if there's anything he needs from you before the gig.

Opening the door to professional courtesy and all that shit."

"Do you have his email?" Laney said to Jeff.

"I never asked for it," Jeff said. He turned to Drix. "Should I send him a text?"

"Call him," Drix said. "He's not your buddy you're meeting for drinks, know what I mean?"

"All right. First thing in the morning," Jeff said.

"Isn't he in New York?" Laney said.

"Yeah."

"There's a time difference. Call him in the afternoon."

Drix sighed and shook his head. "Come on guys," he said.

"What?" Laney said.

"What's this dude's job?" Drix asked.

"He finds artists and represents them," Laney said.

"When do bands play?"

"At night."

"When do you wake up after a gig if you've been out all night?"

"Before checkout."

Drix looked at her and waited.

"Oh," she said. "We should call him now."

"That's my girl," he said and put out his fist.

"You don't think it's too late? It's almost eight in New York," Laney said.

"On a Saturday, which means motherfucker is probably on the clock," Drix said.

"I'll call him then," Jeff said. He got up and went to the kitchen. We could hear him on the phone, leaving a message. He came back in.

"I gave him the band's email, Laney," Jeff said.

"Cool," Laney said. "I should probably get in touch with Omaha."

"Then we should go out and celebrate," Jeff said.

"Can't stay out too late," Laney said. "We still have to go to San Diego tomorrow."

"We're off the tour," Jeff said. "We don't have a gig for a few more days."

"That's where the merch is going to be," Laney said.

"Oh, right," Jeff said.

"It isn't far," I said. "We can drive down and back in the afternoon. Get there before Spectacular Death Extras."

"I don't think they're going to be playing," Drix said.

"Ah, no drummer. That would make sense," I said.

"We're still almost out of money," Laney said. "We've got enough to get us to Denver with gas, and motels, and food."

"Why don't you dudes just hang here for a couple of days and then we'll hump it up to Denver in one shot. Take turns driving and shit."

"You cool with us crashing?" I asked.

"Wouldn't have offered. Can probably get us a gig or two to keep our chops up," Drix said.

"I like this," Jeff said. "Hang on." He stood up and ran outside. He came back in wearing the Viking helmet and had the polaroid camera hanging around his neck.

"Tonight is on me," he said and put his foot up on the edge of the table. He pulled a wad of money out of his pocket and thumbed through it. "Tonight we sail on the *Pequod.*"

"What the fuck is that and where did you find that stuff?" Drix said, laughing.

"It's my ship, and these are my supplies," Jeff said. "Now say, 'cheese,' bitches."

"Cheese bitches," Drix, Laney, and I said, raising our beers as Jeff snapped off a photo.

"Where to?" Jeff said.

"Nadia is working until two if you don't mind that scene," Drix said. "We can hit up Little Pete's after."

Jeff's face lit up. "That is where I want to go," he said. "Does she have friends?"

"Yeah, man," Drix said. "She has friends. Try to keep your boner to yourself in public. I gotta see these people all the time." He looked at Laney. "You cool with that?"

"Yeah," she said. "I'm cool with Jeff keeping his boner to himself."

"I'm going to hit the bathroom before we leave," I said.

I walked upstairs and went in the bathroom. I had to take a dump and there wasn't any toilet paper. I checked under the sink and it was empty except for a can of bleach detergent. The door snapped shut and made a loud bang. I checked the closet. Just some towels. The medicine cabinet looked deep enough to hold a roll—if there wasn't any toilet paper in there I was just going to wait until the club. It wasn't the best spot, but also wouldn't be the first time shitting in a club. I opened one side of the medicine cabinet. The usual—floss and band-aids. I slid the mirrored door shut and slid open the other side. There were about a half-dozen syringes on the bottom shelf. I felt sick. There was a knock on the door.

"You all right in there, dude?" It was Drix.

"Uh, yeah," I said. "Just looking for some toilet paper."

"Here," he said. "Nadia keeps it in the hall closet for some reason. Are you decent?"

I wasn't sure what to do. He'd hear me if I closed the door and he'd see it open if he came in.

"I'm coming in," he said in a sing-songy high voice. The handle turned and the door opened.

He had his hand over his eyes and slowly opened his fingers to peek through. His hand dropped and he was looking at the medicine cabinet.

"Dude," I said and motioned towards the cabinet. "What the fuck?"

He tossed me the roll of toilet paper. He laughed.

"Man," he said, "I don't fuck with that shit. I mean, I know what that shit's all about, but that was a long time ago." He moved towards the sink and closed the cabinet. "Nadia has diabetes. She got diagnosed a few months ago. She keeps some needles here and some insulin in the fridge."

"Oh," I said. I felt better, and a little embarrassed. "Sorry man, I was just looking for some toilet paper and saw those and just thought…shit, man. She ok?"

"Yeah, no worries, brother," Drix said. "I ain't a junkie. Look." He rolled up his sleeves. There weren't any track marks. I know dudes can shoot in their toes and feet, but I trusted Drix and didn't think he'd lie to me.

"All right, all right," I said. "Let me take a dump so we can get out of here."

He left the bathroom. I felt like an asshole for sort of accusing my friend of being a junkie. I decided to let it go. I knew he liked drugs, but I never saw him strung out. He acted like he was on coke once in a while, and the pills seemed to be more a part of that party weekend for him, but in the grand scheme of things he seemed to have his shit together. I still made a note to check the fridge before we left for Denver.

CHAPTER 20

Jeff insisted on wearing the Viking helmet out. He said he paid good money for it and he was going to wear it. We piled into Drix's car and drove around to where Nadia worked. Drix was right—the place was weird. It was decorated in dark purples and reds and blacks, and lots of velvet. It's what I imagined Prince's house would be like if he were a vampire. There were girls dancing in cages on the side of a stage. The girls that danced on the main stage stripped in the burlesque fashion of teasing and engaging the audience—there was a small live band playing old French music with a heavy delta blues percussive vibe. It sounded like a sexual carnival. As far as these places went, it did seem like a classy joint. None of the girls, for their part, had that vacant faraway zombie look. And I didn't see any arm bruises.

We sat in a circular booth and girls came around in little string clothes and brought us drinks. We settled in and watched the dancers on stage and talked about the next few days before we had to split. What clubs we could play. We decided we'd book ourselves under a different name to avoid any trouble with Space Shovel. We weren't too concerned with drawing a crowd since we'd be playing on a Monday or Tuesday, and had just played this town twice in a week. We bounced around the names Death Sentence for Birds and Hot Dog Tranny, though Jeff was lobbying hard for Hot Dog Tyranny.

"One letter," he said. "It makes all the difference. Trust me. It's better."

The band started up an aggressive number that sounded like the best parts of a Nine Inch Nails song. Nadia strode out on the main stage.

"Does she know you're here?" I asked Drix.

"Yeah, man. I texted her at the club and let her know I'd be around for a few more days."

"I mean, does she know you're here at her work?"

"Oh, yeah. Fuck that pop-in unannounced shit. Who knows what kind of shit she'd be getting into that I don't need to see."

I felt kind of weird watching my friend's girl strip. I wanted to see Nadia naked, but I didn't want to see my friend's girlfriend naked. All with Laney sitting right next to me. It was very confusing. It was burlesque, so her nipples were covered and she wore a g-string, but goddamn, she looked naked up there. And goddamn did she have a great body. She writhed around the stage to some industrial-sounding vaudeville number. She finished her routine and went backstage. Jeff turned to us like he was coming out of a daydream.

"If I was a girl I think I'd be a stripper," Jeff said.

"Why's that?" Drix asked.

"If I was that good-looking, and dudes wanted to give me money to simply gaze upon my body? Fuck yeah, I'd take their money."

"She does make good dough," Drix said, nodding. "What about you Laney? Ever think about it?"

"Not really," she said. "I mean I don't care, but it's not for me."

"That's a shame," Drix said. "You got a nice body."

We all laughed and Laney blushed and covered her face with her hands and shook her head. She took her hands down. "Thanks, Drix," she said.

"That's forthright," Jeff said. "You're a real forthrightsman. I like that."

"Ah, I ain't saying I'm lusting and shit. Just calling a spade a spade. That's all. I ain't gonna try and mess with my boy's girl."

Laney stopped laughing, and froze. I looked at Drix in surprise. Jeff laughed out loud and damn near spit out his beer. He tapped Drix on the side. "Yo, let's go get a drink," he said.

"What? I already got one," Drix said.

"Let's go get a drink," Jeff said and motioned towards us with his eyes.

"Oh," Drix said. "Cool."

They stood up and Jeff put his arm around Drix as they went to the bar.

Laney and I sat there. The next girl took the stage.

"So," I said. "How's it going?"

"Pretty good," she said.

We looked at each other and I had no idea what she was thinking. What with my learning about Gerard a few hours ago, our getting kicked off the tour, and Laney receiving a dose of reality about being a full-time manager for a band, this was one hell of a day.

"It's cool Drix is coming with us," Laney said.

"Yeah," I said back. "New York is going to be awesome." I took a drink and leaned back in the booth. "Laney," I said.

"Yeah?" she said.

"Jeff knows about us and doesn't care. It seems that Drix does too."

She didn't say anything.

"In fact, Jeff didn't seem like he'd care at all," I said.

"Oh, that's good," she said.

"Listen, if you got a dude back home and you just want to keep it cool, that's cool. I'd just rather know."

She shook her head. "I don't know."

"If you got a dude back home, or want to keep it cool?"

"We took a break when we both went away."

"Are you getting back together after the tour?"

"I don't know."

"Do you want to get back together?"

She didn't say anything. A girl came around to clear away the empties and see if we needed anything else. We told her we weren't sure. When she left, Laney turned her body towards me. "Paul, I like you," she said. "But this is confusing with Gerard. I wasn't expecting this."

"It doesn't have to be confusing. I don't want things to be weird and don't want to mess with your home shit, that's all."

Laney didn't answer me and was looking around the room. There were girls taking their clothes off. It seemed a little weird to be having this conversation now.

"Let's forget it then. Whatever you decide," I said.

She looked at me. "Is it that easy for you?"

"No. But you're not saying anything."

"Can't we just forget about everyone else for now?"

"Is that what you want?"

She nodded her head.

"Ok," I said. "Forgotten."

"Ok," she said and smiled a quick smile.

We sat there not looking at the stage, not talking to each other. I wished I'd ordered another drink.

Jeff, Drix, and Nadia came back. She had more clothes on this time.

"Yo, we're gonna take off. Nadia got off work early," Drix said. "We're gonna hit up Little Pete's. Her friend is going to meet us there."

"All right," I said.

"Hey, Nadia," Drix said. "This is Laney. She's in the band."

Laney stood up and stuck out her hand. "Nice to meet you."

Nadia shook her hand, but I got the sense she wasn't happy about a girl in the band. Damn near every time I've been in a band with a girl, that's the first thing the other dudes' girlfriends comment on. They don't come right out and say they're jealous, but they are. It's usually in the form of critique—shit like "her singing was a little off" or "her stage presence isn't good." Sometimes they're legit critiques, but it always comes down to probably the only truth I've ever learned: girls don't like other girls. And girls especially don't like cool girls hanging around their men. But fuck it. Nadia was Drix's headache, and she wasn't coming with us.

Drix gave us the keys to his car and he drove with Nadia. We parked around back at Little Pete's and went in. I was expecting the place to be busy on account of it being Saturday. It looked the same as it did on Wednesday afternoon. There were people in the bar scattered about in booths and sitting at the bar smoking cigarettes. The jukebox was playing the early version of “Make It wit Chu” from Queens of the Stone Age with PJ Harvey.

I hit Drix on the arm. “Yo, remember this song?”

In high school we got into a bar for an open mic and played that song when I was still back and forth between guitar and bass. We played it, just the two of us. I was on guitar and vocals, which wasn’t pretty, and Drix played this two-piece drum kit, bass and snare with a hi-hat and crash, and we thought we destroyed.

He smiled. “Of course, man. They kicked us out afterwards.”

“They kicked me out,” I said. “You stayed, motherfucker.”

“Hey, there were drinks there,” he said.

Nadia’s friend was already there, sitting at the bar. She worked at the same club but had off that night. Her name was Emily.

Jeff introduced himself.

“What’s with that?” she said, eyeing up the helmet.

“Oh, this?” Jeff said, moving his eyes up. “I thought it brought out the color of my eyes.”

She laughed at him.

“I knew an Emily once,” Jeff said.

“Yeah?” Emily said.

“She was a middle-aged lady that lived next door to my grandmom,” Jeff said. “She used to have all these disfigured baby dolls done up on stakes on her front lawn. Arms missing and eyes blacked out. One day, a few years ago, she invited me in and asked me to help her move some things out of her basement. We went downstairs and she had this workbench with saws and doll parts, and the light was one of those single light bulbs that hung from the ceiling. There were these coolers that were taped shut and wrapped in cellophane she wanted me to help load into her trunk. I asked what was in them and she told me not to worry about it and patted me on the ass."

"That's a weird thing to say to a girl right away," Emily said.

"Oh, I meant that you're way hotter than her and I don't think you'd invite me over to move weird things out of your basement," Jeff said. He turned away from her and gave me a wink. She followed him with her eyes.

We said hello to Little Pete and I was surprised that Nadia would hang out in a bar like this. She seemed a bit high-maintenance, but she gave Pete and his wife a hug and smiled.

"Where've you been?" Pete said. "Drix isn't keeping you locked up, is he?"

"Working my ass off, Uncle Pete," she said.

We ordered drinks and went to a booth while Nadia talked to Little Pete and his wife. Emily came over and sat next to Jeff.

"Is that her uncle?" Jeff asked.

"Nah. She used to work here when she first came out to LA. Pete's a good dude. I met Nadia here the night I asked her out. She blew me off at the club and then we both ended up here. She thought I was some weird stalking motherfucker, but Pete got my back. Said I came in all the time. We just missed each other."

"Hold on," Jeff said and closed his eyes. He put his finger up. "I almost got it."

"Got what?" Laney asked.

Jeff shushed her. "Bass," he said.

I hummed a walking bassline again.

"Ships that pass in the night and distant voices in the dark," he said. "So on the ocean of life, we pass and speak to each other. A look and a voice," he paused and looked at us around the table, then hung his head and shook it, "then darkness again . . . and silence."

"That's beautiful as shit," Drix said.

"Did you write that?" Emily asked.

"Longfellow," Jeff said. "Henry Wadsworth Longfellow."

"Shouldn't it be 'just below average length-fellow' if you say it?" I said.

"Classic Paul joke," Jeff said. "Classic. Make fun of my war injury."

"You were in the war?" Emily said.

"I'd rather not talk about it," Jeff said. He leaned over towards her and looked confused. He sniffed her. "What perfume are you wearing?"

"Chanel No. 5."

"That's what I thought. I've a nose for fragrance. You smell good."

"Thanks," Emily said.

"Excuse me," Jeff said. "I've got to go take care of some business."

Emily stood up so he could get out. He took his phone out of his pocket and said he'd be right back. Emily excused herself and went to the bar to get Nadia.

"This is fun," I said.

"What, seeing Jeff make an ass out of himself?" Laney said. "We see that every day."

"Not in front of strangers," I said.

"Nah dudes, you got it all wrong," Drix said. "Motherfucker's making his moves."

"Get out of here," Laney exclaimed. "What girl buys that shit?"

"The one at the bar keeping her eyes on the door for him to come back in," Drix said.

I looked over at the bar. Sure as shit, Emily was talking to Nadia, but she kept glancing over her friend's shoulder toward the door.

"Well goddamn," I said.

"If he doesn't start insulting her a little when he comes back I'll shit my pants right here on this table," Drix said.

"Settle down," Laney said. "This band only has room for one pants-shitter."

"And that might be too much," I said. "But, you're on."

"Next round?" Drix said.

"Next two," I said.

"For everybody," Drix said.

"I like this bet," Laney said.

"Deal," I said. We shook on it.

Jeff came back inside and sat down.

"How was business?" Laney asked.

"Business?" Jeff said. "Oh, business is good in flavor country."

Emily came back over and sat next to Jeff. We slid in to make room for Nadia.

"So, Emily," Jeff said. "You work with Nadia?"

"I do," she said.

"How come you weren't there tonight?"

"I work a weird every other swing shift."

"What nights?"

"Every Sunday, Wednesday, Thursday. Every other Friday and Saturday."

"That's confusing," Jeff said. "I wouldn't have pegged you as a dancer. You seem like you'd be a carpenter or something."

I shook my head, just a little, at Drix. He nodded once.

"A carpenter?" she said.

"Ok, maybe not a carpenter, but like someone who uses their body for a living, like a fisherman or something."

"Are you calling me a fisherman?"

"I'm just fucking around. I don't think you look like a fisherman, I just know how well I can dance, and I don't think you're better than me," he said and laughed.

"Shut up," Emily said, almost smiling. "I can dance better than you."

"Maybe so, maybe not," he said.

"Yo," Drix said to Emily. "Is Jeff insulting you?"

She looked confused. "A little, I think."

Drix laughed and looked at me.

"He talks too much," Nadia said and stared at Jeff.

"I like talking," Jeff said and shrugged his shoulders.

"It's cool," Drix said. "It's cool."

Nadia got up to use the bathroom and Emily went with her.

"Motherfucker," I said.

"What?" Jeff said.

"You just lost me a bet."

"With who?"

"Drix. He said you were making your moves and that your next play was to make fun of Emily."

"Of course I was going to," Jeff said. "I'm not an idiot. Seems like Drix here isn't either."

"This is the first time I'm seeing this?" Laney said.

"Up close," Jeff said. "You've been a great wingman, Laney."

"How?"

"We're in a band, so we're already cool. You're a girl and we get along—this says that I can be around girls and act like a normal person."

"That wasn't normal what just happened," Laney said.

"Perception," Jeff said. "Also, you're not nagging me, so it also sends the message that you don't care and we're not together."

"This is bullshit," Laney said.

"You're the best secret wingman in the world. You're a cool, and it makes me gag to say it," he took a deep breath, "good-looking girl." He shook his head and moved his mouth like he just ate something bad. "If I can hang out with you, then I'm probably not that bad."

"I still think it's bullshit," Laney said.

"Yeah," I said. "What's Laney got to do with you making fun of Emily?"

"Man, have you ever gotten laid?" Drix said.

"Not by making fun of girls, which, for the record, wasn't really like making fun of her."

"Don't be a sore loser, bro," Drix said.

"Teasing is the sixth step," Jeff said.

"God," Laney said. "There are steps?"

"Yeah, it's simple. I'm not the first to realize this, and it has been known by many names, but I learned mine from a wise and ancient Algonquin tribal elder."

I leaned in towards him to get a better look at his eyes. They were getting a bit bloodshot. "Dude, how high are you?"

"Very," he said. "The tribal leader told me about 'coco-le-coco-tea' which in English means 'confuse, compliment, leave, confuse, compliment, tease.' "

We laughed at him.

"You laugh, but examine my procedure. First, one must confuse the target to scatter their defenses, hence the weird doll lady talk. Second, one must compliment the target when they are vulnerable, as I did by calling her hot. Thirdly, one must leave, making themselves desired." Jeff put on an airy voice, imitating Emily: "Where did that mysterious man go? Is he coming back?"

"Where's the teasing?" Laney asked.

"Ah, one must repeat steps one and two before the teasing starts. This is necessary to keep the target in a constant state of confusion. You don't want them to develop their own opinions about you except that you're the mysterious guy who says nice things to them—which I did with the poem and war talk, and complimenting her perfume and showing interest in her work. Then, and only then, can you start teasing the target. One must be very particular in what they tease about, and the manner in which they tease. Of course she's a way better dancer than me. I know that. She knows that. But now, subconsciously she wants to prove it because I challenged her. And since I said I can dance too, it shows we've got something in common. This all gives her a small feeling of being in charge—she knows she is better and will want to prove it to me and use it against me. This really all comes down to the two of us getting drunk and fucking each other."

"Wow," Laney said. "This is really disturbing."

"It's just science," Jeff said and took a drink.

We laughed at him again. Drix finished his pint and shook his empty glass at me.

"All right, all right," I said.

"I think I need one too," Laney said.

Jeff brought his glass to his mouth and tilted it back. He held up his thumb.

"This is bullshit," I said. "Let me out then. Let me out."

I went to the bar and ordered more drinks and brought them to the table. Nadia and Emily still hadn't come back.

"Should I get the girls a round too?" I said, looking around.

"Nah, it's cool," Drix said. "She ran to my house to get her medicine. I'm gonna crash at her place tonight while you guys are in town. Give you the place to yourself. This way I can spend some time with the old lady before we hit the road."

"Oh, ok," I said.

"Medicine?" Jeff said. "Everything cool?"

"Yeah, bro," Drix said. "It ain't nothing."

I'm not sure when her going home was arranged between them, and wasn't about to press the issue. As much as I trusted Drix, I still wanted to check the refrigerator for her medicine. That option was gone, and I couldn't exactly ask Nadia if she was diabetic, and to show me her insulin. I also couldn't envision a scenario where bringing it up wouldn't seem like I was prying.

"Thanks for letting us crash," Laney said, looking up from her phone. "That's a big help."

"Yeah," Jeff said. "Thanks, man."

"Did you sort out the merch for tomorrow?" I asked Laney.

"Well ahead of you," she said.

Laney was in touch with the venue in San Diego about picking up our merch tomorrow. Found out that Spectacular Death Extras did cancel there, and every other date until Vegas. Their website had an update about Ryan losing his voice, and posted a link on where to get tickets for their date with Green Day.

"Smart move," Drix said. "It'll give them time to replace me, and with the Green Day announcement, they've still got momentum."

"How can we do that?" I said.

Laney cleared her throat. "Well," she said, "I already sent the Pitchfork write-up to the clubs we're still playing, and all the radio stations that play us. Hopefully, that'll give us some buzz before New York."

"Did dude get back to you?" Drix asked Jeff.

"Not yet," he said. "Hopefully he'll just email Laney so we have his response in writing. And so I don't have to talk to him, because I'm getting shitty tonight."

Emily and Nadia came back. Emily partnered off with Jeff, and Nadia mostly kept to herself, and eventually pulled Drix away from the group to hang at the bar with Little Pete. We had a couple of more drinks before calling it a night. Drix gave us the keys to his car to take back to his place. Jeff said he was going with Emily back to her apartment. That he'd be in touch tomorrow. That left Laney and me. Outside, Laney pushed herself against my body and kissed me. Someone whistled at us from a passing car.

We drove back to Drix's house and she moved her hand up my leg.

"You're going to make us crash," I said.

"I'll go slow," she said.

We were both fairly drunk when we got to Drix's house. We fell on the couch and took our clothes off while grabbing at each other. We fucked hard. Almost angry. When it was done we laid there for a while and didn't talk. She fell asleep. I went upstairs to take a piss. I checked the medicine cabinet. The syringes were gone. I went downstairs and looked at Laney. In my gut I knew the whole thing between us was a false start. An escape or diversion. I watched her sleeping, breathing. I tried to memorize her lines in this moment, her face, her hair—I knew it was probably one of the last times, if not the last. Something had changed. I took a half-smoked cigarette out of the ashtray and lit it and went outside and finished it. I thought of Laney in there, alone. I went inside and laid down next to her.

CHAPTER 21

We got up before noon and there wasn't any message from Jeff. Drix didn't answer his phone. We sent Jeff a text, letting him know we were heading to San Diego to get the merch and we'd be back in a few hours. We sent Drix a text letting him know the same, so they could coordinate without us if they had to. We wanted to leave soon so we'd be back before the evening.

Laney said she was going to get a shower.

"Need help?" I said.

She laughed, "I'm ok."

We showered separately—not that I was a shower-fucker-guy, because that shit is always better in theory. Getting showers together was something to do when you're new, and I was hoping to salvage some of that teenage feeling that disappeared. But we weren't teenagers, and in the daylight, we weren't new. I pushed down those thoughts. In a situation like this I knew it was best to play it cool, give the lady space. It was a fragile thing, too easy to suffocate. And we still had a week and a half to go.

We drove around to a coffee shop. Laney checked her email. Chester from Columbia sent us a message in the middle of the night. *It's all good. 9pm. Fontana's. Next Wednesday. Rock on.*

"Rock on?" I said.

"Maybe he was drunk?" Laney said.

"I like his brevity. I just hope he's not dismissive."

"Or has a ponytail."

"If he has a ponytail I'll cut it off in his sleep," I said. "After we get signed of course."

"Do you think he'll sign us?"

"If we play like we do with Drix and have a huge crowd there? I don't know. But I've never felt this close before. Like something was supposed to happen. Know what I mean?"

"Yeah. I'm almost glad we got kicked off the tour," Laney said.

"Really?"

"Three months ago, we weren't any different than Spectacular Death Extras. We were actually bigger than them when their old manager booked us."

"And this makes you glad?"

"We're doing things our way," she said. "It hasn't been perfect, but seeing how I, how we, shouldn't do things, it kind of puts things in perspective."

I took a sip of my coffee. "Well, I admire your confidence."

She narrowed her eyes. "You still don't think I can manage us?"

I sighed. "I don't want to lie to you. On a national level, dealing with guys like Graham, and BMI and Promos? No."

She didn't say anything.

"I'm not being mean," I said. "We all got your back when it comes down to it, but did you feel in charge with those guys around?"

She shook her head. "Let's just get down to San Diego," she said.

"Laney, there are certain things you're really fucking good at. Shit, I don't even know how you've been able to keep us all afloat and get this set up. But when it comes down to it, are you ready, and do you actually want to sit there and pore over contracts and make sure everybody, outside of the band, is where they should be and doing what needs to be done, night after night? It's a lot of fucking work."

"I know it's a lot of work."

"You should be proud of all you've done so far. But this isn't the same band that started in Philly ten weeks ago. A lot of that has to do with you."

She stared past me and drank her coffee.

"I'm just saying that even a master marionetter has helpers," I said.

She looked at me and laughed a little out of her nose. "They're called a manipulator," she said.

"What?"

"The people who work with marionettes are called 'manipulators.'"

"Oh. But you see what I mean? I just think that having help wouldn't be such a bad thing so you can focus on music."

She took a deep breath and let it out long and slow. "I know you're fucking right. I just don't want to lose control of the band. I don't want to just hand it off to some jerk in a suit."

"I get it. But that's why we would define parameters and make sure the soul of the band doesn't get white-washed. That's what a good manager does. He's the one making sure all of that gets done. And besides, sometimes the only way to keep control is to lose it."

"What the fuck does that even mean?" she said and laughed.

I shrugged. "It seemed like a good spot for nonsense wisdom."

"You hit the mark." She took another drink. "Let's see how the gig goes. If we need a dedicated manager, we'll talk."

"Ok. You know none of this changes what you did and still do, and mean to this band, right? This is your band."

"It's not just my band. You're a part of it."

"Not like you and Jeff."

"This band, right now, has you in it. You're part of it. It wouldn't have become this band without you."

"All right, all right. But this isn't about me," I said and waved her off.

"It's true."

I looked at her, and she stared back. I had the sudden urge to tell Laney to be with me. To forget about her man back home. Whatever muscle makes a man write poems for a woman and start wars over her beauty was flexing somewhere deep in my chest. I knew it'd be a mistake and didn't want to foolishly make some unwanted offering or sacrifice. I looked away.

"Let's get on the road so we can make good time," I said.

"That's such a guy thing," she said. "Making good time."

"What can I say?" I said.

"Let's go," she said and stood up.

"Ok." I stood up and we walked out of the shop to our van. "Why did you know it was called a manipulator?"

She laughed at me. "Remember when Jeff said I wasn't allowed out that much as a kid?"

"Yeah."

"Well . . ."

We drove down to San Diego. Jeff still hadn't texted us. Drix responded and told us to bring him back some tacos from Mexican Fiesta if they were open, and if not, Las Cuatro Milpas would do.

We picked up our merch from the club. The manager was actually pretty chill about the whole thing. There wasn't any love lost between him and Graham. He said Graham was a colossal asshole and not seeing him wasn't going to ruin his day. He also said he worked with Graham a lot the past few years and he always packed out the place and that he'd make it up to him, so he wasn't too worried. We gave him a copy of our EP and our contact information in case we were passing through town again.

We drove around looking for the taco place. The Forever Lost kept restarting and losing our position so we drove around, making progress for a few blocks, and then having to double back.

"We're pretty close to Mexico," I said. "Want to go?"

"Hmm," Laney said. "It's kind of far."

"It's like fifteen minutes away."

"It's more like an hour. And that's just Tijuana."

"Isn't Tijuana Mexico?"

"Remember South of the Border?"

"Yeah."

"That's more Mexico than Tijuana. Minus the possibility of getting robbed."

"It's not that bad, is it? People go there all the time."

"It's a port town. It's not Mexico. Trust me."

"When were you there?"

"A few years ago."

"You didn't go and flash your tits to bros for beads over spring break did you?" I laughed.

"Ew, fuck no," she said. "I've got self-respect. Besides, those people go to Cancun."

"That makes sense. That's where a lot of cruises end up."

"Did you ever go?" she asked.

"Nah. I had already seen a bit of Spain and knew I'd go back in the off-season. Just getting a little wistful since Mexico is right there."

"It is nice, if you do it right," she said.

"One day, I guess. Where did you go?"

"All over."

"With Gerard?"

She didn't answer. I felt like an asshole. That slipped out and it seemed like I was being an asshole on purpose. I didn't apologize. That would make it even worse. Like I was a puppy looking for sympathy. I saw the taco place up on the right. Thank fucking god for that.

"Hey, there's the taco place," I said, trying to be casual about it.

"Cool," she said. "I'm hungry."

The place was closed on Sundays.

Even if it wasn't Sunday we would have missed it on account of it being just past four o'clock when they closed anyway.

We punched in the coordinates for Las Cuatro Milpas.

They were fucking closed too, and even earlier on regular days.

"Let's just start heading back. We'll grab something on the way," Laney said.

"Ok," I said. "I was really hoping to get five milpas."

"Do you know what a milpa is?"

"No. But I wanted five of them."

"Why five?"

"That's the name. The Five Milpas."

She laughed at me. "It's four. Cuatro is four."

"Shut it, Laney."

We took a detour to see the coast before cutting over to the faster highway. We saw a rollercoaster out in the distance. My phone buzzed. It was Drix.

Jeff's bad. Chilling at my place now. Get back soon, he wrote.

What's wrong? I wrote back.

Not sure. He ain't coherent. Talk soon.

We drove back to LA.

CHAPTER 22

We didn't talk much on the drive. I knew we couldn't afford another trip to the hospital. We stopped for gas and switched seats. I drove us back and pulled up in front of Drix's house. We went inside. Jeff was on the couch. His eyes were closed. Laney went over to him.

Drix was in the kitchen with a cigarette hanging out of his mouth. He was rubbing his arms.

"Yo, what's up with Jeff?" I said.

Drix came out to the living room. "Man, dude is whacked out. I got a call from Little Pete a couple of hours ago saying some shit about some dude that knows me, and him being all out of his mind. Like not bad out of his mind, but that dude was looking for me and seemed a little worse for wear. Said he had leaves and grass in his hair and on his clothes."

"What the fuck," I said.

"Dude," Laney said to Jeff. "You awake?"

He moaned.

"How long has he been like this?" Laney asked Drix.

"Since I got him. He finally went to sleep. When I picked him up he kept mumbling some shit about butterflies."

"Do you think we should take him to the hospital?" Laney asked.

"He ain't that bad," Drix said. "He just had too much ecstasy I think, but it ain't nothing to worry about."

"How do you know?" I said.

"Well, he kept mumbling shit about butterflies. And he was definitely drinking. Little Pete said he came in and was cool, besides being a little dirty, and he had a few drinks. No big deal. About an hour later he starts acting all kinds of weird and Little Pete told him he had to go and Jeff couldn't stand. Little Pete was worried about liability, it being broad daylight and shit. He asked him if there was anyone he could call and Jeff was mumbling my name."

"Why do you think it was ecstasy?" Laney asked.

"I did the math. He was cool when he came in. A couple of drinks don't make a motherfucker get this way. I checked his bag and pockets. He definitely had some cookies, but I still didn't think that was it. I saw him last night. He was pretty chill on that shit and was pretty chill on acid last week. I kept looking and found a couple of little blue pills with butterflies on them in a dime bag."

"Where are they?" I asked.

"I took them," Drix said.

"You what?" Laney said and looked away from Jeff and over to Drix. He laughed.

"No worries, chica," he said. "Had to know what he got himself into."

"Dude, you feel ok?" I said to Drix.

He rubbed his arms again, and his legs too. "Yeah, bro. This shit is definitely ecstasy, and pretty strong too," he laughed again. "Shit don't mix well if you ain't ready for it."

"Is he going to be ok?" Laney asked.

"Yeah, he'll be good. Just gotta let it work its way through his system. He'll be ok in a few hours. Motherfucker might have a headache, but he'll be ok."

"You're insane," I said to Drix. "Why did you take shit you didn't know?"

"Had to find out," he said and shrugged.

Laney seemed a little more at ease, but she was still sitting on the edge of the couch next to Jeff. "That was stupid Drix," she said. "What if it was something else bad and we came back here to find you passed out too. Or worse?"

Drix went over to her and put his arm around her. "Ah, shit. I didn't mean to scare you." He gave her a one armed hug. "I been taking all sorts of shit for a long time. I know my limits. I was thinking of him. We're a family now. He'll be fine and I'll be fine. Ain't nothing to worry about."

Drix stood up. "Man, I got to go see Nadia before this shit wears off."

"You ok to drive?" I said.

"Dude, please," he said. He grabbed his keys off the table. "Make sure you give him plenty of water when he wakes up." He looked at Laney. "It's all good."

"Thanks for taking care of him," she said.

"No problem," he said and turned away, and then stopped at the door. "Yo, did you get some tacos?"

"They were closed," I said.

"Both of them?" he said.

"Yeah."

"Motherfuckers are always closed," he said to himself. "You dudes around later on?"

"Yeah, we'll be here," Laney said.

"Cool. I'll catch you later." He left and we heard his car door close and the engine start. He pulled away.

"That was interesting," I said.

Laney didn't say anything and just nodded. Jeff started snoring and we rolled him to his side and put a blanket over him. We turned the TV on and sat there.

"Hungry?" I asked her.

"Not really," she said.

Jeff woke up a few hours later and he was groggy. He sat up on the edge of the couch and we made him drink a few glasses of water. He said he felt ok, but that he just came down hard.

"This is when addicts go out and do more," he said, rubbing his face. "Fuck, man. I need a beer."

"You're drinking water," Laney said.

He sighed. "I know, I know."

"What happened?" I asked.

"I only remember up to Little Pete's. Just seeing it, nothing after," he said.

"Little Pete said you came in and had twigs and shit on you," I said.

Jeff laughed a little. "Yeah, I slept outside."

"I thought you went home with Emily?" Laney asked.

"I did. And we ate some cookies and had some more beer. And then did some other things I won't speak of in front of a lady."

"Drix said you were on ecstasy," I said.

"I was. That was after I left Emily's place."

"Why did you leave her place and sleep outside?" Laney asked.

"It wasn't on purpose. I went out to grab a pack of smokes, and I ran into these guys outside of the convenience store and they were trying to sell me weed. I asked if they had ecstasy because I was going to go back to Emily's and I was in that kind of mood. To make a long story short, I got lost and couldn't find my way back to her house in the middle of the night, and my phone died, so I slept in a park under some bushes. I woke up around noon I guess and was still kind of high, and it was a nice day so I took another bite of a cookie and walked around."

Jeff yawned and rubbed his face again. He took another drink of water.

"Fuck, I could really use a beer," he said.

"Finish your story," Laney said.

"Ok, ok. I just liked being outside and was feeling good, so I swallowed a pill and figured I'd see something I recognized to give me my bearings. I don't remember much until I found the strip and Little Pete's. I remember feeling like you guys were supposed to meet me there."

"Jesus, man," I said. "You didn't have any of our numbers?"

"Fuck, no. Do you?"

"I guess only in my phone," I said.

He pinched between his eyes. "I need some ibuprofen and food," Jeff said. "Can we order food?"

"Yeah, we can order food," Laney said.

We ordered some pizzas and Jeff went upstairs to find some medicine and use the bathroom.

"We've been slipping with keeping an eye on him," Laney said.

"I know," I said. "I thought after the dehydration he would have been better."

"Me too."

"Should we talk to Drix too? Let him know about Jeff?"

Laney nodded. "We don't need Jeff thinking he can keep up, or feeling like he has to."

"Man, I feel like a grown-up," I said.

"There's nothing wrong with trying to protect the people you care about," Laney said.

"I know. It just feels like we're narcing out or something. Like we're having an intervention."

"Let's just lay low these next couple of days and keep our eye on him. We've done it before. I'll talk to Drix if it makes you feel funny."

"It kind of does. It shouldn't, but it does. He's always been this way. Always taking more than everybody else, and always being the most functional."

"More reason to make sure Jeff doesn't start doing the same things if we're all going to be together for at least the next ten days."

CHAPTER 23

We lounged around the next two days and tried not to spend any money. Emily was pissed at Jeff, thinking he fucked her and snuck off on purpose. She blew him off and wouldn't return his texts. He was cool with her not wanting to see him, but he was a little rotten about losing his Viking helmet. He left it at her house and she wasn't going to give it back to him. She said that he took it with him.

"Maybe you lost it," I said.

"Trust me, I didn't lose it," he said. "That helmet saw some things. It's at her house."

Laney avoided me, as far as being naked with each other went. It would have been weird anyway with Jeff around, so I didn't make any moves either.

We played a couple of gigs as Hot Dog Tyranny and Death Sentence for Birds at some small clubs around LA. There weren't many people at either venue, but we played well and moved some merch. We reintroduced "Peoria" back into the set after Drix said we should change up the time signature and keep Jeff off guitar. It brought a new vitality and energy to the song. It felt good to play it, and it was the first time we wrote a song together, even if it was a rewrite.

After our sets, some people said they heard of us when they found out we were Qualia, and some didn't give a shit. Radiohead could probably play a dive in any town and the people wouldn't care. It's a fickle business—the theater of accessibility and all the shit that comes with being on a stage.

Jeff was good. He knew we were keeping an eye on him, like he was shamed into not drinking too much. Whatever worked.

Laney talked to Drix. She told him about Jeff, and Drix understood. Said that it was cool and he wouldn't offer Jeff anything, especially after seeing firsthand how easy it was for him to spiral out of control. Whether he was just giving us our space, or wanting to be with Nadia, he spent most of his time at her house before we had to leave for Denver.

On our last night, after we played an early set, we went to this low-key club where some chick with black hair was playing the ukulele and harp. She closed her set with a song called "Summer's Over." It was a dark and brooding number that ended with the words, "Summer's over, go back to real life, summer's over, and I want to die." It was catchy as shit and I kept humming the chorus until Jeff and Laney made fun of me.

We planned on leaving before noon the next day. It would take sixteen hours if we drove straight. We figured we'd drive as far as we could before stopping for the day. We packed up our van with our gear and Drix's drums. I felt an odd satisfaction in loading up the van and packing everything in for our final jaunt back to Philly.

We waited in the van while Drix said goodbye to Nadia. For all Drix's talk about them being on and off, and her being jealous and screwing around, they did seem good together. I guess you got to be pretty crazy about something or someone to deal with all the ups and downs. Drix gave Nadia a hug and kissed her.

"I'll be back in a week or so," he said.

"Ok," she said. She kissed him. "Take care of yourself."

"You too," he said. "Make sure to take your medicine."

"I will," she said.

Drix got in the van and closed the door. I started the engine.

"See ya," I said out the window to Nadia.

She just stared. I nodded and pulled away.

"Why does she hate us?" I asked.

"It's the eastern European in her," Drix said. "It is her way. She really liked you guys. Well, except Jeff. She really liked Laney," he said and turned around.

"Funny way of showing it," Laney said.

"Not to be like friends or anything," Drix said and laughed.

"I'm happy for you," I said to Drix. "But that's a weird relationship you've got."

"Ain't nothing weird about love, baby," he said.

Jeff laughed. "Who are you, Barry White?"

"It's like that?" I said to Drix.

"Yeah, man," Drix said. He drummed his hands on the dashboard, fast and hard. "You fuckers ready to fuck shit up?"

"Fuck. Yes," I said and put my fist out to him.

"Fucking right on," he said.

After a few hours of driving through the desert and long stretches of highway, and Jeff wanting to stop in Barstow just to say, "We're in bat country," we ended up driving through Las Vegas. Jeff said he wanted to see the strip since we missed Vegas on the way out. We saw a billboard for David Copperfield and Laney got excited.

"Do you want to go to a magic show?" I asked her.

"Uh," she said and screwed up her face, "who wouldn't want to go see a magic show?"

"Not I," said Jeff.

"Not I," said Drix.

"Penn and Teller might be cool," I said.

"He made the goddamn Statue of Liberty disappear," Laney said from the backseat.

"Sorry, Laney," I said. "We've still got twelve hours to go."

She sighed. "We should have left a day early," she said.

We stopped at a red light and watched the people walk up the steps to use the elevated crosswalks. There was a guy dressed like Batman standing on the corner getting his picture taken with tourists and their kids. I noticed all sorts of other people dressed up doing the same thing or performing acrobatics. There were so many people out on the street and this was Wednesday afternoon.

There was a big screen advertising an all-female strip show, high above the main drag, looking down on everything.

"We *should* have left a day early," Jeff said.

The sign changed. It was a picture of Green Day. The bottom of the sign said, "With Special Guests: Spectacular Death Extras."

"Motherfuckers," I said.

Drix looked up. He didn't say anything. The light changed and we drove on, out of the city and back into the desert.

We found a cheap motel outside of Aurora, Utah and set up for the night. We still had to leave early in the morning, for us anyway, to make it to Denver in time for load-in. It was getting late in the evening and we were hungry. We went to a convenience store and bought some pre-made sandwiches. Jeff grabbed a huge bag of pistachios.

"Yo, they have beer here," Jeff said. "Anybody else want any?"

Drix looked at us. "I'm good," he said.

Jeff bought two six-packs. "I'm going to have to drink all of these if I want to get drunk," he said, showing me the cans.

They were 3.2% alcohol.

"Why are you getting them then?" I said.

"They're all like that. Or fucking lower," he said.

We found out from the clerk that state law prohibits selling the good shit at convenience stores. We would have to go to a licensed liquor and strong beer store. The closest one was in Salina and it was closed. We left the store.

"Fucking Utah," Jeff said.

"Yeah," I said. "I thought PA laws were bullshit."

"They're still bullshit," Jeff said.

"We'll be in Colorado soon enough," Drix said.

"Fuck yes," Jeff said. "I'm out of pot. I need to re-up with the kind."

"I got a dude that knows a dude," Drix said.

Laney looked at me out of the corner of her eyes.

Drix must've caught that or felt weird. "Ah, shit. I think I got my states mixed up. I was thinking Arizona. It's all the same down here," he said.

We went back to the motel and ate our food. Laney, Drix, and I watched *Big Trouble in Little China* on TV. Jeff sat up in bed with earbuds in and drank his beer and read his book.

We woke up early and got back on the road. We pulled into Denver right at load in. We got out of the van and went in the club. Jeff went to the bar.

"Your finest IPA, sir," he said to the bartender.

"Why don't we take it easy," Laney said.

"I'm good," Jeff said. "We're only in Colorado for a day."

"We've got a long night still."

"I feel great. Just a little to take the edge off," he said.

"We still have to load in," Laney said.

"I'll help still," Jeff said. "Just need a little medicine."

The bartender brought Jeff his beer. He drank half of it in one pass.

"All right," he said. "Let's go unload some gear."

We brought our equipment inside and met the other bands on the bill. Pre-sales were good. The promoter said the buzz we had from the Pitchfork write-up moved a bunch of tickets the past few days.

Drix said he was going to step out to make a call after we sorted out shit with the promoter. He seemed to be even-keeled the past couple of days. Almost at a distance. He was true to his word and didn't talk about doing extra things around Jeff after mentioning his guy in Denver earlier. I respected that, but I also felt like Drix wasn't being himself on account of it. Like he was tiptoeing and just playing it cool. I remembered when I first joined the band and we were on the road—it took a few days to really warm up to the guys and fit in. I assumed it was a combination of that, and not trying to tempt Jeff.

We went out to grab a quick bite to eat before we played. The place we went to had Rocky Mountain oysters on the menu. I ordered a basket for the table.

"Yo, bro," Drix said. "I hope you're hungry."

"Yeah," Laney said, "I'm not putting those in my mouth."

"That's what she said," Jeff said.

Laney groaned. "I thought those jokes went with Gooch?"

"Yeah, but these are actual balls, Laney. Big ol' deep fried balls."

"Lame," Laney said.

"Come on," Jeff said. He looked at me, and then Drix. Drix shook his head.

"Eat up, dude," Drix said.

"Nope. I'm a vegetarian," Jeff said.

"A bull would eat you," Drix said. "That's your rule, right?"

"Yeah," said Jeff. "And it wouldn't. They eat grass."

"You're eating its ball, not the bull," Drix said.

"Drix is right," I said. "One ball per foul."

"Nope. That's a bullshit argument. I call on my second," Jeff said and looked at me. "Don't be a pussy."

"Whoa, don't try to pull me into this," I said.

"You fucking ordered them," Jeff said.

"He's got a point," Laney said.

"Yeah, he's got a point," Drix said.

I looked at Jeff and then Laney and Drix. "I hate all of you."

I picked up a piece.

"Make sure you get the cocktail sauce," Laney said with extra emphasis on the word "cock."

I dipped them in the sauce and ate one. They tasted like the fryer. And a little gamey. But mostly like fryer oil and cocktail sauce.

"It's a good thing you're not our singer," Laney said.

"That's a very good thing," I said. "But why do you say so?"

"Because it will be tough to sing with all those balls in your mouth," Laney said. She looked around the table with a big smile on her face.

We all groaned and called lame on her.

"Screw you guys," she said. "That was funny."

"You're lucky you're a vegetarian too," Drix said. "Paul, eat another one."

"Fuck you," I said and laughed.

We went back to the club. The first band went on and we chilled out in the green room. It was a packed out house and there were still people waiting outside to get in. That was the first time that happened and it felt good. When it was our turn we fucking killed the set. And then went and sold a shit ton of merch. Drix excused himself from the table and went to hang out with a guy at the bar. He said they were old friends, but didn't introduce us. He came back after a few minutes.

"Who was that?" Laney said.

"Just a dude I did a gig with a few years ago," Drix said. "Just saying 'whassup.'"

We packed our gear and Jeff smoked up with one of the other bands in their van and bought some weed from them. He was better when he had weed since he didn't like to smoke before a set.

"This is good shit," he said, holding up the bag. "I think they gave me a lot more than two eighths."

"Yeah?" I said. "You sharing tonight?"

"Fuck yeah, motherfucker," he said in a high voice.

"Don't get too shitty tonight," Laney said. "We still have a long haul to Omaha tomorrow."

"It's cool," Drix said. "I'll drive first."

He seemed up and awake. The last time I saw him like that was before our set in LA at the Whisky.

"You sure?" I said.

"Yeah, man. I'm good," he said.

We found a motel not far outside of Denver. We wanted to drive further to cut down on time tomorrow, but we decided sleeping longer was more important than a shorter drive. We smoked up out in the parking lot and went back to the room. We watched TV for a little while before going to bed. Drix was sitting in the chair looking at his phone. He said he was finishing up a movie he was streaming from some overseas website and that he'd go to bed in a little while.

In the morning he was still in the chair. His phone was on his lap, and he didn't look like he had slept at all. I planned on driving to give him a chance to rest, but when we left the room he took the keys.

"You all right, man?" I asked.

"Dude," he said. "Always." He slapped me on the arm. "Let's go."

His eyes were a little bloodshot, but he did seem alert, so I assumed he was cool. Still, I paid extra attention until it was time to switch driving partners. When Laney and Jeff took over, Drix and I sat in the backseat. Once we started moving he was out cold.

He woke up when we got to the club. We loaded in and it was the same story as last night. Pre-sales were heavy and then they sold out. Got a big boost after the club and local rock station passed on the buzz from the Pitchfork write-up. Laney invited Omaha out to our gig. She turned out to be a cool chick and seemed genuinely happy for us in a no-hard-feelings kind of way. We invited her to hang out with us backstage and Jeff tried to put the moves on her. She played along but didn't seem like she was buying it. When Jeff went outside for a cigarette she told us she was gay.

"That is fucking priceless," Laney said. "How long you going to let him flounder?"

"Until I get bored," Omaha said and laughed.

"I like you. This is good," I said, pointing to her.

We played a great set again, and sold a ton of merch. We told Omaha to keep in touch, and to let us know if she joined another band. We'd be happy to have them on a bill. Jeff had a few drinks at the bar before we left. It seemed to be better to keep moving and not give him a chance to settle in at the bar. These longer hauls in between gigs helped with that.

The next night in Minneapolis was the same. We started to get our nest egg back and got to pay ourselves again without worrying about the band fund. Laney found a bunch of bootleg videos from our gigs the past few days on the internet. They were getting a lot of hits. That felt good.

We were playing at Reggie's in Chicago the next night. The promoter there sent Laney an email saying they had just sold out and to be ready for a big show.

CHAPTER 24

We had a room in a run-down part of Uptown at some joint Laney booked before we left LA. We got to Chicago early and went to check in and drop off our bags. It was in this old building called the Chelsea Hotel. I thought of the Leonard Cohen song, but that Chelsea Hotel was in New York. I looked around and didn't think there'd be any limousines waiting in the streets. This place was run by some Jesus people who offered rooms to travelers, folks trying to get back on their feet, and seniors in assisted living. There was a coffee/skateboard shop attached to the lobby where people with tattoos worked. We later found out it was a non-profit and the people who worked reception and the coffee shop and the kitchen did so as part of their rent.

When we got out of the elevator I felt like maybe we made a bad choice. The carpet was old, and in the elevator lobby were a broken piano, a rocking chair with a blanket on the back of it, a child's chalkboard and easel, and a tricycle.

"Dude, we're gonna get murdered," Drix said.

"Not by Jesus people," Laney said.

"Yeah," Jeff said, "They never killed anybody."

We walked down the hall past doors with various posters on them. Some had children's drawings and chains of construction paper hands held together by yarn. We could hear canned laughter from a television. The smell of someone cooking with curry hung in the air and on the walls.

"This place is creeping me out," Drix said.

"We'll be fine," Laney said.

When we got to our room there was a welcome note that said, *Welcome Qualia! We hope you enjoy your stay!* There was an attached note with instructions to put all of our used sheets and towels in a duffel bag and leave it in the room when we left tomorrow. It also listed the mealtimes down in the cafeteria. We opened the door to the room and went inside. It was small. My cabin when I was working the cruise circuit was a little smaller, but that was for one person. The room had a bunk bed, a loft with a mattress over the little couch, a bathroom, and a small fridge. I did the math and it looked like none of us would have to share a bed, which was surprising and good. Besides the overwhelming heat, it actually wasn't bad.

Laney said she was going around to the lady's apartment who was in charge of letting the room. We opened the windows to let out some of the heat. I called dibs on the bottom bunk. Laney came back.

"I like this place," she said.

"You don't get a weird vibe?" Drix said.

"Nah. Carol was cool," Laney said. "She said she had a band just last week."

"For dinner," Drix said. "They're probably in a cage in the basement all Hansel and Gretel and shit."

We laughed at Drix. I started to feel more comfortable about the place on the way back to the elevator. We went for a coffee before heading down to Reggie's.

We got there early and loaded our gear in and checked out the venue. It was cool as shit. There was a record store on the second level, and the venue also had a separate dining area and bar for other bands to play apart from the main stage in another building.

They gave us each a meal ticket and two drink tickets. I don't know if they did that for all bands, or because we were on tour, or because we helped them sell out, but it was welcome. Chicago was surprisingly turning out to be cheap so far. We ate dinner and had a drink. We set up our gear and ran a sound check. Jeff and Drix went up to the roof deck to smoke a cigarette while Laney and I went to the record shop.

I found an old 45 of the Dead Milkmen's song "Punk Rock Girl." I bought it and gave it to Laney.

"What's this?" she said.

"A present. I figured we've got a couple more dates left before this tour is over. Now's as good of a time as any. This tour has been real fun," I said. "I'm going to miss it, despite what happens in New York."

She looked at the record. And then back at me. She smiled. "Thanks Paul," she said. She moved towards me, and gave me a kiss on the cheek, and then hugged me. I wasn't expecting that. I hugged her back. We stayed like that for a while before I gave her a hard squeeze and let her go.

"Want to go and play?" I said.

She nodded.

Reggie's was packed the fuck out and I wondered if they oversold the place. People were crammed in tight. The first two bands played well and some of the people in the crowd were there for them. When we took the stage everyone went apeshit. We plowed through our set and saved our last song for an encore. It's a risky business manufacturing an encore. What if the crowd didn't deserve one? We finished up and went backstage, sweating and out of breath. The audience was chanting our name.

"One more?" Jeff said and raised his eyebrows.

"Go team," I said.

We went back out and killed.

We almost got overrun at our merch table, and security for the venue had to come over and make sure people formed a line. We talked, and shook hands, and signed t-shirts and CDs. It was our best night in a long time. Probably the whole tour.

We hung out and had some drinks at the bar, and when it closed we went back to the hotel. Jeff passed around a fat joint in the van before we got out. We tried not to make too much noise on the way up. We got to our room and it was fucking hot. And bright.

We sat on the lower bunk and on the couch. Drix made sure we slid the couch in front of the door.

"What's that for?" I asked.

"Man, this place creeps me out," he said. "I don't want no weird motherfuckers petting us in our sleep."

"Uh, speak for yourself," Jeff said.

Laney looked up the history of the building and the organization that ran the building. They seemed legit all around in recent years, helping out in the community and giving people a place to live. They seemed cool except for the lawsuit a couple of years ago about covering up child abuse and reports of adult spankings in the 70s and 80s.

"Yo, I told you this place was creepy, man," Drix said. "Motherfuckers touching kids and spanking each other and shit."

"It's a church affiliated cult house. Of course they were doing fucked up things to kids," Jeff said.

"Doesn't make it cool," Drix said.

"I'm not saying it's cool," Jeff said. "Just not surprising."

"What's it say about the adult spankings?" I asked Laney.

She told us they claimed it was part of their past and there hadn't been any spankings in a long time. That it was part of repentance during a spiritual immaturity phase.

"Sounds like newspeak," Jeff said.

"Like what?" I said.

He shook his head. "You guys need to read more." He stood up and took off his belt. He walked over to me, grinning and looking sinister. He snapped his belt.

"Ok, ok," I said, "I'll read more, I promise." I pulled my legs up on the bed and turned away.

"Damn right you will," he said and snapped his belt again. "After you've all had your spankings." He whacked me on the leg and said, "Adult spankings, Paul," and gave a high-pitched giggle. He grew serious and turned to Drix and then Laney, and did the same thing. Giggling and saying, "Adult spankings, Drix. Adult spankings, Laney." Laney tried to get away, but there was nowhere to go in the room and he hopped around and gave her a lashing on the leg.

"Ow," she said, rubbing her thigh, "That hurt, asshole."

Drix put his hands up, "Relax dude, I'll be good. I swear."

"You'll be good after your spanking," Jeff said.

"You can't hit me. You're not my real father," Drix said.

Jeff laughed loud at that, and then started spanking himself until he fell on the floor.

There was a knock on the door.

"Oh, fuck," Drix said.

We all went quiet. There was another knock.

I climbed on the couch and looked through the peephole. It was an older man with a real thick mustache. He knocked again.

"One second," I said.

Drix looked at me and whispered, "Dude, what the fuck are you doing? Don't open that shit."

"Relax," Laney said. We slid the couch out of the way and she opened the door.

"Hi," she said.

"I can hear everything," the man said. He looked around the room.

"Sorry," Laney said.

"Just keep it down. All right?" he said. He looked at Jeff, who was still holding his belt.

He left and Laney closed the door. Laney covered her mouth and Jeff snorted out of his nose.

Drix stood up and locked the door and moved the couch back in front of it.

"Let's chill out," he said. "I'm gonna get a cold shower. It's hot as shit in here." He picked up his bag and went into the bathroom. We all got settled in and ready for bed. When Drix came back out his pupils were dilated.

"You cool?" I said.

"Yeah, man," he said and looked towards the door. "As long as motherfucker don't come back."

We took turns in the bathroom and then shut the lights off. After a few minutes we heard a loud snapping, and then Jeff giggling. Drix was in the bunk above me and I could see the glow from his phone up on the ceiling. I fell asleep and woke up from the heat a few times during the night. Sometime before dawn the glowing went out.

We woke up the next morning and showered and left the room. We went to the coffee shop next to the hotel and had breakfast before the drive to Cleveland.

"Yo, we got time for the Rock and Roll Hall of Fame tomorrow morning?" Drix asked Laney once we were on the road.

"Uh, yeah, I think so," she said. "We're in Pittsburgh tomorrow night."

"Yeah, there's time," he said. "Always wanted to go there."

CHAPTER 25

We were tired on the drive, and aside from the limited views of the Great Lakes, there wasn't much to see. Even though it was hot, I was glad it wasn't Texas hot. Drix and I sat in the back since we drove yesterday. He fell asleep, and buried in the pocket on the back of the passenger's seat I found an old magazine that Gooch bought at one of our first road stops after it took us forever to get out of Philadelphia.

We stopped for gas about an hour outside of Cleveland. Drix woke up and yawned.

"We there?" he said.

"Almost," I said. "Getting some gas."

"I gotta take a leak," he said.

He grabbed his bag and went inside the rest stop to use the bathroom.

We bought bottles of water. Laney went outside to pump gas. I was hungry. I took a frozen burrito off a shelf.

"Don't do it," Jeff said, walking over towards me.

"Dude, I'm hungry," I said.

"Laney found this pierogi joint not far from the venue."

"But I'm hungry now."

Jeff took the burrito out of my hand and put it back on the shelf. "Here," he said, taking a small bag of pistachios off a rack, "just grab some nuts."

Drix came out of the bathroom and saw us and walked over. His pupils were dilated again. He noticed me looking at his eyes. He took his sunglasses out of his shirt pocket and put them on. "What's the word, motherfuckers?" he said.

"We're getting pierogies," I said.

Drix looked around, "Here?"

"In Cleveland," I said.

"Oh, cool," Drix said.

We went back out to the van and continued on to Cleveland.

"What's the pre-sale numbers look like?" Drix asked Laney.

"Really good," she said.

"Like really good, or really good for a Monday?" Jeff asked.

"The venue said they'd be surprised if they didn't sell out after the doors opened," Laney said.

"Right on," Drix said.

We pulled into Cleveland and found the venue. There was a big black trailer out back where we should have parked to load in. We found a spot on the street at the edge of the driveway. We walked up to the back entrance and saw a few guys wearing headphones and unrolling cables, and bringing them into the building.

We went into the club. Laney asked one of the guys running back and forth from the venue to the trailer what was going on.

"We're recording tonight," he said.

"For?" Laney said.

"Columbia." He walked away.

We stood there looking at each other.

A guy wearing a white v-neck t-shirt, jeans, and Doc Martens came over to us. He looked young, but when he got close, the small flecks of gray in his hair and the crow's feet around his eyes gave him away.

"Qualia?" he said.

"Yes," Laney said.

The guy smiled and put out his hand. "Chester," he said.

We shook his hand.

He looked at Laney. "You're the manager?"

She cleared her throat, "Yeah."

"Good," Chester said, "we've got a few things to go over and sign. I was hoping to do this earlier, but, we've got time still. We've got time."

He looked at me, Jeff, and Drix. "Load in boys. My stage guys will get you set up."

"What's going on?" Jeff said.

He looked at us, confused. "We're recording tonight and in New York. You guys are fucking hot right now. I want to release a teaser EP and video of your live show. I put this all in an email this morning."

We looked at Laney.

"You got the email, right?" he said, furrowing his eyebrows. Laney shifted her weight from one foot to the other. Chester sighed. Then he smiled. "No worries. We'll sort out management later on. After New York." He looked at Laney and moved his head towards the venue. "Come on, let's talk." They went in the venue.

I looked at Jeff and Drix. "Is this for real?"

"I think so," Jeff said, looking at the trailer. We poked our heads in and saw a giant mixer board and all sorts of rack mounted processors with blinking lights.

"Shit," Drix said. "This is fucking crazy, yo." He smiled at me.

We brought our gear in and set up. The stage crew ran sound and mic'ed our amps and drums. When Laney came back over she got her levels and we ran through a few songs while the engineer made sure things sounded good on his end. When we were done we went to the green room. Laney had four documents, one for each of us.

"What's this all about?" Drix said, scanning the paper.

"It's just a release," Laney said. "Not a record deal. He said we'd talk about that later."

"Hmm," Drix said. "I don't know man."

"Can you send this to your guy?" Jeff asked.

"We're on in two hours," Laney said.

"I thought we were headlining?" Jeff said.

"They shuffled the bill around so some of the suits could check us out."

"Well," Jeff said. "I'm glad they'll be able to get home in time to watch their programs with their families."

I read through the contract. Some of it made sense. A lot of it was jargon.

"What did Chester say?" Drix asked.

"We basically don't own the recordings or the video. We get a small percent back after the label recoups." She looked around at us. "They shouldn't have to recoup much since it's only two nights and we're going live."

"We don't own the songs?" Jeff said.

"We own those," Laney said. "We copyrighted them when we released the EP. We won't own the tapes from tonight and New York."

Drix was reading the contract. "Copyrighting ain't publishing," he said.

"What do you mean?" Laney said.

"You still don't technically own your songs. I mean you do, but you don't. I think. That's why there's lawyers. Shit gets confusing once the paper comes out."

He flipped over the last page and ran his finger down it. "Do you mind if we wait so I can call my guy?"

"I'm cool with that," I said.

"Yeah," Laney said. "That's fine."

"Thanks," Drix said. "It's better to be safe than sorry, know what I mean?" He looked at Laney. "What type of feeling did you get from this guy?"

"He seems cool," she said.

"Compared to Graham?"

"Fucking light years away," she said.

"Cool," Drix said.

He called his guy. Drix had to take a picture of each page of the contract and send it to him.

Laney checked the band's email, and filled us in on what Chester said. He got wind of the buzz we had since San Francisco and wanted to capitalize on getting our live set on tape. He wanted to release it as part of an underground, indie series of EPs from emerging artists he was developing at Columbia. He wanted to pump some of the excitement back into the listener's experience that he felt in the 80s and 90s. Back when the listener could feel like they discovered a new band no one else knew about from listening to a sampler tape or CD. The market was different today with the internet, but if he could keep his finger on the pulse and act fast enough, he could help create that excitement in a tangible way with leaking live EPs and some video from bands before they released an album. Like how a studio releases a movie trailer a year before the movie is out. It puts it in the viewer's mind.

Drix's guy called back and said everything looked fair, but that we shouldn't sign it unless we changed a clause so the rights to the songs reverted back to us after it was released. He strongly suggested we create a publishing company to keep a tighter grip on our music. And that he'd bill Drix for the time.

"How much?" Laney said.

"Like two hundy," Drix said.

"Let me know," Laney said. "The band should pay for it."

Drix nodded to her.

"So, I don't understand," Jeff said. "We'll own the tapes?"

"No," Drix said. "They're your songs. Even though you own the rights, they'll own the tapes. Like if they want to use the recordings, after the EP is out, for a soda commercial or some shit, you should be able to get paid."

"That seems unlikely," Laney said.

"It's the unlikely shit that fucks a motherfucker," Drix said. "Let us not forget that Neil Young got sued by his label for not sounding like Neil Young. Remember that shit? Fucking John Fogerty got sued for ripping himself off. Motherfuckers said he sounded too much like himself in a song he didn't own the rights to."

"Yeah," Jeff said. "But both of those guys sucked balls."

"Dude, you're insane," I said, shaking my head.

"Nah, bro," Drix said. "Jeff's right." He laughed. "But, you see what I mean?"

"What do we do then?" Laney said.

"We tell Chester," Drix said.

Laney went to him and he said he'd have to get the ok from legal, but that it shouldn't be a problem. The limited, one-time release was part of his vision anyway. My stomach growled. And as excited as I was, and as dreamlike it all seemed that we were about to record our live set for a label, I was getting really fucking bored with paperwork. We came here to play a rock show.

Laney said she'd walk around and bring us back pierogies. She thought that we should stay at the venue just in case anything else came up. We saw Chester pacing the hallway, on his phone. He popped his head in, and pulled his phone away from his mouth.

"It's cool, guys," he said. "I'll fix that before we go on." He winked at us and walked away.

"That was easy," I said.

"Thanks, Drix," Jeff said. He held up his pack of smokes to us. We nodded.

We went out back to the van to smoke a cigarette.

The other bands on the bill that evening showed up and introduced themselves. They looked at the gear in the trailer and got excited that the show was being recorded. When Jeff told them that he didn't think they were going to be recorded, they seemed to deflate a little, but were still happy to be playing with us and to record label people.

Laney came back with a bunch of food and we ate it in the green room as the doors opened up and the house filled in. The opening act went to set up their gear in front of ours and run a line check. Chester introduced us to a few people that shook our hands and seemed disinterested in actually talking to us.

"Fucking suits," Laney said.

"They weren't even wearing suits," I said.

"I could smell it on them," she said.

Drix went to the bathroom and he took his bag with him. It was hard feeling like he was being sneaky with drugs since he seemed pretty chill and on the ball, but I didn't like the idea of any of us doing shit behind closed doors. I've seen dudes take a bad turn when they try to keep shit hidden from everyone else. They end up shaming themselves and it spirals from the added layer of feeling bad. I was reluctant to say anything to Jeff and Laney, but decided the worst that would happen would be I'd put it in their ear to keep an eye on him, and it could all turn out to be nothing.

"Have you guys noticed anything strange with Drix the past couple of days?" I said.

"Uh, not really," Jeff said.

Laney narrowed her eyes, "Why do you ask?"

"I don't know. It's probably nothing. He stays up all night and always takes his bag to the bathroom."

"So," Jeff said. "We all stay up late."

"I know," I said. "It's probably nothing, I was just curious. It's probably just me."

"I wouldn't worry about it," Jeff said. "He can handle his shit."

"Just don't want it to be the wrong type of shit," I said.

Chester came in with our contracts.

"Here you go guys," he said. "All fixed up."

We took them from him.

"You ready to play a good show tonight?" he said.

"Yes, sir," Jeff said.

"Good," Chester said. "We might have you do an extra take or two of a couple of the songs, just so we can really capture the best of it. Between tonight and New York we should have a killer set."

"That's not very rock and roll is it?" Jeff said.

Chester leaned against the wall. "I know, I know." He ran his hand through his hair. "Man, if we could have had a few more dates we wouldn't need to, but that's the way these things go now. Even live stuff."

"Nirvana didn't do any additional takes," Jeff said.

"When you're Nirvana you won't have to either," Chester said.

"Touché sir," Jeff said. "Touché."

"Listen, I really like you guys. I did when I heard your EP. No one at the label wants you guys more than me. Trust me," he said. "I know what it's like out there on the road, night after night, sometimes the only people you're playing to is the other bands and their girlfriends. It's fucking hard." He looked us all in the eye, one at a time. "If doing a couple of extra takes and jumping through a hoop here and there is all that separates you from the next level, that will bust you out of the small club scene, it seems a no-brainer, right?"

We nodded.

"Ok," Jeff said. "I was just goofing anyway. We'll do as many as it takes."

Chester pushed himself away from the wall and stood straight. "That's the spirit. I don't think it will take that many if you play as good as you did the past few days. See you out there."

He walked away.

"Dude," Laney said to Jeff. "What the fuck was that?"

"What was what?" he said.

"Why were you giving him a hard time?"

"I was just having some fun, that's all. I told him I was kidding." Jeff stretched and yawned. "Man, I could really, really use a fucking beer."

"We're on in an hour," Laney said.

"I just need to loosen up," Jeff said. "This is nerve wracking."

As much as I didn't want Jeff to drink, he had a point. This was making me anxious as well. Sitting right on the edge. This one performance could mean all the difference. If it was shit, I wondered if we'd get another shot in New York. I was thinking that I could really use a beer too, just to calm down a little.

Drix finally came back from the bathroom. He seemed up and full of energy. He was wearing his sunglasses. He set his bag down and sat on the couch.

"Did you fall in?" Jeff said.

"Had to dump, bro," Drix said.

"Gross," Laney said.

"That's gross?" I said. "Jeff had diarrhea and wasn't bashful about it."

"Yeah," Laney said. "But diarrhea is almost a nice word. It's from Greek and makes me think of rivers."

"*That's* gross, yo," Drix said.

"Whatever, dude," Laney said. " 'Dumping' sounds bad."

"It's the hard 'p' that does it," Jeff said and looked at Drix. "She's right."

"Fuck you guys," Drix said.

Jeff let out a long moan. "I'm getting a beer. I can't take it."

He stood up.

"Jeff," Laney said. "Just fucking wait."

He turned to her. "Take it easy," he said.

"I am. I just don't think you should drink before we play tonight."

"I'm not going to get piss drunk."

"You never start out that way," Laney said. "But that's how you end up."

"What the fuck, Laney?" Jeff said. "This shit is making me freak the fuck out a little. I just want a beer. One fucking beer."

"We're on real soon," she said.

"Which is why I want one, and is more reason to fucking trust me. I won't even have enough time to get drunk, even if I wanted to," he said.

She didn't say anything.

"Do you really want to have this fight before we go play?" Jeff said.

She sighed. "No," she said. "I just don't want to fuck it up."

"Then don't," Jeff said. He walked out.

I stood up. "I'll go with him," I said. "Just to make sure."

Laney nodded.

"Drix?" I said.

"Nah, man," he said. "I'm cool. I'm gonna warm up."

"Ok," I said. "We'll be back soon."

I caught up with Jeff backstage. On our way out to the floor we had to get lanyards with these giant plastic cards attached so we could get back past security.

The room was just about full and we shuffled our way through the crowd. The opening act was going on in a few minutes. We ordered two beers. Jeff picked his up and took a big mouthful. And then another.

"Can you believe her?" he said. "You know she meant she didn't want me to fuck it up."

"She didn't mean that," I said. "She's just nervous like the rest of us."

He finished off his beer and ordered another one and a shot.

"Do one with me?" he said.

"Just one," I said. "I want to be clear up there."

The bartender brought Jeff another beer and the shots.

Jeff held up his shot. "To you, sir," he said.

I held mine up. "To you," I said.

"No," he said. "To you. We wouldn't have made it this far without you. Shit's funny, man."

"What do you mean?" I said. "What's funny?"

"Everything's funny. I think about what it could have been like if you and Drix were in the band when we started. I think we would have made it already, when we were in our early twenties. Instead of now. I think about how much time we wasted trying to find the right drummer and making the right connections. Just a lot of dead end roads we spent a long time on. I kind of feel like this is the shot. Like we won't get another one."

I nodded. "I know what you mean, brother. I know what you mean."

"Don't get me wrong, I mean, me and Laney are still pretty young compared to you. If this all falls through we can still keep going. I just worry about you and Drix, sitting alone eating burnt TV dinners in a one bedroom apartment wishing your kids would remember your birthday and return your phone calls."

"Like we're living together and have the same kids?" I said.

"It's how I've always imagined it," he said and shrugged.

He raised his shot glass again. "No, seriously though. Thanks, man," he said.

"Thanks dude." We shared a look for a few seconds.

"All right," he said. "We should either kiss or do these shots." He cocked his head and leaned forward. "I could pass on the shot, eh?"

I laughed at him. "Maybe later," I said.

We clinked glasses and put back the whiskey.

The house lights dimmed and the opening act took the stage.

Jeff ordered a third beer after he finished his second.

"Come on man," I said. "Let's get back there to warm up."

"When have I ever warmed up?" he said.

"Might not be a bad time to start."

He drank his beer and when he put it down I picked it up and put back a good swig of it. I reached over and dumped it down the drain tray under the taps.

Jeff looked at me and shook his head. "Sacrilege," he said.

"It was an offering," I said.

"You owe me a beer after the show."

"I'll buy you two."

We walked backstage and flashed our passes to get through security. Laney was running scales and Drix was warming up on a practice pad. Laney looked at Jeff.

"Feel better?" she asked.

"Way better," he said. He started jumping up and down in place. "I want to go play."

"Soon brother," Drix said. "Soon. Save your energy for the stage."

I took out my bass and began warming up too. I looked down at my hands running scales and arpeggios, my fingers plucking the strings. Drix was in my periphery and I thought of when we were kids sitting in his basement, smoking weed and listening to classic rock. I remembered, early on, we took a bus ride to a record shop in Manayunk because they had a killer used CD section and weren't shy about selling bootlegs. It was eight or nine years after Cobain shot himself and Drix bought this CD full of Nirvana demos and live performances. It was something like volume eight. It sounded like shit. I picked up a scratched copy of Primus' *Sailing the Seas of Cheese*. It wouldn't play when we got back to his basement and I rubbed toothpaste all over it to get some of the scratches out. It worked a little better but Drix busted my balls because his CD player smelled minty for a few weeks.

That was well over ten years ago. It seemed like another life. I smiled to myself. Jeff was right. Shit is funny. I never thought I'd meet Drix again in this capacity, in this other life. We were two completely different people from when we were kids, but also the same. I was bringing myself down a little thinking about the paths we take and the choices we make, and how none of it has anything to do with us. How easy it is for all of it to go away.

A guy with headphones on poked his head in the green room. "You're on in fifteen," he said and walked away.

I put my bass down and stood up and stretched.

"Pre-show nerve poop," I said. "I'll be back."

Laney chuckled.

"Is that better?" I said.

"It's still got the hard 'p,'" Jeff said. "Fuck, it even has two of them. There's no way that's better."

"It sounds cuter," Laney said. "It's quick." She said the word "poop" in quick syllables, like a bird chirping.

"She's right," Drix said. "Dumping does sound bad when you think about it that way." He stood up and bent over with his hands on his knees, and his ass hanging over the couch. "It's all like, 'ddduuuuuuuuuuummmppp.'" He said it low and slow and really dragging out the middle of the word, his face twisted in a frown.

I left the room and went to the bathroom. When I came back, it was time to play.

CHAPTER 26

The house manager introduced us and gave a small speech to the audience. Letting them know that the show was being recorded and to make a lot of noise when we came out. He got a little weird and I'm not sure if he ever got on a microphone or on a stage before in front of people. He started talking to the lightman and quoting Jim Morrison.

He said, "I don't know if you're aware of it, but this whole evening is being taped for eternity and beyond that too. And so listen man, if you want to be represented in eternity with some uncouth language then I hope you'll stand up on the top of your seat and shout it out very clearly or we're not going to get it on tape."

For my part I thought it was pretty fucking funny. I elbowed Jeff and we watched the guy keep going.

"Was there another opening act?" Laney said.

"Yo," Drix said. "This dude ain't going to stop. If he starts a comedy routine, I'm fucking out of here."

I almost felt bad for the guy. There are people of a certain disposition that given the chance will gladly make an ass of themselves in front of strangers, saying stupid shit, and not even know it. When he was done talking he gave a big yell and punched his fist in the air. He got off the stage and walked past us, smiling and nodding.

"They're all yours," he said. He gave Jeff a hard slap on the back and clapped his hands loud.

Laney looked at me and mouthed, "What the fuck?" I shrugged and smiled.

"All right bitches and Laney," Drix said. "Let's do this shit."

We took the stage. The house was full and they roared. I imagined this is what the Beatles felt like invading America.

We tuned up real quick and started the first song. Drums and bass. Laney entered with her snakey guitar line.

Jeff grabbed the microphone and closed his eyes. He opened his mouth to sing. His voice cracked on the first word. He turned to us and waved us off. We stopped playing.

He coughed into his sleeve and turned back to the mic.

"Sorry about that guys," he said. "I thought I was done with puberty." He touched his throat and looked confused. "Just ignore me if my pants get tight during the show."

The audience laughed. Jeff looked at us quick and widened his eyes and pulled his lips back, showing his teeth, then turned back to the audience.

"Ahh," he crooned. He cleared his throat again, and coughed. "All right, let's try that again," he said and laughed.

Drix counted off the song. Drums, bass, and then Laney.

Jeff was spot on.

We played well. There were two guys with steady cams wandering around the stage and one dude with a handheld who was all over the fucking place. It was kind of weird having a camera looking at you. I did my best to ignore it. I know you're never supposed to look at the camera, but every time I looked up there was a fucking camera. I stayed close to Drix and just rocked out with him, lost in our own rhythm section cocoon while Jeff bounced around stage and Laney moved and danced around with her guitar. We blasted through the set and the audience was loud. A good deal of them sang along to the choruses. We killed our last song and the audience was chanting our name. Chester came over the monitors.

"All right guys," he said. "Let's run 'Half Full' and 'Black Swan' one more time."

Jeff went to the mic. "Cool," he said. "Hey listen guys, thanks for coming out tonight. Since we've got the man in the house recording us, and they want to make sure that they're not wasting your time, they want us to play a couple of songs again. What do you say?"

The audience yelled.

"All right," Jeff said. "But I'm going to level with you." He lowered his voice. "They real reason we have to do the songs again is because the mics that were recording the audience crapped out. They're working now, so let's make sure we really get you this time." Jeff pointed his mic to the audience and they went fucking insane. I've never heard so many people scream so loudly. I smiled and looked at Drix and Laney and then back at Jeff, his foot on the monitor, holding the microphone out over the audience. His body silhouetted in the bright glow of lights. I could see a red exit sign burning through the blackness in the back of the club. He turned back to us and bounced up and down. Drix clicked off the song. When we were done, Chester came back over the monitors. "That should do it," he said. "Good work boys and girl."

Jeff thanked the audience and asked them to stick around for the next band. We went backstage. The house manager was back there and he clapped us on the back as we passed him. He followed us into the green room and closed the door.

"Great fucking show," he said. "Great fucking show." He sat down. "You guys were fucking awesome." The guy was clenching his jaw. He pulled four business cards out of his pocket. They were his personal cards. Derek Parkinson. He handed one to each of us. "Show this to the guys at the bar. It's good for anything. Food, drinks, whatever."

"Thanks man," Jeff said.

"Yeah, thanks," Laney said.

"Don't mention it," he said. He pulled a little bag out of his pocket and what looked like a compact. He set the bag down. It was coke. He poured out a pile on the mirror and cut up five lines. "Let's have a bump," he said and looked at us.

"I'm good," I said. "But thanks anyway."

"Yeah, no thanks," Laney said.

"Come on," Derek said. "Don't be pussies." He looked at Laney. "No offense. It'd be rude to come into my house and not have just a little."

I looked at Laney.

Jeff took the mirror and snorted a line.

"Jeff," Laney said. "What the fuck?"

"I don't want to be rude," he said. "It's just one line." He was sniffing and moving around his mouth. "That's good," he said to Derek.

"I'm glad one of you has manners here," Derek said. "Another?" He said to Jeff.

"Nah, I'm good," Jeff said and sat back in the couch and pulled out a cigarette.

"Come on man," Derek said. "I don't want to do it alone. Just one more."

"Well," Jeff said and leaned forward. "Maybe one more wouldn't . . . "

Drix reached across him. "Hand me that shit, yo," Drix said and took the mirror. He banged the other three lines and pinched his nose and shook his head. He gave the mirror back to Derek. "That one's yours," Drix said.

"Holy shit," Derek said and laughed. "My man."

Derek did his line and stood up. "Drinks on the house," he said. "Go get 'em." He left the green room.

Jeff stood up. "Who's up for a drink? I could really use a drink."

"What the fuck is wrong with you?" Laney said to Jeff. "When did you start doing coke again?"

He looked at her. "When we just recorded a fucking live EP for a goddamn record label. Don't you feel fucking great?" He almost yelled it, and didn't say it mean. I could tell he was up from the coke and feeling good. He smiled at us. "Come on guys," he said to Laney and me. "Just a little celebration. No worries, we're done for tonight. Let's go get a drink."

"We're not done. We have to go sell merch. We'll get drinks later," Laney said and stood up.

I looked at Drix. "You ok, man? That was a lot."

He shook his head and stood up. "Let's go sell some merch to these hungry motherfuckers."

I stood up too. "Ok." He actually did seem all right besides clenching his jaw and talking a little faster than usual.

"I can't wait until we have people to do this for us," Jeff said. "I hate selling merch. Like what the fuck are we supposed to say to people?"

Drix put his hand on Jeff's back. "Bro," Drix said, "you smile and say, 'thank you.' That's it dude."

"So wise, Master Drix," Jeff said. "So wise."

We went to the merch table while the next band was playing. The venue set up a faux barrier around the table with those metal poles that have expandable nylon straps attached to one another. The kind at airports and train stations to keep people in line.

People started coming over and we shook their hands and signed their stuff.

"We're going to have to order more after New York," I said.

"We're not going to have much for New York," she said and tapped a box with her foot. It was damn near empty. I knew we sold a lot these past few days, but I didn't think we went through that much. That was a lot of t-shirts, CDs, buttons, and stickers.

A group of dudes came up to us with a tray full of shots on the side of the rope fence separating our table from the bar. He handed the tray to Jeff, who was the closest. "Hey," one of them said. "You guys rock." He and his crew started chanting, "shots." We each picked up a shot and did one with them. They walked away chanting "Qualia, shots."

Chester came up to our table and was smiling. "Good work," he said. He looked at us like a proud uncle. "I haven't felt this way in a long time. You guys get some rest ok? I'll see you in New York."

"You're leaving?" Laney said.

"Yeah. I've got a long day tomorrow going through the mix," he said.

"You're doing the mix?" I said.

"If I had to wait for the label for everything, nothing would ever get done," he said. "See you in two days. Good work again." He walked away.

The third band finished up and we were just about out of merch except for some stickers. The house manager got back on stage and told everybody to stick around because it was still early and he had a special guest DJ coming in to play music for them. Some people left, but most stayed which surprised me since it was after eleven on a Monday. Laney decided we should walk around the venue and hand out the remaining stickers to people. Somewhere along the way we all got separated and were talking to people. I saw Jeff at the bar with Drix surrounded by people. Laney was talking to a bunch of girls who had pink hair and plaid pants on. Beyond the few random people who recognized me and wanted to talk after I gave out my stickers, I was alone, just walking around the room while some dude was on stage doing what Girl Talk did a couple of years ago. It could even have been Girl Talk. Fuck if I knew what the dude looked like.

I was enjoying my anonymity. I wasn't the singer, so I wasn't the voice or face of the band. I wasn't the hot chick guitar player, and I wasn't the crazy good wild man drummer. I was just a dude laying down the low end, holding it together.

I grabbed a beer from a small satellite bar on the other end of the venue, and found a spot off to the side and watched everybody. I watched Laney surrounded by the girls, and I saw all the young people dancing and drinking. The lovers with sex in their eyes, the drunks with sex in their eyes who would go home alone, the wide-eyed lovers of life, drinking it all in, the scene, the night, the feel of being young and alive and saying "fuck you" to the world in the late hours of the night. I smiled and watched. I hopped up on stage and asked the DJ if he had any Tom Waits. He looked at me like I was fucking insane.

"Who?" he said.

"Dude," I said and looked at my watch, "it's Waits O'Clock, and you don't even know it."

He started typing on his laptop.

"It's cool," I said and walked away.

CHAPTER 27

Laney came over to me and we went to Jeff and Drix at the bar. Their piles of stickers were sitting on the bar next to them, scattered around a bit. They each had a few empty glasses surrounding them and they were both drunk. Jeff was slouched over and slurring, but up and laughing and talking a lot. I'm sure he had to have been down from the coke by now and was making up for it by drinking. Drix seemed a lot better off, but he talked a little bit louder and faster than usual.

I looked at Laney. She shrugged. "It's no use saying anything now," she said. "Let's give them tonight."

"Ok," I said.

I was glad she was going to let it slide. I wanted to have a few drinks myself and I wasn't looking forward to talking to Jeff and Drix about cooling out on the drinking and drugs. If this was the new scene we were going to be around, we wouldn't last long living every night like we were in some 70s or 80s band. I guess any big band really. It's just a matter of saying "yes" or "no" when the stuff is around. When it came down to it I didn't feel like I was in a position to tell my friends what to do. I knew people had interventions and shit like that, but who was I to tell someone to stop drinking so much when I was the one drinking with them? I put it out of my mind and ordered another beer.

Laney said she found a motel about ten minutes away and we could probably get two rooms tonight. When she said that she bumped her hip into mine.

"Two rooms?" I said.

She smiled and winked at me.

We sat at the bar and people eventually started leaving. Drix was telling stories about when he first moved out to LA and got a job with this legendary producer. He wouldn't tell us his name. He said he had to sign a confidentiality agreement and wasn't even supposed to talk about it. I wasn't sure if he was lying, but I listened along anyway.

"So this motherfucker comes into the studio after I set up my kit and we get it all mic'd and he tells me it doesn't sound like it's facing the right way. Like what the fuck does that even mean? He was carrying around a little ficus and whispering to it. I couldn't hear what he was saying, but he'd whisper to it and then say shit to me like, 'the room sounds more purple over here. But it feels more blue over there.' Motherfucker made me break down my kit. Not just move it. I had to fucking break down my kit piece by piece and remove it from the room and bring it back in one piece at a time. He had all these other percussion instruments from around the world lined up on shelves in the hallway and every day he told me to take one home and learn it."

"Why didn't you tell him to go fuck off," Jeff said.

"You don't tell this dude to fuck off," Drix said. "Not when you're just starting out and motherfucker's paying you serious scratch."

"How much?" Jeff asked.

"Dude, I don't even know anymore. I was with him for eleven days. He had this duffel bag full of cash. Twenties and fifties. A lot of hundreds in there. At the end of the day, which could have been whenever the fuck he wanted, sometimes late as shit, like four or five in the morning, he would tell me to go grab a handful and pay myself."

"What?" Laney said. "That's crazy."

"Right?" Drix said. "So, I don't know if it was some kind of test or some shit, and my instinct was to grab as much as I could. That first day I think I ended up with like eight hundred crumpled up in my pockets. The next day I came back and it was the same shit. I had to redo my drum kit, he'd talk to his plant and have me move it."

"What were you recording?" I asked.

"Beats," Drix said. "He just said, 'Play a rock beat. Play a jazz beat. Play a punk beat.' I'd do this for hours, and then he'd say ask me to hit the drums one at a time for a few hours. When we were done for the day, he'd nod to the duffel bag. By day nine I started to think that maybe I died and was in purgatory or some shit and this was how I'd spend eternity. Like maybe I died on my way to LA, or was selling my soul to the devil at the crossroads. I stopped counting when I paid myself. He never looked at me when I took the money and I just loaded up my pockets and stuck it all in a pillowcase in my closet at my apartment. The next day the bag would be full to the top again."

"What did you spend it on?" Jeff asked.

"Rent for a few months, drugs. My car. More drugs," he said and laughed.

"You're putting us on, man," I said.

"Nah, man," Drix said. "That's not even the weirdest part. This dude was so meticulous and abstract with getting the right sounds except for my bass drum. My pedal needed some lube cause it was squeaking. Not a lot. Just fucking enough. I could hear it like a little fucking mouse for a millisecond before the bass hit. Like Bonham's hi-hat pedal on 'Since I've Been Loving You,' but even quieter than that. I went to adjust it and lube it up and dude sees me through the glass in the control room and comes running in with his plant and is all like 'what are you doing?' and I'm all like 'my pedal's squeaking, bro,' and he gets all dark and serious as shit and lowers his voice and stares at me. 'Don't change it,' he said. 'That's your sound.' He nodded slow as he was saying it and went back to the control room."

"Come on," I said. "Tell us who it was."

"No way man," Drix said.

The bartender came over and Drix ordered a round of shots for us.

"On day eleven we go through the same shit again, and I was telling myself if this went on for a few more days I was going to start asking some questions. I was cool for now because I was getting paid and got to work with this dude. But anyway, on the eleventh day I finish up after playing some weird ass Arabic beats I looked up the night before because I was running out of shit to play. He asks me to come into the control room. He nods to the duffel bag and after I grab my cash and say 'goodbye' to him, he turns around and he has a gun in his lap and asks me to have a seat. So, I start shitting my pants a little, even though I didn't think this dude was murderous. But he was fucking crazy, and I feel it's always best to listen to the crazy motherfucker with the gun, so I sat down. Dude slides a contract over to me with a pen and says, 'Sign this. You were never here.' "

"What happened next?" Laney asked, leaning against me.

"I fucking signed it and packed up my kit. Never heard from him again," Drix said and laughed and picked up his shot. "Cheers, motherfuckers," he said. We put back the shots.

Jeff and Drix were wasted by the time we left the club, but Drix pulled it together when we had to load up the van. Jeff fell down in the hallway that led to the back door and just started giggling. We picked him up and put him in the backseat.

The house manager stopped Drix on our way out and they disappeared for a few minutes. When Drix came out to the van he was sniffling and wiped his nose. He was holding a bottle of vodka.

"What's that?" I said from the passenger seat.

"A gift from that dude, Derek," Drix said.

"Vodka," Jeff crooned.

"No more for you sweet prince," Drix said. "We'll save this for later."

Laney pulled away and Jeff fell asleep. She told Drix that we were going to get two rooms when we parked at the motel.

"That's cool," he said, slouched in the back seat.

"Can you make sure Jeff doesn't throw up all over the place?" Laney said.

"It's all good," Drix said. "He'll be fine."

"If he gets up in the middle of the night, he might try to pee on the nightstand," I said.

Laney looked at me. "Why would he do that?"

"I don't know," I stalled. "I was just joking."

We helped Jeff into his room and put him on the bed just inside the door. We rolled him on his side. He was out cold.

Laney stood over him and pulled the blankets over his body.

"He'll be all right," Drix said. "Go. Do things to each other."

Laney blushed.

"So," I said. "Still want to try for the Rock and Roll Hall of Fame before we leave tomorrow?"

"Fuck yeah," he said. "Even just for an hour. Be cool to see."

"Cool," I said. "Night dude." I put out my fist. "Good show tonight."

"Right on, brother," he said and bumped my fist.

We went down the hall to our room and fumbled with the key to the door.

Laney was a little more drunk than she let on, and the whiskey wasn't helping my cause. We made out for a while and somewhere just before dawn we fell asleep.

I woke up hours later and the sun was bright behind the curtains. We were both naked and I was ready and I started kissing her. She woke up and moaned and pulled me into her. When we were done she got a shower and I texted Drix.

She was dressed and drying her hair when she came out of the bathroom.

"My head is fucking killing me," she said.

"I have some ibuprofen," I said and got out of bed and took the plastic bottle from my bag and put it on the table.

"Thanks," she said. I walked past her. "Hey," she said.

"Yeah?" I said.

She looked at me. Then smiled. "Nothing," she said and pulled her hair back.

I got a shower and dressed. Drix still hadn't texted me. Laney said she texted Jeff, and he hadn't responded either. I sent a few more texts to Drix and called. I knew he slept late, but we would have to leave soon if we wanted to make the Hall of Fame before we made our way to Pittsburgh.

Laney and I put our bags in the van and went to Jeff and Drix's room. We knocked on the door and Laney called Jeff. After a few minutes of pounding on the door and yelling "wake up sleepy heads," we heard Jeff moan from inside.

"Hang on," he said. "Hang on."

We could hear him sit up and put his feet on the floor. He walked the two steps it took to get to the door. The latch slid and the handle turned and the door opened. Jeff put his hand and arm across his face.

"Holy mother of fuck-christ-shit-balls," he said.

He closed his eyes. "Oh, my fucking god," he said. "Never again. Never fucking again."

He turned around and sat down on the edge of the bed with his hands on his head.

Drix was in bed on the other side of the room.

"Yo," I said. "Wake up motherfucker. Going to the Hall of Fame today."

He didn't move. I walked over to him and shook his foot. "Wakey, wakey," I said. I moved around to the other side of the bed. The bottle of vodka was on the floor, half gone. I saw his face. I saw a pool of vomit around his mouth and on the pillow.

The next moments were all one unstoppable, indistinguishable swell of events. I remember screaming for Laney to call an ambulance. I remember Jeff looking stunned. I remember scooping vomit out of my friend's mouth and giving him CPR and gagging and spitting and crying and shaking him. I remember Laney's eyes and her putting her hands on my shoulders and pulling me away as paramedics ran into the room, sirens blaring in the parking lot, and how limp Drix's body was as he was lifted on a stretcher and how I jumped in the back of the ambulance as we raced to the hospital.

I sat in a room at the hospital and stared at the carpet. It was a dream and everything was going to be all right. This wasn't happening. This wasn't happening. A doctor came out and told me that Drix was dead.

CHAPTER 28

I filled out paperwork about Drix. The hospital said they had people that would take care of things. I gave them his address in LA and his mother's name in Philadelphia. I thought of Little Pete and Nadia. I thought of his family. I felt like I should be the one to tell them about Drix, but I also didn't want to. I didn't want to say it.

I took a cab back to the motel. I was expecting us all to be arrested and questioned. Laney and Jeff were sitting in the van. There weren't any signs of police or anything around. Like everything was fine. They told me that Jeff dumped whatever drugs he had down the toilet before the cops got there, which was right after the paramedics. The cops didn't even search the room. They asked a few questions and when they heard from the hospital that Drix asphyxiated and it didn't seem like a suicide, they said the room wasn't a crime scene, and they left.

I asked Jeff what he found in Drix's bag. He said there were some pills and a little bit of coke. We drove to a diner and ordered food that none of us wanted. We sat there, quiet.

"Paul," Laney said. "I'm sorry."

Jeff avoided eye contact with me.

Laney said she cancelled at the venue already for tonight, and asked what we should tell Chester.

"I don't know," I said. "I don't know."

We sat there quiet for some time. I ate a little bit of my food. Each swallow was poison. I felt sick. Jeff eventually ate his food. He needed to after last night. He kept ripping up straw wrappers. When he was done, he took another straw and ripped up that wrapper too. He had about a dozen straws in his cup of water. The sun was beginning to make its long arc down and set for the day, but it still had a few more hours to go. The waitress came by and we asked for our check.

Jeff cleared his throat. He made like he was going to say something, and then stopped. He took a deep breath. He looked down at his pile of ripped up paper and put his hands on the edge of the table.

"We could get Gooch," he said.

"Jeff," Laney said quick and loud and looked at him.

My eyes shot to his. My heart started racing and my skin was hot. I wanted to reach across the table and grab him and punch him in the fucking mouth. My arms started shaking. My body started shaking. My face was on fire and my vision became blurry. I ran my sleeve across my eyes and stood up and ran outside into the parking lot. I went to our van and I saw Drix's drums in the back window and I started kicking the van and punching it. I hurt my hand and I thought of Drix pulling me away from the fight in LA, and I turned around and let out one long painful scream and fell back into the van and slid down till my ass was on the ground and I just fucking cried. I sat there and cried until I couldn't cry anymore and my body felt empty. Nothing mattered.

Laney came out and kneeled down next to me. Her eyes were red and she put her arms around me. She didn't say anything. There wasn't anything to be said and I was glad that she knew that.

I heard Jeff shuffling around. I could hear him light a cigarette. He came over to us and kneeled.

"Paul," he said. "I'm sorry. It was a stupid thing to say. We're done. We can just go home now."

I didn't look at him or respond. The words "we're done" echoed in my head. Out of the corner of my eye I saw Jeff reach forward. He was holding out his pack of cigarettes. I took one. Laney rubbed my back and kissed me on the top of my head and stood up. Jeff leaned over and lit my cigarette and sat down next to me.

"I'm sorry," he said and shook his head. "I'm sorry for everything."

I didn't say anything. I thought of the years Drix and I shared and the ones we didn't. The time we'd never get back. He was my brother and he was gone. We made a pact when we were dumb kids, and it got him killed. It was over. It wasn't over.

We sat there and smoked our cigarettes. When we finished, we stood up. I looked at the van and at the small dents I made in it with my foot. I opened and closed my hand. It hurt, but it would be all right. Laney was leaning against the van, and Jeff was toeing the gravel. I took a deep breath. The words "we're done" wouldn't leave me. I took another deep breath. Drix. Motherfucker.

"Did you call Chester?" I asked Laney.

She looked at me. "No," she said. "Not yet."

"Don't," I said.

Jeff looked at me and Laney didn't say anything.

I took my phone out of my pocket. "I'm going to call Gooch," I said and walked away.

I talked to Gooch and he agreed to come up to New York and play for us. I told him he could use Drix's drums.

I told Laney and Jeff.

"It's totally your call," Jeff said.

"You sure?" Laney said.

"Yeah," I said. "If Drix knew we were quitting he'd probably say, 'fuck that shit, yo.'" I forced a small laugh.

We drove away from Cleveland with the sun behind us. We drove away from Drix's body that was cold and dead in a morgue somewhere. The hospital people said they'd contact the next of kin and put them in touch with a funeral home that would take care of transport.

Jeff drove for a few hours. Then Laney. We drove through the night. I hoped we could just drive forever. We pulled into New Jersey sometime in the middle of the night and found a shitty motel across the river from New York.

We checked in and I fell asleep. When I woke up Laney was next to me and Jeff was in the other bed. Gooch was going to come up a few hours early so we could run through the set before we played. Laney contacted the people at Fontana's and they said it was cool to load in and rehearse before our set. We checked out of the motel and drove into New York a couple of hours before we had to meet Gooch.

We parked right in front of the venue and bought three hours of parking.

"I'm going to take off for a little while," I said.

"Ok," Jeff said.

"Do you want us to get you anything to eat?" Laney said.

"I'm good," I said. "I'll be back for practice."

I found the nearest subway and took the line that went to Central Park. I got off and walked through the crowd of people in Columbus Circle and past the vendors selling hot dogs and nuts. Past a stand selling Belgian waffles. I walked past all of it and under a bridge and past where they set up an ice skating rink in the winter and I zig-zagged north until I found myself at a statue of Shakespeare. I walked down the wide path that was flanked by statues of writers and at the end I saw a bust of Beethoven and kept walking, across a terrace and down steps to where there was a fountain with a lake just beyond that. I sat on a bench and looked at the water.

On the other side of the courtyard, a girl wearing a tutu was performing ballet next to a portable radio. I couldn't hear the music well, but it sounded like Debussy. I sat and watched her, the water just behind her. I remembered a field trip I took in high school for English class. We were supposed to go see things from *The Catcher in the Rye* and stuff from a playwright that wrote a story about a zoo. Drix and I snuck off on our own to smoke weed and visit Strawberry Fields. I hadn't thought about that in a long time. I smiled. "Goddamnit," I said to myself and wiped my eyes.

I sat there for a while watching the girl dance. I had to get back for practice soon. I stood up and went to the girl and put a twenty into a bucket in front of her. She did some ballerina move that looked like a curtsey, but a lot more beautiful. I nodded and began to turn away, but stopped.

"Excuse me," I said.

She looked at me.

"Sorry," I said. "What do you call a male ballet dancer?"

She furrowed her eyebrows and pursed her lips and moved her eyes up. Then she looked at me and smiled.

"They are called 'danseur,'" she said with a thick accent.

I nodded to her. She did the graceful curtsey thing again. I walked away.

When I got back to the club I was expecting to see the big trailer that was at our gig in Cleveland. I could see our gear in the van still. I walked into Fontana's and saw Jeff, Laney, and Gooch sitting at the bar with paper cups, steam rising from the top.

Gooch stood up and shook my hand and pulled me in for a hug.

"Sorry," he said.

"Thanks," I said. "And thanks for coming up."

"No worries. I figured I owed you," he said.

"How's Dunk?"

"Oh, you know. He's getting so big."

"Really?"

"No," Gooch said and laughed.

"Should we load in?" I asked everybody.

Gooch took a deep breath and turned to Jeff and Laney.

Jeff rubbed his palms on his legs.

"Yeah," Laney said. "But we have some bad news."

I looked at each of them.

"Fucking Chester got fired," Jeff said.

"Apparently," Laney said, "his whole indie-buzz vision was a little too under the radar at the label and he got canned for spending money on a band the label told him they weren't interested in."

"I thought that was his job?" I said. "To find bands for the label to be interested in?"

She shrugged. "Yeah, me too. I got the feeling there was more to it than that. He said he'd be in touch later on."

"Did you tell him?" I asked.

Laney shook her head.

"So, what are we going to do?" I asked.

"We figured we'd see what you wanted to do before loading in," Jeff said.

I looked around the room. Here we were sitting in an empty club on a Wednesday afternoon, a whole tour behind us, my friend and bandmate dead, a record deal that never was just dissolved, a drummer on loan, and a sold out show to play in a few hours.

I laughed at the absurdity of all of it.

They looked at me.

"Give me the keys," I said.

Jeff tossed them to me.

I walked towards the door.

"Where you going?" Gooch asked.

"To load in," I said over my shoulder.

CHAPTER 29

We rehearsed and it felt weird but we sounded good. We went out for some pho at a place around the corner. Gooch made small talk and we filled him in on some of the stuff that happened after he left. We told him about Graham and about the pot cookies.

I asked him where he went when he left.

"I stayed in San Luis Obispo for a few days," he said. "I liked it there. I found a real cheap motel and then took a bus up to San Francisco for a flight back home."

"Cool," I said.

Laney and Jeff didn't say much. I imagined they had their own struggles to deal with. Their band was just sort of dropped, and I didn't think about it until now, but I thought about what Jeff was going through since he was the one drinking with Drix, and he was the one that was asleep next to him while he was dying. That thought hit me in the gut. I looked at Jeff and his eyes seemed far away.

We went back to the venue and it was packed. The club was in the basement and although it wasn't the biggest place, it was a great place to catch a band in an intimate setting. We didn't play bad, but Jeff lost a step in his stage performance and Laney's playing seemed a little lazy. Gooch played tight and I stood off to the side of the stage and stared out into the crowd. I played so hard that my finger got rubbed raw and started bleeding, and on the outro of our last song I pounded the shit out of the low E string with my fist until the string broke and I had to go up an octave on the A string to finish in key.

I was glad we were out of merch because I didn't have it in me to talk to people. We found a table upstairs and waited until the basement cleared out so we could get our gear out of there. I ordered a beer and a shot. Gooch had one with me. Jeff didn't order anything. Laney said she would drive and had a water.

I drank my beer and my shot and thought of Drix. Jeff was sitting next to me and I put my arm around him and gave him a little hug. He was cold from sweating. He looked at me and I gave his arm another squeeze. He clenched his jaw and looked down.

A dude wearing a polo shirt and khakis came over to our table. Laney looked up.

"Hey," he said. "Did you guys play yet?"

Laney looked up.

The guy sat down next to her. She slid over.

"Yeah, Gerard," Jeff said. "We played an hour ago."

I looked at Laney. She looked at me.

"Ah, damn," Gerard said and looked at Laney. "I thought I'd surprise you."

He looked at me and Gooch. He put his hand out and introduced himself. I shook his hand and then excused myself from the table. Laney followed me with her eyes as I slid out of the booth.

I went to the bar and Gooch came with me. I had another drink and Gooch ordered a water.

"So," he said. "That's Gerard."

"Yeah," I said. "There he is."

"Did you guys hook up?" he asked me.

"Me and Gerard?" I asked. "Not yet. He just got here."

"You know what I mean," Gooch said.

"Was it that obvious?" I asked.

He smiled and shook his head at me. "Ever since Cincinnati."

"You knew about Gerard?" I asked.

"She told me they split up before the tour," Gooch said.

"Well," I said and looked over at the table. Laney was talking to her man, and Jeff was sliding out of the booth. "The tour is over."

Jeff came over to us. "I'm going to go break things down," he said.

"Ok," I said. "I'll be down in a minute."

Gooch went with Jeff and I sat there and finished my beer. I ordered another shot and put it back. I wanted to sleep until we got to Philly.

Laney came over to me and leaned against the bar. I didn't look at her.

"Hey," she said.

"Hey," I said.

She nudged me.

I looked at her.

"I didn't know he was coming," she said.

"It's cool," I said and looked away. "Don't worry about it."

"Don't be that way," she said.

"I'm not any way," I said.

She didn't say anything and just stood there. I finished my beer and pushed my chair away and stood up. She didn't move.

"Let's go help pack up," I said.

She looked at me. Her eyes were soft and the edges of her mouth hung down.

"Give me some time," she said and pushed herself away from the bar. "Please."

I looked at her. I nodded.

We went to load up the van. There was a parking ticket on it that Jeff threw on the ground. When we were done, Laney got into an argument with Gerard outside of the club. He said he drove all the way up here after not seeing her for the summer and that she should drive back with him. She told him that she had to drive back down with the band. We all got into the van and drove off, away from New York and back to Philadelphia.

We dropped Gooch off first and thanked him. He seemed real cool about everything and I had a profound appreciation for his friendship and character. I told him that spending nine weeks in a van brings out the worst and most annoying in people, but when we needed him he came through.

He made a sheepish grin.

"Well," I said. "Except for the whole leaving in the middle of the tour thing."

We laughed, standing there in the middle of the night out front of his place. I told him to take Drix's drums. He said he felt weird about it.

"Just take them," I said. "You need a new set. I can't use them."

"You sure?" he said.

"Yeah," I said. "You would've liked Drix. He was a good dude."

Gooch said he'd borrow them. That I could take them back whenever I needed to.

We left him there and Laney and Jeff dropped me off next. I hoisted my bass cab out of the van. Jeff helped me carry it up the stairs to my apartment. I went back down to the van to grab my bag. Jeff gave me a handshake and a hug. He said he'd talk to me soon.

Laney was leaning against the back of the van. My bag was at her feet.

She looked at me and smiled a half smile. I bent over to pick up my bag and she stopped it with her foot.

"Hey," she said. I stood back up.

She put her arms around me and we kissed and then held each other for a long time before letting go.

I picked my bag up.

"I found this," she said and held out a picture. "It was under the gear."

I took the picture from her. It was the polaroid Jeff took of me and her and Drix in Drix's living room.

"Thank you," I said.

She got back in the van. Jeff pulled away. He laid on the horn while driving down the street. It echoed against the buildings and off the ground and I watched the brake lights of the van glow red and then turn around the corner and then it was gone.

CHAPTER 30

Drix's funeral was two days after we got back to Philadelphia. I saw his mom and sister. I forgot he had a sister. She was three grades below me and looked like him. They remembered me and we hugged and talked, but I couldn't help feeling responsible for his death, and their pain. They didn't invite me back to their house, and I was glad for it. I didn't want to go there—where we jammed when we were kids thinking we could take on the whole fucking world with rock and roll.

Jeff went back to his job at a university doing something in an office. I couldn't imagine him putting on a button-down shirt every day, and hadn't thought about what he did for a living outside of the band. Laney got a job at a coffee shop and started giving piano lessons. I found out from Jeff she started playing the piano a lot since we got back.

I went back to work at the Fire. I ran sound a few nights a week and bartended the others. Within a week it was like the tour never happened. We still had buzz and tried to keep that up, but without playing out in a new city every night it was tough to feel like we were making any more headway. We had some offers to play venues in the tri-state area and a little beyond.

Gooch didn't want to join the band again, but said he'd help us out and fill in for local shows. That got us through the next couple of months. We convinced Gooch that local shows meant anywhere we could drive and come back from within a day or two on the weekend. We hit up Boston, and then DC. We made it as far as Chapel Hill. Gooch said that was stretching it and he wouldn't go that far again since he had to take off work for two days to make those shows.

By the time December came around I was only seeing the guys when we had a gig. I talked to Gooch the most and he talked to Laney more than any of us. He said that she definitely split with Gerard. She didn't call me, or make any mention of it when we saw each other, so I didn't say anything.

We had a gig before Christmas at Johnny Brenda's. We were opening up for this girl from Asbury Park who just got released from her contract. We traded war stories about touring and when we told her about Columbia falling through she went into a half hour tirade against record labels. About how they take, take, take and try to mold you into an unrecognizable product and then give you no support. She got a little worked up and kept saying that not signing was the fucking luckiest thing we could have done. She kept saying, "Fucking luckiest." Before we went on, Jeff called a band meeting.

Jeff took a white box out of his bag and tossed it to me.

"What's this?" I asked.

"My work made me get a new phone if they were going to pay my bill. I figured we could be futuremen together," he said. "And besides, it's Christmas."

"You're using one now, too?"

"Yep. Just don't tap at it with your index finger or the kids will laugh at you."

"Thanks, man. This is a helluva gift."

"Don't get too sentimental. It's old and refurbished." He laughed.

"You guys are cute," Laney said.

"So. I've got some good news," Jeff said and popped a nicotine lozenge into his mouth. "Remember Chester?"

"Yeah," Laney said. "The guy that screwed us over."

"Woah, woah, woah," Jeff said. "I think he was legit. I think he got screwed over and in turn we got screwed over."

"So," Laney said. "The guy that screwed us over. Continue."

"He's at ANTI now," Jeff said.

"Again, so?" Laney said.

"He's putting a bill together for South by Southwest," Jeff said.

"Everybody plays South by Southwest," I said. "Christ, I played there twice. It's full of suits rubbing elbows, jerking each other off over bands that will only ever get played on public radio."

"This is true," Jeff said. "But do you guys want to hear the good news, or bitch about things?"

"What's the good news?" Laney said.

"He wants us on the bill," Jeff said and smiled, and rolled the lozenge around his mouth.

I raised an eyebrow.

"Showcase," he said.

Laney was skeptical and Gooch said he didn't want to drive that far, especially after Chester let the band down once already.

We played that night and said we'd talk about it over the next few days.

The winter came and went. It was March and I stood out front of my apartment. It was cold for it being almost spring. I leaned my bass against my amp and set my bag down. I put headphones in and put on a hip-hop mixtape from some new rapper that just came out. I liked to listen to drum and bass music once in a while. The songs are usually only a few chords, but it's nice to hear the dynamics of what can be done with a groove. I was listening to a real good track that could be a hit. The bass line was good and the lyrics were clever, but it was the drums that stood out. They were fucking tight and sounded huge. I knew it was all pre-recorded samples, but they fucking sounded alive.

I shoved my hands into my pockets and looked down the street. I saw a van turn the corner. The bridge to the song just started and all the instruments except the drums dropped out. The rapper stopped and it was just bass drum, kicking a syncopated rhythm. I heard a squeak.

"What the fuck?" I said to myself and pulled my phone out of my pocket and tried to turn up the volume before the bridge was over. I turned it up all the way and backed the track up. I listened close. Sure as shit, there was a little, almost fucking inaudible squeak just as the bass drum hit. I smiled and laughed.

The van pulled up in front of me and honked.

Jeff and Laney were smiling at me and waving. She wound down the window.

"What's funny?" she asked.

"Everything," I said.

"That's very monk-like," Jeff said.

"Shut up," I said.

Jeff got out and helped me lift my amp in the van. He got in the passenger seat and I sat in the back.

Laney turned around to me. "Hey," she said. She bit her lip.

"Hey," I said back.

"Oh, fuck me," Jeff said and popped a lozenge in his mouth. "There'll be plenty of time for that later on."

Laney blushed and turned around. She tapped at the GPS.

"All right," she said. "If we take turns we should be in Omaha by tomorrow."

I leaned in between the two of them and drummed my hands on their seats.

"Let's go fuck shit up," I said.

ACKNOWLEDGMENTS

My wife, Ellie Miller (and let me tell you, I really outkicked my coverage—miracles can happen!), for her support of my artsy dicking around with bands and book nerds.

My rock and roll forever friends—Jason Gooch, Edward Everett, and Amy Miller—who allowed me to join them on their musical journey. Thank you to Adam Smith for quitting their band, which opened up a space for me. I should note here that the real Gooch is a solid dude, even if he can be a real pain in the ass from time to time.

Joshua Isard at the Arcadia University MFA program encouraged me to write this book. I was deep into Salter at the time and desperately trying to rewrite *Solo Faces*. I'm glad he steered me in a more natural direction. "Why the hell can't a rock and roll novel be literary?" he said. Cohortians Kimberly Emilia, Steve Mazzeo, Elliot Ridenour, Schimri Yoyo, Megan Bowker, and Amber Timlin for their keen eye, encouragement, and lack of hesitation to call me on my bullshit.

Seth Carter—a true friend, comrade, and brother in arms. His sense of the absurd and ability to see what a piece of art could and should be borders on the goddamn mystical.

The truest band I have known, my musical family—Those People: Assad Khafre, Rebecca Miller, Ryan McMurray, Seth Carter (again), Jason Gooch (again, too), and Maxwell Warren. I wrote this book in the middle of a three-year fever dream of rehearsing, gigging, and recording—finishing it in the middle of a 48-hour marathon demo session at Fresh Produce Studios while vocals were being tracked. This book is as much yours as it is mine.

Greg and Siurong of Tailwinds Press.

The Book.Record.Beer. gang: Michael Mehalick—millennial extraordinaire. Nick Gregorio—writer and fellow GERDman. Nick Mehalick—a shirtless Camaro roaring through Alexandria, just as quick to drop knowledge as to pop you in the kisser for your dickassery.

The best damn cheerleaders a writer could ask for: Dave Housley, Andrew Ervin, Paul Elwork, Evan Miller, Chris DiCicco, Matthew Kabik, Zachary Woodard, Britny Brooks, Nick Perilli, Beau and Laura Kegler, Douglas Reilly, Bill "Mayday" Newman, Marisa DeMartino, Kate Marro, The Misses Brown, Taryn Seymour, Mark Matthews, Andrea Duffy, Katie Haire, Robert M. DiCristino, Daniel "Ewok Jedi" Larkin, Aaron Pagoda, Ann Tetreault, Annie and Chris Herman, Timothy Hepp, Taal Aviad, Milo, Lacey, and my biggest fan, Maxine Young.

Mark Ehasz and Linda Ashcom Syzpula for the gift of reading.

Lastly, my mother. I'm not a goddamned savage, jeez.

CPSIA information can be obtained
at www.ICGtesting.com
Printed in the USA
BVHW03s0300070818
523737BV00001B/11/P